PRINCESS TRIUMVIRATE

CATHERINE BANKS

1

THE LABORATORY WE WERE IN WAS SO CLEAN THAT IT WAS ALMOST sterile and yet the various pieces of animals floating in small jars made it feel as disgusting as a dungeon. Two weeks had passed since Prince Marquez of Drimla had tried to use a magical expunger, a device that took away people's magic, on the Kingdom of Crilan. I was able to stop him, but it had cost me dearly.

We set sail shortly after the attack, traveling to Drimla, and began our assault on the small Kingdom. I wanted to be out on the frontlines fighting beside Jared and Finn, but they had ordered me to accompany Faxon on the search of the laboratories. Faxon, my tutor and friend, was examining the other half of the laboratory, his eyes roving over every inch, using his years of knowledge and magic mastery. He was a Seer and while I hadn't asked him exactly what he could do, I knew not to doubt him.

"Find anything?" he asked me.

I shook my head and tossed the notes I had found into a box, which we would take back with us to do more thorough research on. Anger boiled within me and threatened to overflow if I didn't find an outlet for it soon.

Faxon set his hand on my shoulder and turned me away from the desk to face him. "You haven't talked to me in three days. Are you upset with me over something?"

I shook my head and looked at my hands. "I'm not upset with you. You saved me. If anything, I am in your debt."

He tilted my chin up with his fingers and stared straight into my eyes. "You owe me nothing. I did what I did because I love you, Tilia. I would do it again and again, no matter the circumstances."

Tears were bubbling over the edges of my eyelids, but I didn't have anything to say to him.

"Talk to me," he begged.

"I feel useless," I confessed with a sob.

He hugged me, resting his chin on top of my head. "You are not useless." He pushed me back after a moment, hands on my shoulders and said, "You are one of the best fighters in the Kingdom. You could defeat Drimla's forces on your own if we let you."

"Then why are you guys babying me?"

He sighed and dropped his hands to his sides. "You almost died, Tilia."

He didn't have to remind me. I had nightmares nightly, replaying the events of that day.

"That's not something that is easily forgotten," he whispered.

"How would you feel, if you were me?" I asked him.

He flinched, the thought of being without his magic terrifying to him. "I can't imagine how you are feeling, which is why I wish that you would talk to me more."

I felt bad, we had just grown to be very close friends, but I felt hollow. None of them could understand how I felt. None of them were empty inside, missing a piece of themselves that made them feel inadequate.

Faxon hugged me again and sighed heavily. "We will figure

this out, Tilia. I promise that I will not stop until I learn everything that I can about this."

I rested my head on his shoulder and whispered, "You have done enough for me as it is, Faxon. You owe me nothing."

I moved away from him before I started crying in earnest, and resumed my search of the disturbing experiments. What were they doing with these animal babies? They all looked in tact, just small.

"What do you think they were doing with these?" I asked Faxon.

"They could have been doing any number of things. You don't really want to know what is possible with specimens like these."

"Do we do experiments like this?" I asked softly.

He looked up at me and I saw the answer clearly on his face. "Do you think less of me, knowing this?" he asked softly.

I shook my head and tried not to picture Faxon cutting into a small tiger cub. I was not succeeding.

"Anything?" Eric asked as he entered the room.

Eric was a royal from Blith, but he had been so far back in the bloodlines that he never had a chance of taking the throne so he came to Crilan and joined the King's Steel, working his way up and retiring last year. He rejoined after Blith's King worked with the King of Trian to kidnap me. I would have died if not for Blith's Prince waking Eric and allowing him to contact my family. I had picked on Eric when we were kids and now I felt bad about that.

"Nothing out of the ordinary," Faxon said.

"Esmeralda wants you to come look at what she found," he informed us.

"Why didn't you start with that?" I asked indignantly.

"I wanted to make sure you hadn't found something, too," he explained.

I rolled my eyes at him as I passed him by. Eric jogged ahead, leading the way. Faxon walked at my side, a place he took almost daily now. I knew I should be thankful for his protection, but it was becoming increasingly irritating. I hated being treated like a fragile doll, even though I felt that way. Something I also hated.

"Hello," Esmeralda, my aunt and the Queen of Crilan said when we entered the laboratory she was searching in. "You need to see this."

Faxon walked over to her, but I stayed back a bit, next to Eric, so that the two Arch Mages could examine whatever it was that she had found. I would only get in their way if I tried to help.

"Any word on the battle outside?" I asked Eric in a whisper.

"They're down to only about one hundred fighters, but they're not giving up yet."

"Are—"

"They're fine, Tilia," Eric answered my question before I could finish it. He knew I had been asking about Finn, my fiancé and a former pirate captain, and my uncle, the King of Crilan.

Esmeralda was pointing at some writing in the books she had found and then waving her hands animatedly as she told Faxon about her find.

Faxon listened to her while he read and then he set down the notes and ran a hand through his hair. He only did that when he was upset.

"What is it?" I asked, approaching the table where Esmeralda had spread notes all across the top.

"This is a ledger," Esmeralda explained.

Faxon turned away, flames licking up his arms as his anger drew on his power. It was rare that Faxon was angry enough to show it in that manner. What was in there that caused him so much fury?

"It is a record of the money they spent, the dates, and the number of devices that they purchased," Esmeralda continued, but kept an eye on Faxon as he walked away from us to the far side of the room.

"Purchased? I thought they were making these?" I asked her, my eyes wide.

If they weren't making them, then who was?

"There isn't a name or supplier listed," she said, "but we will take all of this paperwork back with us to search more thoroughly."

Faxon punched the wall on the far side of the laboratory and when he let his hand drop, a hole the size of a cantaloupe went all the way through the eight inches of stone, showing the sunshine outside.

I rarely saw him angry and it was slightly terrifying to see a man punch a hole through a wall with only his power.

"I'm going to the field to assist Jared," Faxon said in a growl.

"I'm coming," I said, walking towards him, but one scathing look from him stopped me in my tracks.

"Eric, stay with the Queen and Princess," Faxon ordered him.

Eric nodded and began helping Esmeralda stack the papers and put them into a box for transport.

I watched Faxon leave and only once he was gone did I go help Esmeralda and Eric.

"Are you going to tell me why he's mad?" I asked Esmeralda while we worked.

She shook her head. "It's only a speculation right now and not something of mine to share. Let's just hope that my theory is not in any way true."

"You are beyond infuriating," I growled at her.

"I know that we have to be more open with you, but there are things from each of our pasts that I would hope you never learn about. There are some things that are just meant to stay in the past."

I understood what she was saying, but I was going to be

queen someday, and I would not be able to rule well if I did not have a vast amount of knowledge. I would let this lie for now, but that would not be the last time I brought it up and tried to find out what all of these secrets were.

It took us an hour to finish boxing up all of the papers. It would have taken us longer if Esmeralda had not agreed to my plan of just bringing everything with us now and sorting through it all once we were home in Crilan. There was just too much to go through right now or we would be in the laboratory for a week.

"Do we have any leads?" I asked as I carried a box to the ship. "Aside from your theory?"

"I'm not sure, but Jared still has to interrogate their Arch Mage and he will likely have more answers for us."

I knew better than to discuss the type of interrogation techniques Jared would be using because I didn't want to go down that particularly dark path yet. There were things that were done out of necessity, but I liked having a blind eye to it while I could. I was capable of handling battle and most violent excursions, but interrogation and torture were things I steered clear of.

I stacked my box on top of the one Esmeralda had been carrying and then walked up the stairs from the storage hold and out to the bow of the ship, gripping the railing as I inhaled the salty ocean air. I closed my eyes and focused on the sway of the boat from the gentle waves, the sound of the creaking wood beneath my feet, and the calls of the birds overhead.

"Your beauty continues to grow every time I see you, but when you are on a ship with the sea breeze weaving through your hair, I lose my breath," Finn whispered from behind me.

The edges of my mouth quirked up thanks to his compliment. He was my moon, and his presence brought me peace no matter the turmoil I felt inside.

"Is the battle still waging or did you sneak away for a quick break?" He was the fastest man in the world, able to run across water without breaking the surface. I would not put it past him to take a trip to ensure I wasn't getting into trouble and then go back to the battle.

"The men of Drimla have finally accepted their defeat at the hands of the Dragon of Crilan and the King," he whispered and slipped his hands around the sides of my waist until they were clasped together on my stomach.

"Best not let the King hear your blasphemy," I teased him.

He and Jared had been quibbling off and on about whether or not Finn should have taken the title of Dragon when Finn defeated Jared at the tournament.

Finn turned me around and pinned me to the railing with his hands on either side of my body. "What troubles the most beautiful woman in all of the Kingdoms this night?"

I opened my eyes and tears slipped down my cheeks silently despite the pain they left in their wake. "I'm trying to cope, but—"

He crushed our mouths together in a toe-curling kiss. When he had his fill, he leaned back and said, "We will figure this out eventually, but you must be patient."

I knew he was right and yet...

"If you didn't have your speed, what would you feel like? It's been two weeks and I feel even worse," I admitted to him.

"I understand it's tough, and I would do whatever I could to go back in time and change things. I hate seeing you hurting like this."

"I know," I whispered. I leaned my head against his chest and listened to his steady heartbeat.

"After we finish up today, we will talk more, okay? I don't like cutting you short when you're opening up about everything, but I do need to go back and help Jared."

"Finn," I whispered around the lump that had formed in my throat. "Do you—" I couldn't ask him. I could not ask him the question I had been thinking about every day because I was terrified of his answer.

"Do I what?" he asked softly. He pushed my hair to the side and kissed my cheek.

"Do you think we could sneak away tonight? Just for a little while. They're babying me and I am going to explode at any moment."

He smiled and kissed my forehead. "Whatever you want, my love."

With that, he disappeared, his speed taking him off the boat and to wherever it was that he was meeting Jared.

I looked up and saw Eric lingering at the other end of the ship trying to look anywhere, but at me.

I scowled at him as I approached. "How long have you been there?"

"Faxon ordered me to stay with you," he reminded me.

"Where's Esmeralda?" I asked, letting my annoyance at his presence drop. It wasn't his fault that Faxon had ordered him to stay near me and he did not deserve to have me take out my frustrations on him.

"Below deck. She said she wanted to talk to the chef about tonight's meal."

"Were we given any orders?" I asked him.

He shook his head.

"Well, we better go find Esmeralda and see if she has anything for us to do. She most likely does."

He nodded in agreement and together we searched the lower levels of the ship for the Queen. This ship was built only a few years ago, but the wood it had been built from was old, very old. The wood smelled heavenly, and as we walked I found myself running my fingertips along the grooves and drawing in deep breaths. It smelled like home, my first home, with my father.

"You miss sailing, don't you?" Eric asked me.

I nodded. "You ever look back on your life and wonder what might have been had circumstances been different?"

He laughed. "I don't know anyone who doesn't."

"I wonder what would have become of me had I not been taken to Crilan. Would I be a captain of my own ship? Would I be working under my dad still? Or would I have given it up and taken to land for a man?"

"Our lives would have been incredibly different without your influence. I doubt I ever would have joined the King's Steel. And I probably would live in Blith still. Without you I would be a much different man."

I stopped walking and turned to look at him. "Really?"

He nodded, wholly serious. "Honest truth."

I found it strange to know that I had effected Eric's life so much. The knowledge that without me beating him up that summer, he might never have become a Commander was startling.

What would life have been like for Esmeralda and Jared? Would Faxon be different? Surely, they would not have had as much trouble.

"Why are you scowling?" Esmeralda asked me as she approached down the hallway.

"Nothing. Do you have a task for us?" I didn't want to tell her what I had been thinking about.

She held up a basket that she was carrying. "I got food for us, and for Jared and Finn. I was going to find a place in the castle to eat and see if I could convince the boys to come join us."

"I can take the food to the castle and get everything set up while you go find Jared and Finn," I offered.

"Do you want me to search for Faxon?" Eric asked.

Esmeralda shook her head. "It's best if we just leave him alone for now. He'll come get food when he is hungry." She handed me the basket and said, "Eric, stay with Tilia."

"I don't need a babysitter," I grumbled at her, but didn't really put any emphasis on the statement since I knew my protests would not matter. They had been falling on deaf ears for two weeks now.

"Finn would flip his lid if he knew that I let you wander off into an enemy castle by yourself. Besides, I have the ability to teleport to Jared, so I won't be walking through the castle or risking myself to an enemy attack."

Eric gripped my elbow lightly and tugged. "Come on, let's set up and then we can pick the best pieces for ourselves to eat."

After we climbed up the stairs to the main deck, walked off the boat, and to dry land, I felt my irritation shoved down by a mass of numbness. I had begun to depend on the numbness. Being numb was much easier than caring or feeling. It wasn't until Eric dropped his hand to open the door that I realized he had kept hold of me the entire time. Was he afraid that I'd try to run away? Where would I go?

Two of our soldiers monitoring the hallways of the castle stopped and bowed to me. They were from the King's Steel, the division of our fighters who focused on fighting instead of magic, and based on their assignment, were likely a warrior rank. Jared had brought his top men with us, hand picking each one for the assault.

I dipped my head to them in acknowledgment and continued on our way in search of the dining room.

"Are you happy that you rejoined?" I asked Eric.

He frowned, a crease forming in his forehead. "That's a complicated answer."

"I thought it would be yes or no."

His hand gripped the pommel of his sword and he said softly, "I would rather not discuss it right now."

What had gotten in to him? Had something happened after he rejoined that was making him regret his decision?

"Are you okay?" I asked him softly.

He took almost a full minute to relax and said, "I'm fine, don't worry about me."

"If something happened—"

"Tilia, nothing happened. I just don't want to discuss everything right now."

I let the topic drop because obviously, he didn't want to talk to me about whatever it was. Fine. I had my secrets too. I could understand his desire to keep some things private.

"Where is their blasted dining room?" I asked angrily. It felt like we had been walking for an hour.

Eric pushed open doors as we walked, but so far, they had only been bedrooms, a library, and a small office. We stopped on the far end of the castle, having walked the entire length of it and still not found the dining room.

"Could it be upstairs?" Eric asked.

"Who puts a dining room upstairs?" I asked with a shake of my head. "Our luck they will have hidden it with some secret passage way where you can only enter if you have a preserved lamb's head."

Eric barked a single laugh and his shoulders relaxed. "Maybe they don't eat normal food and exist on the blood of goats."

I pretended to gag and clutched my stomach.

"Well, let's head upstairs. I saw a stairway not too far back." Eric said. He led the way and I followed silently behind him.

This castle was set up awfully peculiarly. I had not seen a counsel room or even a ballroom downstairs, not to mention a war room or throne room. Did they not host balls? Could it be possible that they set up their castle more like most people set up their homes? How did they hold court?

The stairs were curved and as we walked up, round and round, I began to feel dizzy. Eric leaned a hand against the wall and stopped in front of me. "Tilia, is it effecting you, too?"

"Yes," I gasped, the air in my lungs felt like it was being pushed out of me. It felt as if the walls were closing in and squishing all of my breath out.

Eric looped his arm around my waist and together we slowly took one step after another back down the way we had come. My ears were ringing and my head pounded painfully.

I touched the ring Faxon had given me and whispered, "Help."

"It's not weakening," Eric gasped and collapsed to the ground on his knees, leaning back against the wall of the stairway.

"We. Have to. Move," I grunted out and pushed on his shoulder.

He slid down a step on his butt and I stumbled down behind him. If the damn staircase wasn't curved, we could have tumbled the rest of the way down just to get away from the spell or barrier or whatever was causing this.

"What rats did we catch today?" an unfamiliar voice asked loudly behind me. His voice echoed around us and pain stabbed into my skull with each word. Someone grabbed my hair and jerked my head back so that they could look at my face. Cognac eyes stared at me with madness etched in their core. "A princess! How interesting. You will be fun to play with for a little while."

He released me and someone else grabbed my arm. My hands were shaking, but I forced them to grab the Dragon's Tooth, the sword I had been given by Jared. The Dragon's Tooth had the head of a roaring dragon on the end of the pommel, a wing that crossed over your fingers, and a claw on the bottom and was said to feed on its master's enemies blood. I pulled the Dragon's Tooth and stabbed the person behind me before they could tie my hands with the rope I could see in their grasp.

"Not. Taking me," I growled. "Never again."

The person behind me fell against the side of the staircase and clutched at their wound. I had managed to stab them in the stomach even while being disoriented.

The first man had tied Eric's hands together behind his back and left him lying face down on the stairs. He turned to me and smirked. He looked familiar. Did I know him? Maybe I had met him at one of our balls before.

"I suppose it makes sense that you would not want to be kidnapped again. You have had a rough two years. Sadly, you are powerless to stop me."

"Bring it," I snarled. I didn't have my magic, but I would not go down without a fight.

He lifted his hand and my entire body froze. A mage! No. No! I couldn't protect myself from a mage now! I didn't know what to do. Where was Faxon? I had called for him! Did the ring no longer work either? Why hadn't we tested this out before we left home?

"No!" I squeaked, barely able to do more than breathe.

The man's cognac eyes flared brighter as though a candle had been lit behind them, and I felt a tickling sensation all over my body. A Seer! I had experienced this once before and that was when Faxon had used his abilities to See how much magic I had.

"You're a very interesting girl, Tilia." He turned his head to the right as if he could see through the wall, which he very well might have been able to do, and then sighed heavily. "Sadly, my time to play with you is gone. Very soon I will see you again. I have no doubt about that. And when I do, your precious Faxon will not be able to save you from me. For now, I will leave you with a gift for Faxon."

He placed his palm against my forehead and it burned. I screamed in pain. It felt like he was stabbing my entire body with thousands of needles at once. I clenched my eyes closed and continued screaming as tears streamed down my face.

"Tilia!" Eric yelled.

I couldn't move. He had paralyzed me and I could do nothing, but endure the pain. What had he done to me? Why did this needlelike pain continue nonstop? Why couldn't I move?

My throat burned for oxygen as I screamed and screamed. Why? Who was this man and what had I done to earn this from him? Of course, I knew we had taken over the country, but we had taken all of their mages, or so we had thought.

"Tilia!" Faxon yelled.

I wanted to see him, but my terror and pain had blinded me. I wanted to do something besides scream, but I couldn't.

"What's happening to her?" Finn asked.

Someone touched me and it burned my skin with an audible hiss.

"No!" I screamed and sobbed.

Faxon whispered something in a strange language, and the pain stopped. I sighed and fell into sturdy arms that kept me from hitting the stone stairs below. Blessed darkness surrounded me and I fell into a deep, dreamless, and painless sleep.

PEOPLE WERE TALKING. I wasn't sure who the people were, but I could hear them whispering angrily back and forth to each other. I was lying on the hard ground, what felt like stone, but my head was resting on something warm and moving. It must have been a person.

A hand slid down my hair and then down my cheek. The hand smelled like salt and pine.

"Finn?" I whispered.

"Shush, don't speak, Tilia. You're safe now," Finn told me with clipped words.

He was angry.

"What happened?" I asked and opened my eyes.

The room was dark except for a fire on the far side where a large table with chairs was with Eric, Jared, and Esmeralda around it. Faxon was staring into the fire with his hands clasped behind him. I hadn't seen this room before, so it had to be on the second floor or in a different building.

"Don't move," Finn whispered. "Just rest for a bit longer."

The floor was hard and cold, but it was nice to rest with my head on Finn's leg, as he repeatedly stroked his hand down my hair.

I closed my eyes again, and Finn exhaled a deep breath.

"You don't remember anything about what the man looked like?" Esmeralda asked.

I thought she was talking to me a moment, but Eric answered. "No. I know I saw him, but when I try to remember, it's only a blur. I remember that we were heading upstairs and as we went, there was a strange spell or something that made me dizzy and made it feel like the air was being pressed out of my lungs. We tried to go back down the stairs, but someone came and tied my hands. Then Tilia started screaming after he touched her head."

I remembered now. That's exactly what had happened. I sat up and everyone turned to face me, except for Faxon. Esmeralda rushed over and reached out towards me, but I jerked back in fear.

Surprise and sadness crossed her face and she lowered her hand. "How are you feeling?"

It took me a few seconds to calm down from the fear her hand coming near me had caused. "I don't know. I...I remember exactly what Eric does, but I feel strange."

"Do you remember what he looks like?" Jared asked from where he was still sitting at the table.

"No," I whispered.

"Are you in pain?" Esmeralda asked.

"No, but I do not feel normal. I can't explain it. There's just something off. Something wrong with me."

"Can I inspect you?" Faxon asked. He had not turned around from staring into the fireplace, but still stood rigid with his hands behind him.

"I..." I stopped talking because the thought of him using his magic on me suddenly terrified me. This was Faxon. Why was I scared of him?

"You're shaking," Finn whispered and rubbed my arms.

Esmeralda reached out towards me again and I scrambled back from her.

"No." I ran from the room and ran blindly down the hall and into a different room. I slammed the door closed and ran to the window looking for an escape. It was raining outside which was perfect considering all of the emotions whirling around inside of me. There was a patio one floor down and then the ground below that, which were two jumps I could easily make.

"Tilia!" Jared called.

I pushed on the window trying to get it to open, but it was stuck. I growled and pushed harder, straining with the effort and after a moment, the window groaned and flung open. The door to the room I was in opened and I leapt out the window and down to the balcony below without looking to see who it was. I landed on my toes with bent knees and looked up to see Jared look down at me, eyes wide.

"It's alright, Tilia. You know I won't hurt you. I don't have a lick of magic, remember?"

He talked to me like I was an idiot. I knew he didn't have magic, but he was married to Esmeralda and she had magic.

I turned and jumped down to the ground. The rain had made the rocks slippery and caused me to slip and fall on my butt.

"Ow!" I grunted.

I got to my feet and ran as fast as I could away from the castle and onto the ship. As soon as I set foot on the ship, my need to escape disappeared. I collapsed on the deck and drew in deep breaths. What had that been about? Why had I been scared of them? Why had I run away from my family?

The rain pounded down on me, soaking my clothes, and making me shiver from the cold.

"Princess!" the Captain of the ship yelled in surprise. "What in the name of the Mother are ye doin' on the deck in the pouring rain?" He lifted me up with his arm under my shoulders and carried me to the kitchen where a fire was roaring and where most of our men were eating dinner.

Without being asked, they brought a chair next to the fire and someone grabbed a blanket to drape around me. One of the Commanders, I was pretty sure his name was Riley, held out a cup of steaming liquid in front of me.

"It's hot chocolate, your favorite," he informed me with a soft smile.

I lifted shaky hands to the mug and took it from him with a silent nod. The mug was exceptionally warm and after a few sips my hands stopped shaking.

"Anton, report," Riley ordered.

A man in the back jogged from the room without a response.

"You feel better?" Riley asked.

I nodded and took another sip of the delicious chocolate drink.

The ship's Captain handed Riley a plate of food and a fork and then disappeared.

"Can you hold this and eat?" Riley asked.

I couldn't talk yet, but I held out the mug towards him and he traded me, giving me the plate with a fork on top. Everyone was looking at me. I couldn't blame them. I no doubt looked like a lunatic.

"Oy," Riley snapped loudly. All of the men turned away from me and the only pair of eyes left looking at me were Riley's. "Better?"

How had he known?

"Fire's going in her quarters," the ship's Captain announced.

It was the only ship I knew of that had fireplaces in the four main quarters. I rarely used it because I was afraid it might catch my entire room on fire if we hit a storm.

"Why don't we take you to your room where you will have a little more privacy?" Riley suggested.

I didn't mind being in the kitchen with the King's Steel, but I did not protest as he lifted me in his arms and carried me. I held onto my plate of food tightly to keep from spilling on Riley. That would be a terrible way to repay the man who was helping me in my moment of lunacy.

"Did you know when I joined the King's Steel and was sent to the castle, that the very first fighter I saw in the arena was you?" he asked me. His voice was smooth and rich with a hint of an accent that I could not place. It was relaxing just to hear him speak.

I shook my head slowly.

Why couldn't I break free of this feeling? Why was I so scared?

Riley continued as he ascended stairs and walked down the hallway that led to my room. "I had just arrived and I had actually gotten lost going to my room when I heard swords clashing. I went to the arena and peered through, but remained hidden from whoever might be in there fighting. I thought I would find the King practicing since it was so late, but instead I found a girl no older than twelve fighting the Queen. Not only was she fighting the Queen, but she was holding her own against the notoriously fierce Queen of Crilan."

He pushed open my door and set me on my bed. "Sit there one minute."

I watched as he took a blanket from the end of the bed and laid it on the ground in front of the fire which had warmed my room significantly already. He put another log on the fire and then picked me up and set me down on the blanket. He took the blanket they had draped on me in the kitchen and replaced it with a new one from my bed.

After a few moments of silence, he took a piece of bread from my plate and held it up to my mouth. "You have to eat."

My brain was refusing to act properly. What had that man done to me?

Somehow, I opened my mouth and chewed on the bread he had offered me. He smiled and as soon as I swallowed the bread I felt something within my body ease apart, like a knot unraveling.

Function returned to my limbs and the fog that had settled in my skull disappeared.

"What? What did you do?" I asked him in shock and lifted my hands to touch my face.

"A little kindness goes a long way towards helping a person on the road to recovery," he said with a smile.

"Are you a mage?" I asked softly.

He shook his head. "No, Princess. I don't have abilities like Faxon or Queen Esmeralda."

"But you have abilities?" I asked to clarify.

He shrugged. "I do not have ones that I control, but I have been told that I am rather good at helping people relax and begin to heal after a traumatic event."

I realized shamefully that I had not thanked him. "Thank you," I whispered and hugged him.

He patted my back. "You're welcome."

"Tilia," Finn said angrily from the bedroom door.

I leapt up and spilled my plate of food all across the floor.

"Oh," I gasped.

"What's going on?" Finn asked, his glare directed straight at Riley, who didn't look the least bit worried.

"The Princess came back a bit soaked, so we gave her some food and helped her get to her quarters where the Captain had started a fire for her," Riley explained. He turned and faced me. "You alright now?"

"Yes, thank you again, Riley."

He winked at me since Finn couldn't see with his back to him and said, "Anytime." He turned towards the door and nodded at Finn. "Chief."

Finn stepped aside and let Riley leave the room with a deep scowl on his face.

"It's not what it looks like," I said quickly, stepping over my words as I tried hurriedly to explain myself. "I don't know what that man did, but somehow Riley was able to reverse it, or get rid of it, or suppress it, or whatever."

Finn walked towards me and the scowl turned into a frown of worry. "Jared said that you jumped out of a window and then off of a balcony."

I flinched. "Um, maybe."

"What were you thinking?" he asked softly, but not accusingly.

"I felt terrified of anyone with magic. I don't know why. I know that Faxon and Esmeralda would never hurt me, but the thought of them using their magic on me horrified me so much that I felt that I had to run away."

He lifted his hand out towards me slowly, as though he were waiting for me to flinch away from him. I stepped forward into his arms and buried my face against his chest.

"Why did it take you so long to find me?" I asked him softly.

"Jared made me wait," Finn growled.

"Wait?" I asked, confused.

"He thought you needed some time to yourself or to run off your fear," he explained, "but obviously, you didn't want to be alone."

"Are you jealous?" I asked and looked up at him beneath my eyelashes.

"If he had tried to kiss you, he would have lost a hand," he whispered as he bent down and kissed me on the lips.

"Jared wouldn't be too happy about that," I whispered back, my heart racing as my hormones reacted to him. I didn't like men who were possessive of women, but as dumb as it made me, I enjoyed knowing he felt so strongly for me and essentially claimed me as his. I blamed it on my pirate upbringing since we were so possessive of our prized jewels or other gifts. The greatest compliment was to have a pirate covet you more than his treasure.

"What wouldn't Jared be happy about?" Jared asked from behind Finn.

"Removing a man's hand for trying to kiss me," I answered.

"Depends on who it was," Jared said grumpily.

"A Commander," I answered.

"That would be a predicament," Jared said. "Are you calmed down?" he asked me.

Finn stepped to the side so that I could see Jared. "Yes."

"You kill someone?" he asked.

I shook my head. "Riley helped me."

Jared smiled. "Ah, that's where the topic of dismemberment came from. Did he try to kiss you?"

"No, Finn's just being jealous," I answered.

Finn rolled his eyes at me, but didn't dispute the statement.

"Well, I am glad that he was able to help you," Jared said. "Are you up to seeing Esmeralda?"

I was about to say yes when my heart started beating faster and sweat slicked my palms. What in the name of the Ocean God was going on with me? Hadn't Riley fixed me?

"What type of spell does this?" Finn asked Jared softly.

"I've heard of people becoming afraid of magic users after being attacked by one, but this is extremely odd," Jared whispered. "And I have never met someone who Riley hadn't been able to help."

"I know she won't hurt me," I choked out. "I can't. Control it."

"Sit down," Jared ordered me.

I obeyed.

He took my hands and when he felt them shaking his eyes widened. "Close your eyes and think about your father's ship."

What did Dad's ship have to do with this? I did as he asked and slowly the shaking stopped.

"Now, picture your Aunt."

I pictured her face and recalled the way she looked when she laughed and yet my hands began to shake.

"Remember the time that Faxon and she saved you after the bomb that Marquez used," Jared ordered me.

I recalled the bomb that took my magic from me and how Faxon had saved me from the small island I had transported Marquez and myself to. After he had found me, Faxon had teleported me back to the castle and he and Esmeralda had healed me. I had almost died. If not for them I would have died.

No matter how hard I tried to think positively about them I

also recalled their terrifying feats and the pain that man had made me endure.

I jerked my hands away from Jared and clutched them to my chest. "I can't."

"I was afraid of that," Jared said with a sigh.

"Can't they fix it?" Finn asked Jared.

Jared rested his hand on my shoulder and said, "For now we will let Tilia have some space. We are sailing out at first light. What matters is that you are alive and safe. We can deal with everything else later, okay?"

I nodded and turned to face the fire, so I wouldn't have to see the sadness in his eyes.

Finn and Jared whispered together outside of my room and then Finn joined me on the floor in front of the fireplace.

"Would you like me to stay here tonight?" he asked softly.

I did not want to be alone, but at the same time I did not want to be coddled any longer. I needed to buck up and deal with this somehow. "No, I'll be okay."

"Okay, I'm next door so I can be here faster than you can blink if you need me," he reminded me.

I nodded and continued to watch the flames dance along the logs.

"I love you."

I turned and smiled at him. "I love you too, Finley."

He brushed his lips across mine and left my room, shutting the door behind him.

2

AFTER FINN LEFT, I STOPPED A CREWMAN WALKING BY AND ASKED him to have Riley come see me. I paced back and forth in my small room as I waited. Finn was right next door, so we were going to have to either leave or be very quiet. I didn't like sneaking around behind Finn's back, but I had a feeling that he would be too jealous to let me work with Riley.

I opened the door, ready to flag down another person and found Riley with his hand raised, about to knock on the door and a plate of food in his other hand. "You—"

I put my hand over his mouth and put a finger to my lips so he would know to be quiet. I looked right and left down the hallway and pulled him inside my room, shutting and locking it behind him.

"It's not gone," I whispered to him. "I thought you had fixed me, but when Jared asked me to see Esmeralda I got scared again."

"I didn't say I fixed you, Princess—"

"Call me Tilia."

"Tilia. I said I helped you begin to heal. Your brain is what has to finish the healing."

"How?" I asked in exasperation. "How do I fix this? I don't want to be afraid of them. I don't want to not be able to look at them."

"First, you need to eat." He held out the plate of food and I realized that I hadn't cleaned up the food I had dumped on my floor earlier. "You eat and I'll clean," he offered.

"No, you don't need to—"

"I insist," he interrupted.

I sat on my bed and ate the food on my plate while he picked up my mess. I did not like him cleaning up after me, but it was pointless to argue with him. He seemed as stubborn as Jared.

"What am I going to do?" I asked him sadly as I ate.

He finished cleaning and then tossed another log onto the fire. "What happens when you think about them?" he asked and turned to face me.

"I try to picture the nice things they have done or how they look when they are laughing, but I end up picturing them doing terrifying things. I mean, they are things they have done, but right now it's terrifying to me."

"Hm, okay." He sat down on the floor in front of me.

I did not like being higher up than him, so I joined him on the floor. I finished the food he had brought and set the plate on the floor next to us. Was it wrong of me to seek out his help? Should I have waited until tomorrow? I didn't want to spend another day afraid of my family.

"Are you afraid of anyone who has magic? Try picturing someone else you know who has magic," he suggested.

I pictured Eric and although I felt nervous about him I wasn't terrified.

"So, it still bothers you. Well, now we know it's not a spell that makes you dislike a specific person or persons."

I supposed that was a good thing. I would have hated being scared of Faxon and Esmeralda the rest of my life.

"Are you perhaps afraid that they will do the same thing to you that the other mage did?" he asked me.

I had not thought about that.

"I do not specifically think that," I informed him, "but I suppose it is possible."

"Do you know who stopped whatever happened to you?" he asked.

"Faxon," I whispered.

"So, the rest of the night I want you to picture him saving you from the pain that the other mage caused. It could help."

"Okay." I was not confident in that idea, but anything was worth a try.

He stood up and asked, "Are you going to be okay by yourself?"

I nodded. "Yes. Thank you."

He bowed and said, "Goodnight, Princess."

He closed the door behind him as he left, and I changed out of my still wet clothes into warm sheep wool lined pajamas. As I snuggled underneath my covers, I did as Riley had suggested and pictured Faxon saving me from the painful spell. My fear grew and decreased constantly and by the time I fell asleep, I was exhausted physically and mentally.

Something woke me during the middle of the night and I wasn't sure what it was until I opened my eyes and saw someone standing in front of my fireplace.

"It is my fault that this happened," Faxon whispered. He bent down and put a new log in the fireplace, the original fire having died, and used his magic to start it. "Somehow, he knew that you were special to me. Somehow, he knew that hurting you would hurt me. I won't let that happen again. I won't let him win by using this spell to push us apart. You mean too much to me." He spun around and I gasped at his mad expression. "I will kill him for this. I won't run off to find him, but when we do meet, it will be the day he regrets ever touching you. I promise you, Tilia, he will pay for the pain that he caused you and for making you fear me."

"Faxon, I..." I could barely talk. My body was shaking in fear and the room suddenly felt very small with him in it with me.

His gaze softened and he knelt on the ground and then bowed until his forehead touched the floor. "Forgive me, for I have failed you once again. All my life I have been so sure of myself and yet, twice now, I have failed to protect you. I do not deserve the title of Arch Mage nor do I deserve your respect."

I wanted to tell him to stop being stupid. I wanted to tell him that this was not his fault. I wanted to stop shaking like a leaf in the fall.

"I also beg for your forgiveness for what I am about to do," he said and stood up.

"What...don't..." I stammered in fear.

He pinned my arms down with his hands and straddled my body to keep me from moving. "Whether you would hate me for this or not, I do not know, but I hope that you understand why. I cannot bear to see you look at me with such fear any longer. Your terror hurts me more than words ever could. Everything will be better when you wake up tomorrow, I promise. Tomorrow, all of this will be as if it had never happened." He bent forward and kissed my forehead. "I love you."

I opened my mouth to scream, but nothing came out. Something burst within my head and the pain was so intense that I almost threw up. Faxon climbed off of me, standing beside the bed as I gasped for air like a fish out of water. He took the ring he had given me from my finger and whispered, "Memoria."

My body went rigid, and then numbness and darkness enveloped me.

A WARM HAND stroked my cheek as birds called to each other outside. I opened my eyes and Finn smiled at me. "Good morning."

I smiled at my handsome pirate, and scooted back on the bed so that he could climb on with me. He lay down on his back and I rested my cheek on his chest. "Good morning, Finley."

"So, how are you feeling today?" he asked me as he ran his fingers through my hair.

"Wonderful. You?"

He leaned back to look at me. "Wonderful?" he asked skeptically.

I nodded. "Yes, why wouldn't I be?"

He frowned and opened his mouth to say something, but Faxon opened the door and said, "Wake up, sleepyhead. It's time to eat."

"Be right there," I told him and stretched my arms up over my head.

Finn watched our interaction and said, "I'll meet you at the kitchen." He shut my door behind him and I heard him yell, "Faxon!" as he walked away.

What was wrong with Finn? He seemed mad at Faxon for something.

I shrugged and changed clothes, brushed my hair and went through my morning routine. I looked down at my hand and felt as though I was missing something. I had Finn's ring on, Esmeralda's bracelet that she had given me for my birthday, and my necklace that my father had given me. I wasn't missing anything. Weird.

I skipped down the halls to the kitchen and smiled at all of the King's Steel warriors who were gathered to eat. They looked at me strangely and I wondered what was going on with everyone. I spotted Jared, Esmeralda, Faxon, Eric, and Finn talking together at a table, heads leaned forward conspiratorially.

Faxon noticed me first and smiled wide as I walked over.

"What's going on?" I asked.

Faxon waved his hand. "Boring stuff. How was your sleep?"

"Good!" I said happily. "I always sleep better on a ship."

"I'm glad," he said with a wide smile.

Why was he so happy?

Esmeralda reached her hand out towards me with an odd look on her face. "Good morning."

I reached across and gripped her hand. "Good morning. Are we heading out soon?"

Her eyes widened and she turned to look at Faxon who was smiling like he was proud of something. I felt out of the loop.

"What's going on, really? You are all acting weird." I asked.

"Do you remember—" Jared started to ask, but Faxon interrupted him.

"Where we put that scroll we found yesterday?" Faxon asked.

"In the locked box that you were keeping with you," I reminded him.

He knew that. Faxon never forgot anything.

"Right!" he said and leaned back in his chair. "Of course, it's in there."

Jared scowled at Faxon and folded his arms across his chest.

"Hello, Princess," a male voice that sounded vaguely familiar said beside me.

I turned and smiled at the Commander. I knew his name... Riley! "Hi, Riley."

"You seem better today," he commented.

"Better? Was I sick last night? I don't remember being sick," I said and felt my smile slip a little.

"You were a bit emotional yesterday, remember?" Faxon jumped in to say.

"Yes," I mumbled. Why was he bringing that up in front of Riley?

"Well, Riley here has the rare ability to help people with that. You probably don't remember because you were really tired, but once he sat with you a bit, you perked right up."

Now I knew something was up. Faxon never spoke like this.

Riley raised an eyebrow at Faxon, but didn't speak.

"Um, well I guess, thanks," I told Riley.

"No need to thank me," he said and smiled. "I'm just glad that you are feeling good today. I hope that my advice last night helped."

"It must have," I said since I had no idea what advice he was talking about.

"You should eat," Finn told me and slipped an arm around my waist.

He was jealous of Riley? What had gotten into everyone today!

"You're all acting weird," I told them.

"It's nothing," Faxon assured me. "We're all just glad to be heading home."

"It will be good to be back in Crilan," Esmeralda said and smiled at me.

I spooned some food onto my plate, not paying attention to what it even was and ate while I processed everything. My family was definitely hiding something from me. I had no idea what it was...oh right! Faxon had been mad yesterday because of something they found out. I would have to corner him and convince him to tell me.

"Well, I will leave you to your meal," Riley said. "If you need my help again, don't hesitate to ask."

"Thank you," I told him despite not knowing what he had done.

I ate while everyone stared silently at one another and then dismissed myself to go up to the main deck. The cool ocean mist eased my worries and I shoved aside my family and their odd behavior to enjoy being on the sea. It was hard to believe that it had been more than eight years since I sailed on my father, the King of the Pirates' ship. I wondered what the old man was up to in their new town, the life of piracy behind him now. It still amazed me that he had given up his title to settle on land. I never thought I would see the day. I honestly thought he would die on the sea.

I wondered what Cristoff was up to. That man was a handful, but he was hilarious and had died to save me. I considered writing to him, but wasn't sure how Finn would feel about that.

The ship's crew moved about quickly as we prepared to set sail. Their calls and routine movements were relaxing to me. The salty air further relaxed me to the point that I stumbled over to lean against the center mast and sat down with my back against it. I tied a rope around my waist, securing myself to the mast, and closed my eyes. With my eyes closed I heard everything more sharply and smiled as two crew members argued over the proper tying of a knot.

Wind blew my hair around my face, so I took the time to braid it to help keep it out of my eyes. The Captain yelled something and then I heard the plank dragged up onto the deck. The ship rocked a moment and then we were sailing. The wind pressure increased and despite the cold I was smiling.

"Afraid we're going to have bad weather?" Finn asked.

I opened my eyes and he smiled at me as he sat down.

"It's better to be prepared."

"I don't think I have ever seen a pirate tie himself to the mast when there wasn't a storm before," he teased me.

"Well, if I fell asleep as we left dock and we entered a storm without me knowing, I could be tossed overboard before I realized what was happening. Then, I would either drown or be left behind."

He shook his head. "Never. I would jump in and save you."

I smirked at him. "While that is reassuring former co-captain, I would rather stay dry."

"You keep using this title, but I never agreed to it."

"You keep fighting it despite knowing it was truth."

"Perhaps you are too stubborn to see the truth."

"Right back at you."

We stared at each other a minute and then laughed together. He scooted closer to me and took my hand in his, rubbing one of my fingers.

"What happened to your ring?" he asked in shock and lifted both hands up to inspect them.

"I never had a ring on that finger, Finn."

He opened his mouth and then closed it and scowled. "I see."

"You *see* what?" I asked.

"I was mistaken, that's all," he said. "I was thinking of your other hand." He took the hand with his engagement ring on it and ran his thumb across the top of my hand. "Every morning I wake up and have to pinch myself to believe that I will soon be married to a beautiful princess."

I leaned forward to kiss him, but the rope kept me a foot away from his lips.

He laughed and asked, "What's wrong, former co-captain?"

I grabbed his shirt and dragged him forward to kiss him. "Nothing. Everything is right in this world where I get to kiss you each day."

We leaned back and he continued to rub my hand as the ship sailed deeper into the open ocean.

"You think Duke's bored out of his mind at home?" Finn asked.

"No, that horse of mine is probably enjoying being able to eat grass nonstop and will most likely have a grass belly when we return." Duke was my horse, his coat, mane, and tail the same color as my golden hair. He was large, a mix of the types of horses that had been used for battle in the old days. Whatever his breeding was, he was my gentle giant.

"I wonder what progress they have made on the town," Finn pondered softly as he thought about his former crew and my father's who had banded together to form a town where they could live in peace and leave piracy behind.

"Do you miss living with them?" I asked him softly. Part of me knew he had to, but I also wished that I was enough to make him not care. Selfish and narcissistic as that was.

"Sometimes," he admitted, "but life with you is what I want. Jared's teaching me so much new information about tactics and war and politics that I am enjoying myself too much to really think about them. And that also makes me feel bad. I don't want to forget them."

"You'll never forget them," I assured him. "They will always be a part of you, just like my father and his crew are still my family." He nodded, but stayed silent. "Would you like to visit them when we get back?"

He smiled. "I would like that."

"Good! We can make a trip to see them and spend a few days enjoying the rowdiness of our crews."

"Sounds wonderful," he said and kissed me quickly. "I'm going to go find Jared and see if he needs me for anything."

"I'll be here!" I called after him.

I closed my eyes and resumed my peaceful morning of doing absolutely nothing. The sound of a broom on the deck sweeping back and forth grew louder and louder and seemed as though it was right next to me. I opened my eyes.

A crew member that looked to be in his late thirties was sweeping the deck near me. He had on pants that were torn almost up to the knee and a billowy shirt. His beard was thick and hung down almost to his belly button, looking as though he had not shaved it his entire life. He stopped sweeping when he noticed me and stared at me in surprise. "There a storm?" he asked. "Captain didn't mention a storm."

I shrugged. "I don't know. I figured I would fall asleep here and thought I had better tie off to be safe."

He nodded and resumed sweeping. "Good idea. You're smart."

"Thanks."

"You seem to enjoy the ocean more than the rest of your group," he commented. "Well, that fiancé of yours loves it too, but you definitely love it most."

"Yes, we're former pirates," I told him truthfully.

He stopped sweeping and stared at me with wide eyes. "What?"

"My fiancé was a captain of a pirate ship and I sailed with him for about four months," I told him since I couldn't tell him about my dad.

"You don't say. And now he's going to be the prince?"

"That's the plan," I said with a smile.

"And you're not worried that he'll revert to his old ways?" he asked me, crossing his arms and leaning on the handle of his broom.

"No. He and I go out and sail occasionally, but he doesn't feel like he has to go out plundering anymore."

"A retired pirate becoming prince." He scoffed. "Never thought I'd see the day."

"You and me both," I told him and laughed.

"You aren't like most royals," he said.

"How so?"

"I'm from Blith," he said.

I laughed and waved my hand. "No more needed to be said. I met the King of Blith."

"I take it things didn't go well?"

"He let King Priam of Trian kidnap me and take me to Trian where he was planning to execute me."

He gasped. "That's why Crilan blew up the Capitol and took over their Kingdom?"

I nodded. "They came to rescue me."

"That fiancé of yours go too?"

"Yes, he broke me out of the prison."

"Good man. I guess I'll give him a break on being a former pirate."

"Glad to hear it," I teased him.

"Tilia," Faxon called. "Are you hungry?"

Was I? How long had I been here? It couldn't have been more than an hour.

The crew member resumed his sweeping, moving away from me.

"Is it lunchtime already?" I called back to Faxon.

"Yes."

"Oh."

He walked over to me and sat down. "I enjoy spending time with you while you are on a ship. You're much more at ease here."

"It's nice to be on a ship every once in a while."

"So, how would you feel about joining me on my continued hunt for information about these devices?" he asked.

"I thought that was the plan?" I asked him.

"It was, but I didn't know if you still wanted to, after seeing how boring it could be."

"Do you know where we are going next?" I asked and adjusted my butt on the deck.

"I have to do a bit more research and examination of the things we're bringing back home with us, but I think we might be headed to Judby."

"I've never been there! Are we going diplomatically or

stealthily? Or are we blowing things up?" Personally, I preferred the last two options.

"We're going in disguise," he said. "Any objection to that?"

"No, but how—"

"I will take care of the disguises."

"Disguises for what?" Finn asked.

"For our trip to Judby," I answered.

"I'm coming," Finn told Faxon.

"Finn, Jared told you—"

"I'm not letting her go outside of Crilan without me. This has nothing to do with your strength, Faxon, but you know exactly how I feel. You wouldn't want her to go without you either."

Faxon frowned, but nodded. "Fine. I'll discuss it with Jared. Your speed will likely come in useful for our objective."

"What is our objective?" I asked.

"Research first, and then plan development next."

"Okay," I said with a sigh.

"Lunch time!" Esmeralda yelled.

"How is it lunch time already? I swear I've only been out here an hour," I muttered as I untied myself.

Finn and Faxon looked at each other in that weird way that men do when they communicate without words, and then turned their gazes on me.

"You've been out here three hours," Finn told me. "I left you out here two hours ago."

"No. You were just here," I responded nervously. If that was true, why was time off for me?

"You probably dozed off and didn't realize it," Faxon assured me and put an arm around my shoulders as we walked towards the stairs that led below deck. "Don't worry about it."

Finn didn't seem to agree with him, but his theory was likely right. I did fall asleep much easier on the ship.

"What's for lunch?" I asked as we headed to go below deck.

"Fish and rice," Esmeralda said from below us. It was too dark to see inside, but I assumed she was at the bottom of the stairs.

"Yum," I said happily.

"When we get back to Crilan I'm buying a pound of chocolate," Finn informed me.

"Are you going to share the chocolate?" I inquired and headed down first with Finn behind me and Faxon behind him.

"No. You can buy your own pound," he replied indignantly.

"I would rather buy a dozen cakes," I said and practically drooled.

"Stop it. You two are making me want sweets," Faxon groaned.

"Can't you make some with your magic?" Finn asked Esmeralda and Faxon.

"I wish," Esmeralda muttered. "I've been trying to figure out a spell for that since I realized I had magic."

"Have I ever told you about the time that your aunt tried to skewer me with a spear?" Faxon asked me.

"What!" I shrieked.

Esmeralda sighed. "You'll never forget about that, will you?"

"I have a scar from it," Faxon reminded her.

"You would have never been in danger, had you given me what I asked for in the first place," she snapped.

"What happened?" Finn asked.

We entered the dining area and sat around a table. Jared was talking with some of his men at another table, but excused himself to join us.

"Some dignitaries from one of the other Kingdoms, I can't even remember who anymore, came to visit so the former King threw a party," Faxon began.

"You guys sure do love parties," Finn noted.

"Don't interrupt," Faxon ordered him. "Being the princess,

Esmeralda had to dance with the sons of these people and those men kept her occupied most of the evening."

"They smelled terrible," Esmeralda commented and then shuddered.

"The King knew that these people loved sweets, so he had a whole assortment brought in from all across the Kingdom. They were amazing! Jared and I spent most of the evening gorging ourselves on the sweets, as did many of the others in attendance. By the time Esmeralda was able to steal a moment to herself, she walked over to us, we were standing by the display where the sweets had been," Faxon said.

"Had been?" I asked in shock.

Esmeralda snarled, "Exactly, Tilia."

"I had one last truffle in my hand and Esmeralda tried to steal it from me," Faxon recounted as though he were a victim.

"He'd already eaten several dozen of the sweets," Esmeralda told me. "But he refused to give me that last piece."

"It was *my* piece," Faxon argued.

"Then what happened?" Finn asked.

Faxon turned away from glaring at Esmeralda to look at us. "She tried to steal it from me, even used magic on me, but I refused to give in. She was screaming at me in the ballroom and everyone was watching us, horrified. A guard walked over to tell us to go outside, but as soon as he got close to us, Esmeralda snatched the spear he was holding and stabbed me with it."

"No!" I gasped in shock.

"She did," Jared nodded. "I watched the whole thing."

"And he didn't even bother to help his friend," Faxon said.

"There was no way that I was going to choose a side on that fiasco. Plus, I was trying to ensure she didn't stab me," Jared explained with a laugh.

"I jumped away from the lunatic princess, and ran out of the ballroom. She chased me all throughout the castle and I made a wrong turn in my attempt to flee and she cornered me in a hallway. Then, since my time was up, I popped the truffle in my mouth and swallowed."

I laughed and Esmeralda glared at me, not looking amused. "He ate the damn truffle right in front of me and smiled with pieces of the chocolate on his teeth!" she yelled.

"She almost skewered me to the wall, but I dodged her strike and ran past her and out of the castle," Faxon ended and pulled his shirt down to reveal a scar on his shoulder. "But I still bear the mark of her rage from that day."

"Maybe you will remember not to be so selfish," Esmeralda said.

"Would you have really stabbed him?" I asked.

"Of course, I would have. Not like he would have died," she replied nonchalantly.

"You could have killed him if you hit anything vital," Finn said.

"Not likely," Jared answered. "She has terrible aim with spears."

Everyone laughed at that, even Esmeralda.

Finn excused himself to get our food and I stared at the table top. Something was missing. What was it? Had I left something in my room?

"Tilia," Esmeralda whispered. "What's wrong?" she asked and set her hand on top of mine where I had absentmindedly been rubbing my right ring finger.

"I don't know. I feel like I forgot something or something is missing," I admitted. "I don't know what it could be."

Faxon's eyes darkened and he walked away from the table without a word.

"I am sure you aren't missing anything," Esmeralda assured me.

Jared scowled at her and folded his arms across his chest, but stayed silent. He seemed irritated.

"Did I do something?" I asked quietly.

Jared turned to me and asked, "What do you mean?"

"Everyone, you all and the King's Steel, are acting strange. Everybody keeps looking at me like I'm crazy. I know that I haven't been the most level headed with what happened, but it seems like it is something else entirely."

"How do you feel inside?" Esmeralda asked me with a soft voice.

"Hollow," I admitted.

"Do you think that perhaps all of these strange feelings that you have been having, are due to you missing that part of yourself? You rubbing your finger and feeling like you are missing something? It could all be connected."

That was a really good and likely theory.

"Are you certain that there is not anything else that you haven't told me?" I asked her.

She leaned back in her seat and said, "The only item I've kept from you, I explained during our search of the laboratory."

"Food," Finn announced and set a pot of rice in the center of the table.

Faxon set a plate of cooked fish beside the pot and then handed us all plates and utensils. "Eat up!"

The sour expressions everyone had been wearing disappeared as they talked and joked over lunch. Esmeralda was probably right; I was causing myself undue worry from missing my magic. And yet, I felt as though there was something else. There was something in the back of my mind, barely a spark, which kept nagging me to ask more questions. I shoved the thoughts down and joined in on the conversation with a smile on my face. There would be plenty of time for self doubt once we were home. It wasn't fair of me to continue to ruin their days with my problems.

3

"Are you certain that you won't let me come?" Faxon asked me for the hundredth time that morning.

"I am going with Finn to visit my father. I do *not* need a guard with me. We are not going sailing or leaving Crilan."

"I know, but I would just—"

I stopped him with a raised hand. "I know that you're worried about my safety, but I am capable of protecting myself and Finn can run us to safety if it's something I cannot handle."

Faxon sighed loudly and looked up at the ceiling. "Fine."

"Have you made any progress on the Drimla notes?" I asked him and folded a shirt before putting it in my bag.

"Yes and no. I still have zero idea who the seller of the devices was, but I did learn that they used all of the ones they had except for the one Marquez had, during trials."

I stopped folding another shirt and turned to Faxon. "They used them against their own people?"

"Their prisoners," he explained. "They took them to uninhabited islands."

How terrible!

"They would tie the prisoners to trees at varying distances and then set off the device," he continued.

"They used it to determine the range of the device," I summarized.

Faxon beamed proudly. "Exactly."

His normally beautiful hair was knotted and dirty and the skin under his eyes was darkening weekly.

"You should take a break too while I'm gone," I suggested. "You're looking worse every day."

He scrunched his face up and said, "Thank you for pointing out my ugliness."

I rolled my eyes at him and resumed packing. "You know darn well that you aren't ugly, Faxon. Stop being nonsensical."

"I guess you might be right. I have been rather tired lately," he conceded.

"Faxon, why don't you court women?" I asked softly without looking at him. I had been wondering this for quite some time, but aside from Esmeralda's opinion that he didn't want anyone to be close to him because of his enemies, I wondered what the truth was.

"I have enemies all over, Tilia. Enemies that will hurt or try to destroy anyone or anything that gives me joy. A wife would be a primary target for them. A pregnant wife would be vulnerable."

"But you're the strongest mage in existence! You could protect her."

He looked at the ground and said, "I've learned that I am not as strong as I thought I was. I have failed you and you were hurt due to my inability to protect you."

"What happened to me is not your fault," I assured him.

"We never should have let you go to Marquez. I should have gone and obliterated the prince myself."

I took his hand and whispered, "You can't blame yourself for what Marquez did."

"It's not only that incident," he snapped and then ran a hand through his hair.

"What else are you talking about? You saved my life and risked losing your magic to bring me home. There hasn't been anything else that has happened that you could have prevented. You saved me when Griffin was deceiving Jared. I should be apologizing to you for making you save me."

"I won't let him harm you," he growled. "I will do whatever I have to in order to keep you safe."

"Him? Who?"

"Them," he amended. "Whoever they may be."

"You're worrying yourself needlessly, which is making me worry for you. So now, we're in this cycle of worry that has no end!" I said in exasperation and threw my hands up into the air.

He laughed and pulled my arms back down. "Point taken. I'll stop worrying so much and take a break while you're away."

"Promise?" I asked with a glare.

"I promise."

"Tilia," Finn said. "Let's go." He looked down at Faxon and my joined hands and stared at Faxon silently.

"I'm almost done," I assured him. "I was just convincing Faxon to stop worrying and working so much, and take a break while we're gone."

Faxon released my hands and turned to Finn. "Jared said you wanted to speak to me?"

Finn nodded. "Tilia, I'll meet you at the barn, okay?"

"Okay," I agreed. I resumed packing and hoped that whatever had happened between them would be fixed soon. I couldn't have my mentor and my fiancé arguing or hating each other.

I couldn't even think of a reason why Finn would be mad at

Faxon. Maybe he wasn't mad and I just read the situation wrong. Maybe he wanted advice from Faxon about something.

I sighed and rubbed my temples with my fingertips.

"What's troubling you?" Esmeralda asked.

"Men."

She laughed, tossing her head back, and then threw an arm around my shoulders. "That is something that will never go away."

"I could become one of those fanatics who seal themselves away from men," I suggested.

"And every day you would think about the men you had known and why they had acted so strangely."

"Do they fret about us as much as we do about them?" I asked her.

She shrugged. "I don't know the first thing about men and their ridiculous minds and emotions. Ask me about their battle strategies or point a man out and make me determine his fighting abilities and I'm your woman. Ask me what a man's thinking and you might as well ask me what a horse or a fish is thinking."

"They discuss their feelings just as much," I muttered.

"Is something going on between you and Finn?" she asked with genuine concern.

"No. It's Faxon."

"Faxon?" she asked softly.

"He's been overly protective since the incident, but ever since Drimla, he has been even more crazy. He even tried to convince me to let him come with us to the Lost Port."

The Lost Port was the name of the town my father and the other pirates had restored. It had gone from a few shambled buildings to a thriving town with visitors each day. They were farming the land, fishing the sea, and some even discovered they had talents with carving and blacksmithing.

"I warned you about his past," she reminded me.

"I know, but I had no idea it would end up like this. I just wish he would relax. He's making me paranoid by being so paranoid."

"In time, he will relax, but it hasn't been that long since the incident."

She had started referring to Marquez' attack with the device and my almost death as 'the incident'. I think it made her feel better than to say what happened.

"I hope so."

"Are you all set?" she asked me, changing the subject.

"Yes."

"Behave while you're gone," she ordered me.

"I promise."

"And when you get back we're going to sit down and discuss your wedding," she said with a smile.

My wedding. To Finn.

"Okay."

"You look terrified," she said with a laugh.

I couldn't tell her why, because she would just tell me I was being ridiculous. I wasn't sure whether I was or not, but I couldn't change the fear inside of me. The fear or rejection and loneliness.

"It's just a lot to plan," I lied.

"That's what I am here for," she reminded me and hugged me. "I'll see you when you get home."

I slung my bag over my shoulder and headed out to the stables.

Finn was already mounted on his horse, Twist, a horse with a midnight coat and a single white star in the center of his forehead. He was mild mannered, but when he wanted to, he was the fastest horse I'd ever seen.

Duke nudged my shoulder when I approached him and

nickered at me. I rubbed his face and kissed his muzzle. "Hello, handsome." I mounted him and turned to Finn. "You ready?"

"Always," he replied with a smirk and then squeezed his legs around Twist's sides. Twist trotted ahead and Duke immediately followed.

"So, what did you need to talk to Faxon about?" I asked as nonchalantly as I could, even looked around at our surroundings like I didn't care.

"Nothing important," he replied shortly.

"Liar."

He sighed. "I asked him for help on something. I'm not going to say anymore about it."

"Why not?" I asked and felt my anger stirring.

"Tell me what you wanted to ask me on the ship the other day," he said. "What you actually wanted to ask me, not what you made up when you decided not to ask."

Dammit. How did he know?

I remained silent and so did he. Now my curiosity was even higher. What could he have needed to talk to Faxon about that he wouldn't want to tell me? What would he need help with?

No answers came to mind, which infuriated me further.

The silent ride dampened my mood to the point that I almost considered turning back and staying in my room for a week.

Finn slowed Twist until we were riding side by side. "I don't like when we fight," he told me.

"Then you should tell me what I wanted to know," I snarled. I wanted to end the fight, but I was too angry to let it drop. Everyone was constantly keeping things from me and it was bull.

"Are you going to stay mad at me the entire trip?" he asked quietly.

"Yes."

"Tilia."

"No! Start talking and then I'll adjust my mood. You hate being kept in the dark just as much as I do."

"It's a secret," he said. "A surprise. Okay? I don't want to tell you yet what I'm doing."

"And what about the other things you've been hiding from me?"

"That's the only thing, Tilia," he assured me.

I didn't believe him. I don't know why since everyone assured me that there were no other secrets, but I felt it in my gut that something was amiss.

"Are you going to talk to me now?" he asked me with a pout.

"Esmeralda is going to make me plan our wedding when we return," I blurted out.

He looked at me like he was waiting for something else. "And?"

"What do you mean, 'and'? That's a big deal."

"Don't you girls usually plan out your wedding when you're young? I know my sisters did."

"Hello, raised on a pirate ship," I reminded him as I pointed at myself.

"Right..." he said with a frown.

"You're going to help me," I informed him.

He laughed. "Nope. That's the bride's job."

"And what, pray tell, is your job?" I grumbled.

"Showing up."

"Impossible. You're simply impossible."

He laughed at me and we finished our ride in silence, but this half was at least comfortable.

We neared the town and I was shocked to see they had planted several more fields of crops and there were more houses as well.

"Looks like the town has grown," Finn noted.

"I wonder if they gave your house away," I teased him.

"Your dad promised to leave it for us to use to visit them," he explained.

"I wonder how the old badger is doing," I said with a wide smile, talking about Sedgwick, the ship's doctor.

We urged the horses to trot, and rode into the center of town to find it bustling with activity. There had to be a hundred new faces walking around. It looked like a thriving port town now.

We tied the horses to a post outside the tavern and surveyed our surroundings. Most of it looked the same, but there were so many more people here.

"Tilia!" Cristoff yelled and lifted me into a spinning hug. "You're back!"

He set me down and I smiled at him. "I'm here for a bit, to visit."

He smirked and said, "How is it possible that you're even more beautiful than the last time I saw you?" He kissed my cheek and Finn cleared his throat. "Hey, Finn," Cristoff greeted him and shook hands.

"The town seems to be doing well," Finn noted.

Cristoff nodded. "Captain's done a helluva job setting everyone up for jobs and figuring out skills everyone is good at. We have visitors everyday coming to shop from us."

"Can it be?" Sedgwick asked behind me.

I spun around and threw my arms around him. "Sedgwick!"

He hugged me and then gripped my chin to look in my eyes. "Tilia, I'm so happy to see you."

"How've you been?" I asked him.

"Gettin' old, but I'm still alive." He touched my cheek and asked, "Something's happened to you. What's wrong?"

"Where's Dad?" I asked excitedly, ignoring his question.

Sedgwick took my hand and placed it on his bent elbow. "I'll show you the way, m'lady."

Finn walked behind us, saying his hellos to men he knew, and we made our way through the variety of people to a large building right by the docks. Sedgwick pushed open the door and I looked around the large room. It had several chairs around the perimeter of the room, two in the center in front of a large desk, and Dad's deck chair behind it. Dad looked up from the papers he had been signing and a smile split his face.

"My girl!" he boomed and walked around the desk to hug me tightly.

"Hi, Dad."

He held me at arm's length and continued to smile. "How are you?"

"Good. How are you?"

"Can't complain. Business is booming!"

"I saw," I agreed. "You've done an awesome job here."

He turned and shook hands with Finn. "How are you, Finn?"

"Good, Captain," Finn replied with a smile.

"Your house is still yours. We locked it up to keep people out, though. You'll have to find Bernard for the key."

Finn nodded and asked, "Tilia, are you okay staying with your dad while I go look for Bernard?"

"Yeah," I agreed.

He paused and looked at Cristoff, "Don't let her out of your sight."

Cristoff smirked. "You don't have to tell me twice."

"Finley!" I growled.

"No arguing. If I'm leaving, then Cristoff is staying with you. He can die and come back to life protecting you."

Finn left and I yelled at the now closed door.

"Everything alright?" Dad asked quietly.

I turned and stared at him in disbelief. "You don't know?"

I couldn't believe Esmeralda hadn't told him. I knew they hadn't told many people about the devices, because they didn't want to cause mass panic, but I thought she would have told my dad.

Cristoff sat in a chair by the door and Sedgwick sat in one of the chairs in front of Dad's desk.

"Don't know what?" Dad asked nervously.

"Sit," I said since I didn't want to see him throw a chair or something if he got mad about what happened.

He obeyed and waited for me to begin.

"After the tournament, Prince Marquez from Drimla, threatened to use a device on Crilan that would steal everyone's magic."

"That exists?" Cristoff asked, fear edging his words.

I swallowed and whispered, "Yes."

"What happened?" Sedgwick asked me.

"He said if I agreed to leave Finn for him, that he wouldn't use it. I went to him under that rouse, but was really going to steal the device and leave him. He must not have believed my act, because he activated the device while he was with me and in front of Finn and the King and Queen. I couldn't let him take their magic, so I teleported us to a small island not far from Crilan. It's uninhabited and far enough away that I hoped the device wouldn't reach our people."

I had started crying. I hadn't realized it until Sedgwick handed me a handkerchief.

"I tried to teleport myself away again, but he was a mage, too. I killed him, but I didn't have enough magic to return and..." I fell into the chair beside Sedgwick and sobbed, "It's gone. My magic is gone."

Sedgwick knelt in front of me and hugged me. "Child, I am so sorry."

"I feel so empty. I feel so—"

Sedgwick moved aside as my father sat on his knees to look at me. "I know this must be heart wrenching for you, Tilia.

You're a strong woman and when you were on our ship you did just fine without your magic. You'll do fine once you've adjusted to life without it again," he assured me.

Just hearing my dad's confidence in me made the pain lessen. If he had such faith in me, then why didn't I have it in myself? I was always sure of myself before this. And he was right, I survived fine without magic. I could figure it out again. I had known this was a possible consequence when I offered to go to Marquez. I had really hoped it wouldn't happen, but I had known going in.

"Did you find out if they had more devices?" Cristoff asked.

"They didn't have any more, but they were not the ones making them. They only purchased them. We still do not know who is making them, but Faxon is trying to find out."

Dad returned to his chair and leaned his chin on his fist. "We can do some searching for you as well. We still have connections out there and there's bound to be at least one rat who transported these who will talk. I'll send word to a few of my people and let you know if I hear anything useful."

"How much damage can one device do?" Cristoff asked.

I could understand why he would be worried about losing his powers especially. Without his power, he wouldn't regenerate his health and might stay dead.

"We aren't positive yet, but Faxon said that he believes if that device had gone off in the Capitol, all of Crilan would have been effected by it."

"The entire Kingdom?" Sedgwick asked, eyes wide.

"Come on, let's get you some food and something to drink," Cristoff offered and opened the door.

"We'll catch up with you once our daily duties are finished," Dad promised me.

I followed Cristoff out and he led me around the building and into a small alley.

"Cristoff, where are you—"

He crushed me to him in a hug that pushed all of the air out of my lungs. "You saved all of us and no one knows. If you hadn't sacrificed yourself, we all would have lost our magic."

I patted his back and was glad when he loosened the hug. "I know."

He looked down at me and the heat in his eyes was alarming. "I'm in your debt, Tilia. Whatever you need, you let me know."

"Cristoff, you don't owe me anything."

He shook his head adamantly. "I owe you a debt. I always repay my debts."

"Fine, I'll find some way to free you of your debt." I would make it stupid and simple so he wouldn't have to worry about it anymore.

"Tilia, you're too good for Finn," he whispered.

I rolled my eyes. "Cristoff—"

He stopped my protest by kissing me. I tried to jerk away, but he was holding me still.

As soon as the kiss started, it ended, but only because Cristoff was now being held against the wall beside me with a sword to his throat.

"Touch her like that again and you won't heal fast enough from the damage I inflict," Finn threatened him.

"Finn, don't. Cristoff knows better. He won't do it again, right, Cristoff?" I asked, trying to defuse the situation.

I still couldn't quite believe he had kissed me. I knew he liked me, but to kiss me when he knew I was engaged to Finn? What had gotten into him?

"You know you aren't good enough for her, Finn. You know that she deserves someone better. Someone who doesn't have the twisted past that you have," Cristoff growled.

So not helping things.

"Someone better, huh? Someone like you maybe?" Finn growled and dug his sword in enough to draw blood.

"That's enough," I ordered them. "Stop it right now. I don't know what got into you, Cristoff, but knock it off now."

"Do you even know about his past?" Cristoff asked, flicking his eyes towards me. "Did he tell you?"

He hadn't, but I wasn't going to admit that in front of Cristoff.

"Tell her, Finn. Tell her why you ran away from your Kingdom. Tell her why your half-brother hates you. Tell her why—"

"That's enough!" I yelled.

Cristoff stopped and looked away.

"Come on, Finn. I need to eat and so do you. Cristoff can take some time to cool off or sober up. Whatever it is that he needs to do," I ordered them.

Finn lowered his sword and took my outstretched hand. As we walked past Cristoff, Finn whispered something to him that made Cristoff clench his fists and jaw.

ᐧ I waited until we were out of the alley and several buildings away before asking, "What did you say to him?"

He looked at me, his face still a mask of fury, but didn't reply.

"What did you say?" I repeated.

"I told him to remember this the next time he thought it was a good idea to try to kiss you. And to remember whose bed you shared every night."

I rolled my eyes and sighed. Typical. He was still holding his sword and practically vibrated with anger.

"I'm sorry, Finn. I didn't—"

He shook his head. "It's not your fault. I told him to stay with you knowing that he wants you. It's my fault. I should have known better than to trust that dog."

I wanted to ask him about what Cristoff had said, but now probably wasn't the best time. We went into the tavern and

Finn's entire crew was there. I hugged and greeted everyone and they made room for Finn and me at a table.

"Hungry or thirsty?" Bernard asked.

"Both," I replied immediately.

"So, we hear that you got yourself engaged to some loser," Tristan said with a smirk.

"Yeah, we heard he's a real piece of work and that you felt bad for him so you agreed to it," Bernard agreed.

Finn normally would have taken their teasing in stride, but after our interaction with Cristoff, he couldn't take it. He slammed his fist on the table, knocked his chair over in his haste to get up, and went up to the bar top.

His men looked at him in disbelief and then at me.

"What was that about?" Tristan asked.

"Best not tease your former captain too much tonight," I informed them quietly. "He's in a foul mood."

"You need anything from us?" Tristan asked softly.

I shook my head. "He will cool off soon. In the meantime, why don't you boys update me on what I have missed since we were last here?"

The men told me story after story. I ate and drank while I listened to them and as the night turned to morning I still hadn't heard everything new. As my eyelids grew heavy I realized that Finn had never come back to sit with me.

"Bernard!" I called since I couldn't see him around all of the men.

He pushed his way through and crouched beside my chair. "Yes?"

"Where's Finn?"

He looked down a moment and said, "He said he needed some time alone. Told me if you wanted to go to sleep that I could take you to the house."

He'd left me alone? What could have made him so mad to leave me alone?

"Alright, I'm falling asleep in my chair," I admitted to everyone. I stood up quickly and immediately regretted it. Apparently, I'd had a few too many drinks. "Whoa."

Bernard picked me up and laughed. "I've got you."

"To the house!" I ordered him loudly.

The men laughed at me and I waved to them as we exited the building.

Once we were clear of the people near the tavern I asked, "Why is he so mad?"

Bernard shrugged. "I don't know what happened. He wouldn't tell me."

If Finn had not told Bernard, then I wouldn't tell him either. If Finn had wanted him to know, he would have told him.

"What do you know about his past?" I asked softly.

I knew that Cristoff had said all of that on purpose. He wanted to drive a wedge between us or make me doubt Finn. Or perhaps even make Finn doubt himself. Yet, I still had to know what he was talking about. We hadn't really discussed his past much and I wanted to know everything about Finn.

"He's had a strange life, Tilia. It's not my place to divulge the Captain's story. Plus, there are many things I do not know myself."

He was dodging the question, but it was better that I learned the entire truth from Finn anyway.

"My dad and Sedgwick never came to see me," I realized with shock.

"Rocco's mighty busy these days," Bernard told me. "I'm sure he was working until he fell asleep, and he'll be sorry to have missed spending time with you when he wakes up tomorrow."

It was unlike him to not even send a messenger to let me know that he wasn't coming or that he would be delayed.

I looked up at the stars overhead and wondered why Cristoff had acted the way he had. His harmless flirtations were one thing, but this was unlike him. Or so I had thought. I had to admit to myself that I hardly knew him.

"Here we are," Bernard said as he opened the door to the small house that Finn had built. Bernard deposited me onto the bed and pulled a few blankets up to cover me. "You going to be okay?" he asked.

"Yeah. Thanks, Bernard."

"You're welcome, Princess."

"If you see my dad will you let him know I went to bed?" I requested.

"Will do," he assured me and left, shutting the front door behind him.

It wasn't much later when I felt someone slide into bed beside me.

I rolled over and smiled at Finn. "Hi."

He brushed his lips across mine and pulled me closer so that he could wrap his arms all the way around me. "I love you, Tilia."

"I love you, too, Finn."

He exhaled and relaxed further. I didn't know if I should say something to him or ask where he went or if I should just leave him alone. I decided on leaving him alone and allowed myself to fall asleep.

Finn woke me up the next morning with a plate of food in his hands.

"How long have you been awake?" I asked him as I rubbed the sleep out of my eyes.

He shrugged. "I'm not sure. You didn't notice when I got out of bed, so I figured you were tired and needed to sleep. So, I went and cooked you some food."

I ate a few bites of the eggs he had brought and then asked, "Are you ready to talk today?"

He clenched his jaw and then nodded. "Yes, it is time that I told you everything, even if I had hoped never to discuss this."

I finished my food and set the plate on the side table. Finn adjusted himself on the bed and took a deep breath. My heart rate increased as I prepared to hear what he had to say, not knowing what I was in for.

"Where I'm from, magic is part of our everyday lives. Everyone has magic there, not like here where some don't have it. Our speed is not magic, we are all descendants of the God of the Sea, and we are all born with the ability. No one leaves. No one *can* leave. The ruler there is a tyrant. He forbids anyone from leaving the land, makes his people create whatever he wants, not what we need. He has no queen and instead chooses to have a harem of women. These women don't choose this life. He takes whoever he wants, even if they're already married or engaged or single. He doesn't care. If he sees a woman and he wants her, she becomes his. There have been rebellions, but he quickly stamps them out. His soldiers are brain washed into believing that he's the rightful ruler and that he is the reason the land is so prosperous. They think that he is our god's chosen one.

"He doesn't allow his harem to conceive children because he believes that the children would try to rise up against him. He requires the women to drink a special potion that he brews himself to ensure that they remain sterile. Once he decides a woman is too old for him, or grows tired of her, he gives her to his soldiers. When I was six years old, he took a girl from our town. She wasn't more than twelve and her parents fought against him. My father was one of his soldiers and I watched as he slaughtered the parents of this girl without so much as an ounce of remorse. I decided then that I would leave that place. I didn't care how or where I ended up. Anything would be better than there."

He paused and rubbed his temples. I sat still, letting him collect himself so that he could continue. So much already explained why he would want to leave and join the pirates.

"The day I was set to escape, one of my sisters was outside with me and the King saw her. He tried to take her and I fought back. My own father came and tried to stop *me*! He didn't care that the King was taking his daughter. He didn't care what would happen to her. I refused to let it happen to her. I killed my father and gravely wounded the King, but not before the King killed my sister. I ran while the King was down, and I never went back."

Now I was confused. Why did this make him a bad person? Why would Cristoff think that I would view him differently? He tried to protect his sister. That wasn't a bad thing.

"Finn," I whispered. "I am so glad that you escaped."

He looked up at me in disbelief. "You don't think I'm terrible?"

"You tried to save your sister. There's nothing wrong with that."

"I got her killed."

"It was better that she died while you tried to protect her, than her living a life being raped by a man that she hated."

"I killed my own father."

"Do you really think that you shouldn't have killed him? Do you think there was a way around that?"

He shook his head. "I wish there had been."

I hugged him and kissed his cheek. "You shouldn't be ashamed of your past. Anyone would agree that what you did was right. Do you think Jared would have acted differently than you?"

"I should have stayed and killed the King."

"His soldiers would have killed you. If they were as blind as you say, there was no hope for them."

He hugged me and whispered, "You have no idea how glad I am that you don't think I'm a terrible person."

"I honestly do not understand why Cristoff would think that I would think differently of you for this. If anything, it just proves how good of a man you are."

"You truly are amazing," he whispered. "And Cristoff was right about one thing. You are too good for me."

"Don't be ridiculous. You're perfect for me."

Someone knocked on the door three times rapidly. Finn and I looked at each other a moment and then he leapt up and opened it.

Bernard looked at me and said, "It's your father."

I was instantly glad that I had slept in my clothes and shoes as I ran out after him. "What happened?"

"I'm not completely sure. I heard he fell in the warehouse and some boxes fell on top of him, but others are saying it's his heart. I don't know."

"Where's he at?" Finn asked Bernard.

"His office," he answered.

Finn scooped me up and the wind pressed against me as he ran to the office and inside. Everyone spun around at our sudden appearance, but once they saw who it was, they all turned back to watch as Sedgwick worked on Dad.

I walked forward and stood next to them. Dad's face was pale and he looked like he was barely breathing. Blood had pooled on the ground beneath his desk where he was lying.

"What happened?" I asked Sedgwick quietly.

"Heart attack and then he got buried by boxes," he replied without taking his hands off of Dad and using his magic.

"Will he be alright?"

"I'm trying, Tilia. I can heal most of him, but I don't know if I can repair his heart."

I bit my lip to keep from crying and Finn pulled me into his arms. The room was beginning to fill up and while we normally would run everyone out, nobody bothered. We stood in tense silence as Sedgwick worked and hoped for the best.

Faxon! Faxon could heal him. I reached towards my right ring finger and frowned. What was I doing? I couldn't contact him. What was wrong with me?

"Finn," I whispered since it felt like we shouldn't talk loudly. "Can you get Faxon?" He was fast, but I didn't know how long it would take him to get to Faxon. I knew Faxon could teleport once he was with him back though.

Finn kissed the top of my head and disappeared.

"Where is he going?" Cristoff asked me.

"To get Faxon," I answered without taking my eyes off Dad.

How could this have happened? He wasn't that old. He should be healthy.

Time passed slowly, like walking through mud. I sat down in a nearby chair and gripped the arms.

Dad's body began shaking and Sedgwick growled.

Faxon appeared beside me with Finn and immediately walked to Sedgwick. "Prognosis?"

"Heart attack, crushed by boxes. I've been healing his body, but I don't know anything about the heart," Sedgwick admitted to him.

"Finn," Faxon ordered, "take Tilia out of here."

"No, I want to stay and—"

Finn took my arm and pulled me up. "Come on. Faxon will take care of your dad."

I obeyed only because I knew he was right. If Faxon couldn't save him, there was nothing more for us to do.

We walked outside and I kicked a rock as hard as I could. "Ah!" I yelled. "I hate being helpless!"

"We're all helpless here," Finn told me.

I stomped around. I needed to move or I would explode.

"I could have learned healing though. I could have been as good of a healer as Faxon. I should have listened to you. I shouldn't have thought I was strong enough to defeat Marquez."

"You did defeat him," Finn reminded me.

"I should have listened and I didn't. I was too focused on keeping you out of harm's way."

Finn stopped walking and looked at me in shock. "What?"

"I knew that you would volunteer to do it because of your speed. I couldn't let him hurt you. I would rather lose my power a thousand times than have you killed," I admitted to him.

"Tilia," he whispered. "I can't believe—"

"I knew the possibilities when I volunteered. But here I am, still complaining. I saved everyone and I know I should be happy for it, but I'm not. I lost my most valuable asset."

"While your magic is impressive, your fighting skill is definitely your most valuable asset," Finn assured me.

"I'm a selfish woman and I can't stand myself. I need to find the person who is responsible for building these devices and kill them."

"We will," he promised.

"Are you sure that you won't reconsider staying here while Faxon and I go to Judby?" I asked him.

"No. I am going and nothing you say will change my mind on that."

"If something happens to you—"

He gripped my chin lightly and met my eyes. "Tilia, we are better together. If something happens to you and I am not there, how do you think I will feel? We can accomplish so much more if we stay together."

He was right. I knew it. And yet I wanted him to stay behind. To stay safe.

"Would you like to spar? It might take your mind off things while Faxon helps your father?" Finn asked softly.

I nodded. Fighting was a good idea and Finn was fast enough that I knew I wouldn't be able to hurt him. He led me to the arena that they used for fighting and unbuckled his belt with his sword and tossed it aside.

"Hand to hand," he told me. "You've been slacking on it and you need to step up your game to make sure that if you're disarmed, you can still protect yourself."

I set the Dragon's Tooth on the ground beside his sword and faced him.

"Don't let me hurt you," I ordered him.

He nodded and held his fists up. I released the pain I had felt since losing my magic, the anger at myself for being naïve and stupid, the fear over it all. I released it all and let my body act on instinct. Life moved on whether I wanted it to or not. I couldn't dwell on things. No matter what I wanted or what I thought that I should have done, none of it mattered to the rest of the world. The bastard who was creating and selling the devices was still doing it. The people who were purchasing and using these devices were still out there. I had to cleanse myself of my failures. I had to cleanse myself of the feelings and regret. I had to focus on what lay ahead and what I needed to do. I couldn't become a good queen if I dwelled on the past. Like Esmeralda had said, "There are some things that are just meant to stay in the past".

Finn blocked all of my attacks, but I felt the fractured pieces of my life, of my soul, sealing together again. I wasn't perfect. I wasn't necessarily good, but I was me. I had to be the best me that I could be. I had to be the best soon to be wife for Finn. I had to be the best princess for Crilan. I had to be the best that I could to ensure the safety of my family and my people.

I gasped for breath and held up a hand to Finn. "Break," I begged.

He nodded, disappeared, and then returned with water. "Here."

I drank the water greedily and took deep breaths.

"How do you feel?" he asked me.

"Better," I admitted.

"Tilia," Faxon called from outside the arena, "your father is asking for you."

I jogged out of the arena and followed Faxon into the office. Dad lay on the table, but his skin wasn't as flushed as it had been.

He smiled weakly at me. "My girl, there you are."

"I'm here," I said and took his giant hand with both of mine. Somehow the size of his hands hadn't seemed to change as I grew older.

"He's going to live," Faxon informed me. "But he's going to have to take it easy. His heart isn't as strong as it used to be and he can't pretend to be a young man anymore."

"It's terrible getting old," Dad complained.

"He's going to be on bed rest for a week minimum and after that he's going to have to use a wheelchair to get around. The heart attack has weakened him," Faxon explained.

"But he's going to live?" I asked.

"Yes, he will live," Faxon said and rested his hand on my shoulder.

"Men, let's go. We've got to take the Captain to his house," Sedgwick ordered.

Several of the men gathered to carry Dad. Faxon and I moved out of the way to give them enough room. Dad wasn't a small man and it was no easy task taking him to his house at the other end of town.

Faxon waited until they had all left before wiping a stray tear. "I'm sorry that I couldn't do more," he said. "But there are some things that even mages cannot heal."

I threw my arms around him and hugged him tightly. "Thank you. You saved him."

He hugged me back and whispered, "Of course. I only wish I could have done more."

"You've done your best," I countered. "That's all that I can ask of you. You didn't even have to come."

"Of course I did," he snapped. "I told you that I would do almost anything for you."

"You do too much for me," I whispered back.

"If I had to save your life every day until my last breath, it wouldn't be too much. You saved me and saved my magic. It only seems fair that I would use my magic for you in any way possible."

"Are you going to go back now?" I asked him instead of commenting on his statement. It seemed insane to me that he was so devoted to me when two years ago, he didn't even speak to me.

"Yes, but if you need me just..." he paused and then added, "...just have Finn get me."

"Thank you again," I said as I stepped back.

"Stop it. No more thanking me for doing what I should be doing. Now, go find someplace to relax and take your mind off of everything," he ordered me.

"Yes, sir."

He smiled and then disappeared.

Finn was waiting outside for me and asked, "Did Faxon leave?"

I nodded. "He went back home. Thank you, Finn. If you hadn't gotten Faxon, Dad might not have survived."

He kissed my cheek and led me towards the tavern. "Faxon told me that he wants to leave for Judby in a few days. Are you up to leaving so soon?"

I wanted to stay with my dad, but he was likely to refuse to be mothered. Plus, he had plenty of people here to worry over him.

"Sure," I said, "The sooner we find the person making these devices, the better for the world."

"Agreed."

We ate and drank with our pirate family and I felt almost normal again.

4

SINCE OUR VACATION HAD NOT GONE AS PLANNED, IT DIDN'T bother me too much that we ended it early.

Jared was waiting outside when we arrived at the barn and dismounted. I thought maybe I was in trouble for something, but he nodded at Finn and said, "We need to talk."

Finn kissed my cheek as he walked by, and followed Jared into the castle.

I took my time brushing Duke down and then Twist, since Finn was busy. After I put their tack away, I fed them each two carrots and an apple, which they both appreciated.

"What could that be about?" I wondered aloud.

"Maybe he is challenging him to another duel since he lost the last one," Natalie said.

I spun around and wrapped her in a tight hug. "I've missed you!"

She hugged me back and said, "I've missed you as well. You never seem to have time to visit the fields anymore."

She pouted at me and I tugged her hand. "Come to my room. I have a gift for you."

"Is it that handsome man you went on that trip with?"

She was talking about Eric.

I laughed loudly. "No."

"Dang."

Natalie followed me inside, giggling about her crush on Eric, but we both clammed up when we stepped inside and Eric was there talking with Esmeralda.

"Hello, Natalie," Esmeralda greeted her. "It's been awhile since I've seen you."

Natalie curtsied. "Afternoon, Your Majesty."

"Natalie this is Eric. Eric, this is Tilia's friend, Natalie." Esmeralda introduced them.

Eric took Natalie's hand and kissed the back of it. "It's a pleasure to see you again, Natalie."

She curtsied and said, "I'm honored that you remember me."

Esmeralda winked at me, and I held in my laugh. She must have figured out that Natalie liked Eric.

"I'm taking Natalie up to get the souvenir I have for her," I explained.

"You should stay and join us for dinner," Esmeralda offered to Natalie.

"Thank you. I would love to," Natalie agreed.

I took her hand again and dragged her away from Eric and up the stairs to my room.

She flopped backwards onto my bed and sighed loudly. "I can die happy now."

I laughed at her and took out the gift I had, which was inside a small box.

She sat up and opened the box I handed her. Her eyes widened and she gasped, "I can't take this."

I took out the pearl necklace I had made while sailing with Finn and put it on her. "I found these pearls on an island and made this just for you."

"It's gorgeous!" she touched it gingerly like it might break.

"I'm glad that you like it."

"Like it? I love it!" she yelled and hugged me tightly.

"Well, hopefully you will forgive me for my long absences. I am leaving tomorrow on another mission and I do not know how long I will be gone this time."

"Have you started planning your wedding?" she asked.

"No, I have not had time."

"You are as bad as the King," she teased me.

I sat on the edge of my bed and said, "Does it make me a bad person to be excited and terrified about getting married at the same time?"

She sat next to me and patted my leg. "I believe many women feel that way. At least you are a royal in Crilan, where you get to choose your suitor."

Something about the way she said that made me turn to her.

"What do you mean?" I asked softly.

She shrugged. "There are other Kingdoms that make their royalty marry a royal from another Kingdom for treaties or whatever other stupid political reasons there are. And a few where father's basically sell their daughters to the highest bidder."

I had heard of arranged marriages for royalty, but not the latter one.

"Where do they sell their daughters?" I asked.

"I don't remember, but I know it happens," she said and then plastered a great big smile on her face. "Can we go watch the recruits training?"

She loved to watch people fighting and sparring, but refused to let me teach her to fight.

"Sure," I agreed.

We skipped down the stairs smiling the whole time, but I couldn't forget what she had said. Did that happen in Crilan? I thought I had heard them discussing a law banning that, but I didn't pay too much attention to their political discussions. I would have to ask Esmeralda later.

The arena was filled with the sounds of clashing swords and I felt my heart speed up at the thought of fighting. I needed to find more time for practicing, especially now that Faxon didn't need me for magic lessons anymore.

After we found our seats atop the fence of the arena, I looked out over the new recruits. Half of this batch were women, which was abnormal, but a nice surprise.

Today I was shocked to discover that Riley was instructing them. Why was he here?

He walked over to me and bowed. "Princess."

"Hello, Riley," I greeted him with a smile.

"How are you this day?" he asked. He was smiling, but I could see the edges of his eyes were pinched. What had happened between us? He said he had helped me, but I didn't remember anything about it.

"I'm well. Commander Riley, this is my friend Natalie."

He bowed to her. "A pleasure to meet the Princess's friend."

"There are quite a few women in this batch," I commented.

He turned and surveyed the recruits who were sparring with a sword and shield. "Yes, it seems that many have been inspired by the feats of the Queen and the Princess," he told me without turning around to face me.

"I hardly think I've accomplished feats," I mumbled. No one knew about me killing Marquez and saving the Kingdom.

"You claimed a Kingdom," one of the women in the arena said, stopping her sparring to look at me. She was tall, thin, and had amazingly thick black hair.

"Oh, that. Right," I said with a grimace. I had forgotten about killing what had been left of Trian's royal family after they tried to kill us with chimeras.

"And you cut the King," another girl, this one short and petite with two silver earrings in her left ear.

"That she did, but she hasn't defeated me yet," Jared said as he entered the arena. Everyone bowed to him and he waved them up. "No need to bow."

"I may not have defeated you, but my fiancé has," I teased him.

He turned and glared at me. "You are not him. Now, hop down here," he ordered me.

"Kick his butt," Natalie cheered as I walked towards him.

Riley took my spot on the fence next to Natalie and began whispering to her. What was he talking to her about?

"Recruits, take a break," Riley ordered them.

"So, what will my lesson be today?" I asked Jared as I stretched out my legs and arms.

He walked around the arena, looking at the sand and then at the recruits. He stopped when he came back around to me and asked, "What do you struggle with the most?"

Not having magic.

I didn't really have something I struggled with aside from specific weapons. "I guess certain weapons," I admitted.

"She's never used an ax," Finn told Jared from the fence.

I hadn't seen him arrive, but if he had been moving fast, then that was not surprising.

"Axes, huh?" Jared asked.

"And spears," I said.

"She's also terrible with bows and arrows," Natalie told them.

I turned and gaped at her. "Hey!"

She shrugged. "You are."

"Good, okay. Well, I think your new lessons will be to learn how to use these weapons to their fullest capabilities," Jared said.

"And my lesson today?" I asked. He hadn't brought me out here to talk. I knew Jared. He wanted to fight and I had a feeling that he didn't want to fight Finn right now.

"No lesson, just sparring," he said with a shake of his head.

I drew the Dragon's Tooth and waited for him. He drew his sword and bowed to me. I returned the bow and then stood at the ready. He was fast, not as fast as Finn, but faster than me. If I had any hope of defeating him I would have to watch for his tell, the movement that gave away his next move.

"No holding back," he ordered me.

"Never," I agreed.

He rushed me and I blocked his strike with my sword and danced away before his leg could connect with my shin. He smiled and I lunged forward, extending the Dragon's Tooth as far as I could. He deflected it easily, but it gave me a chance to move closer and invade his personal space. I punched his stomach, but he expected it and tightened his stomach muscles to absorb the blow. He swung at my head with an open palm and I ducked down, too late, I realized that he was forcing me low so he could kick me. His knee clipped my jaw as I rolled away from him and up to my feet.

"You've gotten faster," he complimented me.

"Sparring with Finn does that," I replied.

Jared attacked and the speed and number of hits forced me to release my mind and free my body. It felt like time slowed as we hit, blocked, and struck each other again and again. There was nothing, but Jared and I and the sound of our fighting and breathing. It felt like an eternity had past and yet only a matter of seconds at the same time.

Jared's fist connected with my jaw at the same time that my heel hit his shin, which made his hit weaker. It still hurt, and I stumbled back a step before resuming our fight. I didn't know if the recruits were talking, or if Natalie was cheering, or whether Finn was still there or not, but I didn't care. I loved this!

Sweat dripped down my back and gathered beneath my hairline. I felt more alive in these moments than I had since Marquez' attack. I smiled at Jared and he returned my smile, knowing that we shared a love for this adrenaline and ecstasy.

Faster than I wanted, I felt my body slowing. My breathing was rapid and my heart was pounding faster than normal. I felt dizzy and lightheaded. What was wrong with me?

I stumbled forward and Jared stopped his punch in the nick of time, almost smashing my nose with his fist. "Tilia?" he asked with concern.

"Submit," I told him and tried to smile.

"You've really improved," he told me proudly.

"Thanks," I whispered as I headed towards the edge of the ring.

"That was amazing," Riley commented. "You're incredible, Princess."

I wanted to respond to him, but my focus was wavering. The dizziness made the fence swirl around in front of me and I wasn't sure where the ground was anymore.

I tried to take deep breaths to ease the feeling. I tried to focus on Jared in front of me to assure myself that I was not actually spinning in circles. Nothing worked. I gasped for air, but my lungs felt as though they had shrunk.

"Faxon!" Jared yelled loudly.

Finn grabbed my shoulders to keep me upright, but his touched burned and I screamed in pain.

Faxon appeared in front of me, but his face changed and he didn't look like Faxon. His face was different and his eyes were the color of cognac. He said something, but I didn't hear him. My body felt like it was on fire inside and out.

"Tilia!" Natalie yelled fearfully.

Faxon, but not Faxon, reached for me and the fear consumed me. I felt my eyes roll up into the back of my head and then I felt nothing.

I DREAMED about the cognac-eyed man. We were in a stairway in Drimla and he was whispering to me. He told me he would see me soon and I wouldn't have Faxon to save me. He touched me and put something in my head. Who was he? Why was I dreaming about this man?

The dream dissipated, but I still could not wake up. What had happened to me? Had this man put something in my head?

I dreamed about Finn and watched him fight Carlos the Crusher again. I felt warm hands on my face, but it wasn't Finn. The dream changed to one about Faxon. He was bowing to me and asking for forgiveness for failing me. Then, he had me pinned on a bed on the ship we sailed on when we attacked Drimla. "He will pay for the pain he caused you. You mean too much to me. I love you." He took a ring from my finger and then the dream shattered.

I woke up gasping for breath and looked at my naked hand. I remembered now. He had given me a ring for my birthday, one that let me communicate with him. Where was it? Was the dream real? Had he taken it from me?

I looked around and got my bearings. I was in the healing room. Finn was asleep in a chair next to the bed I was on, snoring softly. Had he stayed with me while I was unconscious?

Faxon was on the other side of my bed, sleeping in a chair as well. He looked incredibly peaceful as he slept. I wished that he could look this way more often. He had so much to deal with and it wasn't fair to him. I reached out towards him, but when I touched his hand, something shocked me.

"Ow!" I yelped.

He opened his eyes and I sighed with relief that they were not cognac eyes. "You're awake," he whispered.

"How long was I out?" I asked softly, trying not to wake Finn.

"A week," he whispered. He stood and waved his hand from my head to my feet as he examined me with his magic. "Everything appears normal again."

"Faxon," I whispered. "Why did you erase my memory?"

He froze and I couldn't tell if he was even breathing. "What?"

"I dreamed about *him* and you. I saw you take the ring and use a spell to erase my memory."

"It was the easiest way to protect you," he told me.

"Why did you take my ring?" I asked.

"To protect you."

"From what?"

"From him."

"Who is he?"

"We don't talk about him," he told me. "Just know that he is a dangerous man from my past."

"How does taking the ring protect me?" He wasn't making any sense.

"As a Seer, I have several abilities. One of which is being able to sense who created an object, like the ring. He knew you were special to me because he knew that I had made that ring for you. If you hadn't had the ring, he would never have known."

"He said he was going to *play* with me even before he used his power to look at me. He was going to hurt me before he even knew you were there," I assured him.

"He hurt you and used that spell on you because he discovered I made you that ring. If you had not been wearing it, then he would have toyed with you, but not to that extent. He wanted to hurt me by making you terrified of me."

"You fixed me," I reminded him.

"Only because I was able to remove your memory and in the process remove the thing he planted in you."

"The thing in my head?" I guessed.

"How'd you know that?" he asked me.

"I dreamed about there being something in my head."

He narrowed his eyes at me and then the tickling sensation covered me as he looked at me with his power.

"What are you doing?" I asked him nervously, and tried not to squirm.

"You shouldn't have been able to see that. Normally that's only something people with powers like mine can do."

"I don't have magic, remember?" I growled at him.

"Are you mad at me?" he asked after he stopped his inspection.

"A little, but you did what you thought was best and I'm glad that I hadn't continued to be scared of you and Esmeralda."

"I'm sorry, Tilia."

"Can I have my ring back?" I asked him.

He shook his head. "It doesn't work without your magic."

"I was afraid of that," I admitted to him with a sigh.

He hugged me tightly and whispered, "I am so sorry."

"Stop apologizing. You didn't do this, he did. By the way, why did I have that weird attack?"

"He had another small piece in your head that I didn't see the first time."

"Are there any more?" I asked and held my breath for the answer.

He shook his head. "No, I thoroughly inspected you, as did Esmeralda."

"Do I still get to go to Judby with you?" I asked softly.

He laughed and kissed my cheek as he stepped back. "Yes."

"What's going on?" Finn asked as he woke up. He stretched with his eyes closed, but once they opened and he saw me, he leapt up out of the chair and hugged me tightly. "Are you okay?"

"I'm perfect," I assured him.

"I was terrified," he whispered. "I couldn't do anything and you..."

I patted his back and whispered, "I'm fine, Finn. All better."

"I'm going to go update Esmeralda and Jared. They're out doing drills with the new recruits," Faxon informed us as he walked towards the exit. "I'm glad that you're better."

"Thank you," I told him sincerely.

He bowed and then left.

"Something is different about him," Finn whispered to me.

"He's afraid," I realized softly. "He never got close to anyone, aside from Esmeralda and Jared, and he's realized that even with all of his powers, something still happened to me that was out of his control. He doesn't like it. He is afraid that he won't be able to protect me again or that I'll be killed by his enemy."

"What enemy?" Finn asked and picked me up. He carried me out of the room and down the hallway towards the stairs and to my bedroom.

"I don't know. He was the one who attacked us in Drimla. Faxon knows him, but he won't tell me how."

"Are you really okay?" he asked and looked at me with eyes full of concern.

I set my hand on his cheek and said, "I am. I feel better than ever."

He pushed open my door and then kicked it closed behind him. "You scared me," he snarled and kissed me.

I leaned back from the kiss and said, "It wasn't exactly a picnic for me either."

He tossed me on the bed and then pinned me with my hands above my head and his legs on the outside of mine. "You slept for an entire week," he told me. "I think you were faking it."

I knew he was teasing me and I smirked at him. "Maybe I just needed some time away from you."

His mouth popped open and he yelled, "That's it!" He lifted the hand that wasn't holding my wrists and wiggled his fingers.

"No!" I yelled. "No tickling!"

He lowered his hand and immediately began tickling my sides and stomach.

"Ah!" I squealed and struggled to escape his grip. "Stop!" I begged between laughs and gulped for air.

"Surrender," he ordered me.

"Never!" I yelled and he increased his tickling.

I was laughing so hard that I was crying now and gasping for breath.

He stopped his assault, hand raised above me, and wiggled his fingers. "Surrender?"

"Compromise," I said. "A kiss and no more tickling."

He leaned forward slowly and barely brushed his lips across mine. He sat back up and said, "Nah!" and resumed tickling me.

"Finn!" I yelled.

"Say it!" he ordered me.

"You're a butt!" I yelled between laughs.

He continued his attack and I finally could not take it anymore.

"I surrender," I said.

He stopped and I stared up at his smiling face with a smile of my own. Even with everything that happened, he still found time to make me laugh and smile.

"You're amazing," I told him.

"You're stunning," he replied and kissed each side of my neck.

I pulled him down so that he was lying flat on top of me and then rolled until I was sitting on top of him and he was on his back. His eyes sparked with mischief and heat, but I used his vulnerability to grab his ribs and start tickling him.

"Cheater!" he bellowed and squirmed under me.

"Say it!" I ordered him as I continued to tickle him.

In all reality, he could get out from under me easily, but I appreciated him not using his speed.

He grabbed my wrists and pulled me down until my face was just above his. My hair surrounded our faces like a curtain, hiding us and making this all the more private and intimate.

"You're mine," he whispered. "And I won't ever let you get away."

My heart fluttered in my chest and warmth spread throughout my body. I kissed him deeply and he responded in kind and sat up with me in his lap. I slipped my hands up beneath his shirt and ran my fingertips across his warm flesh, enjoying the way his muscle felt beneath my hand. He pulled his shirt off and I kissed his bare shoulders and chest. He slid his hands beneath my shirt, gripping my back and stroking up and down my sides. At least twice on our sailing adventures, I had been forced to strip in front of him, but both times had been out of necessity.

I climbed off of the bed despite his protests, and slowly lifted my shirt over my head. He watched me intently and when I dropped the shirt, he walked to me, his muscles flexing as he moved, and stared down at me in silence.

He untied my pants and slid his hands beneath the waist-band and pushed them down. I stepped out of them and he moved back, his eyes roving over my body slowly.

A slow predatory smile spread across his face and he whispered, "You are perfect in every way imaginable."

The blush that had begun to warm from his silent stare disappeared as he kissed me and pressed our naked chests together. He was incredibly warm and I felt petite when he held me like this. I reached down to untie his pants, but he took my hand and lifted it to kiss my palm.

"No," he whispered.

"Finn," I complained.

He lifted me up so that I had to wrap my legs around his waist as he kissed me and walked to my bed. He lay me down and kissed every inch of my body, even making me turn over so he could kiss his way from my shoulders to my toes.

He rolled me back over and said, "There's no need to rush things. We have a very long time together."

I opened my mouth to tell him I knew that, but he flicked his tongue out at the same time that he used his hand lower and it tore a gasp from me instead of words. I arched my back as pleasure swept through me and he didn't stop.

I thought I knew what pleasure was until he scooted down. I gripped the sheets of the bed and moaned softly. Pressure had begun building since he had begun and right when I was sure that I couldn't take it any longer, the pressured spilled over.

"Finn," I whispered breathlessly.

He smiled at me and said, "This is nothing compared to what our wedding night will be like."

He pulled the blankets up over us and wrapped himself around me while I tried to remember how to talk.

"Can we get married tomorrow?" I asked finally.

He laughed and squeezed me. "Good things come to those who wait."

I didn't want to wait.

5

Esmeralda made us wait two more days before she agreed that I was fully recovered, and reluctantly allowed us to leave for Judby.

Faxon tried unsuccessfully to convince Finn to stay behind once more. Finn refused and we set sail at dawn the next day. Finn and I ran around the ship, happy to be sailing again and climbed up and down and around everything.

Faxon watched us with silent amusement.

Our disguises were surprisingly non-magical and even more surprisingly, fairly convincing. Most people didn't know what we looked like anyway, but these disguises definitely helped. I had to leave the Dragon's Tooth behind because the sword was just too recognizable. I knew that, but I felt bad for leaving it sitting in my room. The replacement was a good blade, but it just wasn't the Dragon's Tooth.

"She's pouting again," Faxon commented.

Finn stopped the carving he was working on and looked at me. "Why?"

"I miss my sword," I admitted with a sigh and plopped down on the deck next to the barrel Finn was sitting on.

"I'm sure the sword will be perfectly fine while you are gone and no doubt will be right where you left it when you get back," Finn assured me.

"I know."

Finn had a new pair of axes, their wooden handles were wrapped with leather and the heads shone in the sun. Jared had made them by hand for Finn and presented them to him right before we left. Finn looked like he had been given an island, he was so happy.

"What are you carving?" I asked Finn, tilting my head back to look up at him.

"You will see it when I am finished," he chastised me.

It was only the fifth time that I had asked him.

"Sounds like you need to do some meditation," Faxon told me.

I sighed, more than anything irritated that he still made me meditate when I didn't have my magic anymore, but I obeyed.

I scooted my butt forward so that I wasn't touching Finn or the barrel, and set my linked hands in my lap. I closed my eyes, inhaled and exhaled, and relaxed everything. The sounds of the ocean and our ship grew louder, sharper, and I began to separate each sound, focusing on the sound of Finn cutting into the wood in his hand, the sound of Faxon's breathing, and the sound of the ship cutting through the water. I turned my focus inward, searching for any speck of a spark that could still be there...

Nothing.

Despite my frustration and sadness, I let the feelings wash away and reminded myself that I had saved Faxon and Esmeralda. I had done something many would never have done. Peace spread through me and I relaxed.

After a few more moments, I stood up and stretched.

Faxon nodded approvingly. "Good."

"How many Seers are there in the world?" I asked him.

"As far as we know, three. Me, my enemy, and Eric."

"Eric?" Finn yelled in shock.

Faxon nodded. "I thought you would have known that."

"That's why he said that he could see through my disguise and see what I looked like. I thought it was just an ability, but it makes sense that he would be a Seer to be able to do that," I commented.

"He still has a lot to learn, but he refuses to work with me. He thinks he should focus on the King's Steel instead of working on his magic."

"He would be able to help the King's Steel better if he could use more of his magic," I said.

"I've been trying to tell him that, but he won't listen to me. Maybe he will listen to you."

"Doubtful. He has been keeping me at arm's length and refusing to talk to me," I admitted.

"Ah," Faxon said and looked at the pebble he was holding.

"Oh," Finn said after he stopped his carving. "You didn't tell me that."

I shrugged. "I didn't know I was supposed to."

"Tilia, he would only be doing that if he was interested in you," Finn told me.

"I don't think that is it," I argued. "It has something to do with his return to the King's Steel. Something happened that he is not happy with."

"He doesn't like knowing that Finn is higher rank than him and can give him orders," Faxon informed me.

"Do you know that for a fact? Or are you just guessing?"

"You can think what you want, but men are pretty similar and we are pretty easy to understand," Faxon told me.

"He's right. You haven't noticed, but he does not like seeing us together. He almost always finds a convenient excuse to leave when you and I are in the same room," Finn said.

"When we went on that trip to Blith we went over the fact that he and I are just friends. And that was when I was not with you, Finn."

Finn cringed at the reminder.

"Perhaps he, as your friend, saw how upset you were over Finn and grew to dislike him on your behalf. If you had not needed me to treat you and look after you when you came home that night, I might not have been able to stop myself from finding Finn and disintegrating him," Faxon told me.

Finn looked at Faxon in shock and then at me. "Why did he have to treat you?"

I looked away and pretended to be mesmerized by a cloud passing by overhead.

"She walked through a storm to the castle and was drenched when she arrived," Faxon informed him. "Had I not healed her, she would have become sick and her fever would have gotten worse. If I had still been with Jared and Esmeralda she could have died."

"Died?" Finn asked. "Are you serious?"

"Why would I joke about her death?" Faxon snarled at him.

Finn looked at me and I shrugged. "I told you that I could die on land. Besides, nothing happened. Faxon was there and he took care of me."

He shook his head in disbelief and went back to his carving. He kept carving it from different sides so I had no idea what he was working on.

"How much longer until we get to Judby?" I asked Faxon.

"Probably a day and a half," he answered.

"Why couldn't we teleport again?" I grumbled.

"Because I could teleport us right in front of someone important or someone who could report it to others and then we would get caught," Faxon said.

"You would not let them catch us," I replied with a roll of my eyes.

"No, but still."

"I think he just wanted to escape Esmeralda," Finn teased him.

"Why?" I asked curiously.

"She's been making him go through all of those boxes of papers even though we have someone assigned to it who has the ability to read faster than normal."

"It's torture!" Faxon yelled.

"Has any more information come up?"

"Nope. Most of the stuff we found was regarding their experiments with trying to crossbreed animals. I don't know why they were so focused on trying to create new animals, but that was a majority of their work," Finn answered.

"Creepy," I mumbled.

"You don't know the half of it!" Faxon yelled. "They were trying to cross a crocodile with a horse! What on earth would that be useful for?"

"Well, if it had a horse's body and the crocodile's leathery skin, it would make them harder to injure in battles. Or if they could figure out how to give them the long breathes of a crocodile they could have horses with riders under the water waiting to attack people," I guessed.

"Tilia," Faxon said in shock. "I'm going to tell Esmeralda that you should look at the notes."

"No!" I said loudly. "You are not tossing the burden off on me."

He waved his hand dismissively. "That's not what I am trying to do. Maybe you can see a connection that I cannot. I had not even considered what you just said."

"I don't want to be bored and read a bunch of creepy notes," I whined.

"If you could discover what they were up to though..."

Faxon didn't need to finish his statement. I understood what he was trying to say.

"I will try it for one day and then decide if I will keep doing it or not," I said, giving in.

He smiled. "Wonderful."

"I'm not helping you," Finn told me.

"I didn't ask you."

"You would just distract her anyways," Faxon said.

Finn swiveled his eyes towards me and gave me a smirk. Smug jerk. I would not admit it to him, but just that look made me warm and want to lock ourselves in a room for a week without any distractions.

I hurried away from him before Faxon noticed my change in attitude and leaned against the rail. The water was cold and dark through here. If someone could hold their breath and create a light that water wouldn't extinguish, they could go to the bottom of the ocean. What was down there? Were there strange animals? Or was it just littered with sunken ships and skeletons of drowned sailors?

"Has anyone ever gone to the ocean floor?" I asked Faxon.

"What do you mean?" he asked, clearly confused by my topic shift.

"I know that you can create a light source that water does not extinguish."

He nodded.

"And I have heard that people can make a bubble of air stay around their heads while they are underwater."

He nodded again.

"So, has anyone used that to go to the bottom of the ocean to explore the floor?"

"I tried once," he admitted. "But there was a group of sharks and well...things didn't end up the way I thought it would. I surfaced and never tried again."

"You let sharks chase you away?" Finn asked with a laugh.

"There were ten of them!" Faxon countered.

"Why didn't you just kill them?" I asked.

"I was intruding on their home. They didn't deserve me to kill them just because of my curiosity."

"There are stories of parts of the ocean so deep that no man can survive reaching the floor," Finn said.

Faxon nodded. "I've heard that as well."

"Oh, we've been near one before," I told them. "When I was on Dad's ship he sailed to one area and we dropped a can on a string to the bottom. When we pulled it up, it was dented. They say it is because there is too much pressure that far down and it would just crush our bones."

"Fascinating," Faxon said.

"The first time we tried to put a can down it only made it halfway before something bit through the string," I recounted with a laugh. "Dad wanted to jump in and kill whatever had ruined his experiment, but we tried again and that was a successful drop."

"What's your least favorite part of the ocean?" I asked Finn.

"Whirlpools," he said instantly. "We almost got sucked down into one when the former Captain was in charge."

"How'd you get away?" I asked him and sat down to listen.

"I honestly have no idea. I was too busy cowering and clinging to the ropes on the mast to do anything else," he admitted.

"That must have been terrifying," I said. I could not imagine going through something like that.

"It was. So, what's your least favorite part?"

"Mermaids," I said.

Finn and I locked eyes and then started laughing. My hair had grown out fast and I was able to braid it again.

"Mermaids?" Faxon asked. "Did I miss something?"

"A mermaid attacked her while we were in the Fire Ring," Finn explained.

"She tried to drown me," I added.

"Yes, but the mermaid did not win and Tilia injured her enough to escape."

"What did she look like?" Faxon asked.

"Like someone crossed a shark with a woman," I told him. "Her face was hideous."

"I wonder if it was a crossbreeding."

"I don't think you could do that," I said despite the churning feeling in my gut. If someone was able to do that, what else could they create?

"Let's play a card game," Finn suggested.

"Okay," I agreed.

Finn went down to his cabin to get cards and Faxon picked at his fingernails while we waited.

"I am surprised that you have never seen a mermaid," I whispered.

"I searched all over, but they have always eluded me."

"Maybe if you throw me overboard we can catch one."

"Let's not try," Finn said with a scowl as he returned.

"Maybe they're jealous of women's faces and so they drown the pretty ones," Faxon said and smiled.

"Finn's a better-looking woman than that mermaid," I grumbled.

Finn pretended to fan himself and batted his eyelashes. "I think I'd make a lovely lady."

I laughed loudly and clutched at my stomach.

"I disagree," Faxon said. "You would make a wretched lady."

"Well good thing I'm a man then," Finn said.

He shuffled and then dealt the cards and we played until the sun set. After eating a meal together, we went our separate ways, heading for our last night's sleep before we infiltrated Judby.

I lay on my back staring up at the wood above me and wondered what Judby would be like. It was a rarely discussed Kingdom, which was odd in and of itself, but even Esmeralda and Jared did not discuss it. Was it because of Esmeralda almost being killed there? Maybe it brought up bad memories so they avoided it.

Perhaps the entire Kingdom avoided it because they knew what had happened there to Esmeralda and that Jared had split it up. What would Finn and I add to the Realm of Olanze once we ruled? Would there be grand tales about us and our feats? Or would the Crilan name shrink once we took over?

I had to ensure that did not happen. I had to grow as much as I could before I took over the throne, so that Crilan would continue to thrive and people would still view us as a mighty Kingdom.

WE HAD JUST FINISHED lunch when Judby came into sight.

"Finally!" I exclaimed happily.

I jogged to my cabin, grabbed my bag, and met up with the guys on the main deck. Our disguises were on, and I found it difficult not to laugh at Finn. He had a beard glued to his face and ratty looking clothes. He looked like the men you often saw who were too old to sail anymore, but still clung to their past by hobbling around the docks and telling their tales.

"Stop staring at me," Finn ordered.

"But you're so ridiculous looking," I told him and started laughing.

"Me? You look like an old crone," Finn countered.

He was right. I had fake grey eyebrows on, powder through my hair that made it appear grey instead of blonde, and was wearing a hideous brown dress that was baggy enough to hide my sword.

"I still think you're beautiful," Faxon said and winked at me.

Finn rolled his eyes, but didn't take the bait.

The ship docked and the three old crones walked off the boat together. Faxon looked so convincing that I wondered how often he did this. We shuffled between all of the sailors and we muttered excuses as well as curses when we bumped into people. Faxon went to the left while Finn and I continued right. We had agreed to meet back up at the castle at sunset.

"This town is certainly busy," I mumbled in my old lady voice.

"Too busy. Too many people," Finn complained, sounding like the King of Blith.

We shuffled into the housing district and sporadically stopped to catch our breaths and listen to what people around us were saying. Most of it was just boring gossip about his wife cheating with her husband and blah blah. We weaved through the houses until we reached a tavern that was full of rowdy people. Finn tried to walk inside, but a man near the door stopped him.

"Whoa, Grandpa. This isn't exactly your type of establishment," the man, a brute at least six and a half feet tall, said.

"My wife is thirsty and this is the nearest place," Finn told him.

The man looked at me and I tried to look as pathetic as I could.

"Alright, but don't say that I didn't warn you."

"Thanks, sonny," I said and walked into the tavern.

There weren't as many people as I would have thought for how loud it was, but I found us a table in a back corner, out of the way should any fights start, but close enough to listen in on most people's conversations. I sat with my back to the wall and made sure to note where all of my exits were.

Finn hobbled up to the bar and ignored a couple guys making rude comments at him as he ordered. Once he had our drinks, he hobbled over, *accidentally* spilling a bit on the ground as it sloshed around in the mug.

"Whoops," he said to me and set the mugs on the table.

"You old coot," I grumbled. "You spilled half my cup."

"I could have spilled it all," he argued with me. "Or not gotten you a drink at all."

Some of the people around us laughed at our arguments and quickly they relaxed. Two little old people were nothing to fear, and that was exactly what we were going for. It didn't take long for a group of people to come in and start heavily drinking. There were five men ranging from teens to late thirties and they looked like a typical group of bandits. Finn noticed them, too and we sat quietly to listen to what they were discussing.

"Who's working tonight?" one of them asked.

"Boss picks since it's that *special* shipment," another answered.

"Why's he get to pick? Why can't I be part of it?" the youngest looking one whined.

"He picks because he is the boss, you derf."

They all had strange accents. Were they from here? Or had this *boss* brought them here.

"When's the shipment comin'?" the second asked.

"Sunset like always. Dock on the back o' the castle."

"That's the third shipment this month," the young one said. "What are they gettin'?"

"Word is they're stocking up in case Crilan tries anything. They don't want to get turned to ash like those people in Trian did."

"I still can't believe Priam thought he could kidnap the Princess. Don't he know Crilan's King and Queen is crazy?"

"'ave you seen the Princess of Crilan?" one of them asked.

Finn's shoulders tensed and I patted his knee under the table to tell him to calm down and not react.

"No, 'ave you?" the young one asked.

"She's gorgeous! I saw 'er fighting with the Queen once. Thought I might be seeing things. She moved fast and knew how to use the sword. I doubt Tamal here could beat her."

"I've seen her fight, too. She's good." The one who must be Tamal said. "But it wouldn't be long before she threw her sword and her dress at my feet and begged for me to take her."

The men laughed and jeered and teased him.

Finn clenched his hands into fists and slipped them beneath the table. I was having a hard time not saying something to them myself.

"I heard that bloke she's engaged to was a pirate and the only reason he gets to marry her is because he defeated the Dragon of Crilan," the young one said.

"No one's defeated the Dragon," Tamal said.

"He did," I said in my old lady voice.

They all turned and looked at me in shock, noticing us for the first time.

"What did you say?" Tamal asked.

"That boy defeated the Dragon."

"How you know?" the first guy who had spoken asked.

"Saw it. We just got back from there," I told them honestly.

"You saw it?" the young one asked. "What was it like?"

"He moved faster than a man should and he cut the King a few times before pinning him on his back."

"No way."

"I don't believe it."

"Why would the old bag lie?"

"Oy, I'm not a bag, ya child," I grumbled.

"What 'bout you old man?" one asked.

I looked at Finn and realized he was pretending to sleep. I kicked him and said, "Eustace! The boys are talking to you!"

He jerked his head up and snorted. "Wha'? Who's talking?"

"Never mind, go back to sleep, old man," I grumbled.

"Someone defeated the Dragon. Never thought I would see the day," Tamal said with a laugh.

"Gentleman," a voice greeted them as he walked in.

Fear constricted my throat and it became hard to breathe. Finn linked our hands together and I couldn't take his reassurance to calm myself down. It was him. *Him.* Why was he here? Did he know I was here? Had he followed me?

I had begun to shake and Finn's eyes widened. "What's wrong?" he whispered.

"'ey Boss," the young guy greeted the man.

He turned and looked at them and I ducked my head before his cognac eyes could meet mine. There was no doubt, it was him.

"We need to leave," I whispered to Finn in a shaky voice.

Finn stood, being sure to strain as he did it and tossed some coins on the table. He reached over and helped me stand, and then put his arm around my shoulders as we hobbled out the side door.

As soon as the door closed, Finn picked me up and ran through the town to the side of the wall surrounding the castle. He set me down and knelt in front of me as I tried to control my panic.

"Tilia," he whispered. "Talk to me. Why are you so scared? Was it that man? Do you know him?"

I didn't want to tell him who he was because I was afraid he would try to confront him. If he did that he would not survive.

"Where's Faxon?" I asked.

"Here," he said and stepped around a large rock near us. "What's going on?"

"He's here," I told him. "*He* is *here*!"

His eyes widened and he took my hands in his. "It's okay. Did he see you?"

"He looked at us, but I don't think he used his ability. I didn't feel that tickling sensation. He might have just assumed we were a couple of old people. I don't know."

"Okay, calm down. I'm here, right? I won't let him hurt you again," Faxon assured me.

"Again?" Finn asked. "Who was that guy?"

"Faxon, a group of guys called him 'Boss'. They were talking about a shipment coming in on the castle docks. They said it was a *special* shipment. Third one this month. It has to do with being prepared if Crilan attacks," I recounted for him.

Faxon rested his hand on my cheek and whispered, "Breathe, Tilia."

I took a deep breath and let it out slowly. The terror subsided and I relaxed.

"Thanks," I whispered.

"Hey!" Finn yelled. "Fill me in, right now!"

"Shush," Faxon ordered him. "Let's find somewhere to talk and I'll fill you in." Faxon took my hand and led the way around the castle wall, towards the ocean. He peered around the corner and then led us away from the wall and towards the open field. "Tilia, sit down."

I obeyed, but still clutched Faxon's hand.

"That man has been causing trouble across the Realm of Olanze," Faxon told Finn. "We don't speak his name because it could draw his attention. Yes, that can happen."

"Why is Tilia terrified of him?" Finn asked.

"Because he's the one who hurt her on Drimla and implanted those things in her head that made her terrified of

93

magic users and made her collapse in the arena last week," Faxon explained.

Finn's hands clenched into fists and he asked, "Why aren't we attacking him then?"

"We can't attack him. We have to find out what he is up to first," Faxon said with a roll of his eyes.

"If he's dangerous, then we need to stop him before he causes anymore damage," Finn countered, his lip pulling up slightly into a snarl.

"If we stop him now we might lose our best lead for finding out who is creating these devices," Faxon argued.

Finn and Faxon glared at each other in silence.

"Faxon is right," I told Finn. "We have to observe. We need to find out who the creator is. If we find and kill the creator, then there will be no more devices available for purchase."

"Exactly. And I'll destroy the ones that are here," Faxon said.

"Can you destroy them without setting them off?" I asked nervously.

"Yes. Don't worry, there's no risk of setting it off accidentally," Faxon assured me. "When did you say, the shipment was coming?" Faxon asked.

"Sunset at the docks on the back of the castle."

"Okay, we'll observe from afar and then once I've determined who the seller is or how *he* is involved, we will go in and destroy the new ones. Then I will teleport to their storage and destroy the others."

"What am I going to do?" I asked.

"You and Finn are going to apprehend the people who are working with them," Faxon said.

"What if he is there?" Finn asked.

"I will handle him. Neither of you are to engage him. Understand?"

Finn and I nodded.

"Good."

"I'm going to scout good lookout spots," Finn said. "I'll be right back."

He disappeared before I could say anything and Faxon sat down beside me in the grass. "You okay?"

"Peachy," I grumbled. "I don't like being scared like that. I couldn't do anything. How am I going to be able to protect the Kingdom, if one man makes me seize up with fear?"

"We all have something that scares us," he whispered. "You just have to learn how to overcome the fear or use it to your advantage. Like when the chimera attacked us and they used your fear against you. Jared uses fear to make himself angry. He gets mad that he is scared and it makes him incredibly mad, and then he kills things to release his anger. I think you should be able to harness your fear in the same way. Hopefully, you'll be a little more level-headed than Jared. Sometimes he goes a bit off the edge in those moments and it is hard to bring him back down."

"Is that what happened here, when he found Esmeralda?" I asked softly.

Faxon nodded. "Indeed, it is. I think he might have destroyed this entire place had that farm boy not been kind and given him water for Esmeralda."

"What do you do with fear?" I asked.

He sighed. "I'm what Esmeralda lovingly likes to call, 'broken'. I don't really feel fear."

"Never?"

He frowned and said, "Only twice in my life."

"What happened?"

"The first was when I found you, after the device took your magic."

That wasn't a particularly fond memory for me either.

"The second was when you were afraid of me. You looked at

me as if I was a monster. It hurt me more than I can express, and I was terrified that you would continue to look at me like that."

"Perhaps our relationship is a bad thing for you," I whispered sadly.

If I was the only cause for his fear and for the problems he had experienced lately, then maybe it was best if we distanced ourselves. It hurt to even consider it, but I would do what was best for Faxon.

"Quite the opposite," he said. "You've given me life again. I *feel* for the first time in a decade. I was growing weary of life, and then Jared asked me to tutor you."

"I don't want to hurt you," I told him honestly.

He hugged me against his side and said, "You have done nothing to hurt me."

"But he could use me to hurt you. I would feel responsible."

"No. Whatever he does is his doing. You are my shining star in the blackest of nights, Tilia. I will not let you go without a fight."

I leaned against him and closed my eyes. Esmeralda was right, his friendship was one I would cherish forever.

He kissed my forehead, one of the few spots that wasn't affected by the disguise and whispered, "You're going to make a wonderful queen."

"I hope so. I have huge shoes to fill."

"Esmeralda does have big feet," he muttered.

"Ha!" I said and sat up. "I'm telling her that you said that."

"I'm back," Finn said as he appeared in front of us. "There's a spot on the other side of the docks that has enough cover we can stay there and watch everything."

"Lead the way," Faxon said and stood up. He held out his hand for mine and I let him pull me to my feet.

We entered the city again and merged into the stream of people.

"I hate these eyebrows," I grumbled.

"Maybe you should pluck them occasionally," Finn teased me in his old man voice.

"I'll pluck my eyebrows when you stop whistling at those young girls!" I argued back.

"Stop bickering, you hags," Faxon ordered with a croak in his voice. "I can't go anywhere with you two."

"You're the one following us around," Finn spat.

"Well I need *someone* to pay attention to me," I griped.

"Better him than me," Finn mumbled.

"Goat!" I yelled.

"Hag!" Finn yelled.

"Idiots!" Faxon yelled.

People laughed at us, but let us pass by with no concern. We walked to the far side and then Finn led us to the spot he had found. It was surrounded by thick, tall grass with a boulder behind us to protect our backs. We hunkered down and ate some dried meat while we waited for the sun to finish its descent.

As soon as it dipped below the horizon, a ship pulled up to the dock and four men came out of the castle and helped set up the plank and tied the ship. Two of the men were from the tavern, but the others were new faces. The people from the ship carried two crates carefully to the dock and the waiting men, but none of them was *him*.

"He's not here," Faxon said and exhaled a sigh of relief.

"Same plan?" Finn asked.

Faxon nodded. "I'll freeze them, take the devices out and destroy them and you tie up the rest. Then I'll release them and you guys run."

"I can run," Finn smirked.

I rolled my eyes. "Let's go."

Faxon ran ahead of us and the men spotted him when he

was next to the first man. Faxon waved his hand and magic rippled out like a wave and froze everyone that it touched. I ran to the nearest man and tied his feet and hands together while Finn worked on the next one. We ran from person to person until we got to the ones carrying the box. Faxon had already taken the devices and I watched in shock as he tossed them up into the air and made them disintegrate. We tied the remaining people and Faxon turned to us and nodded.

"See you in a few."

"Be safe," I ordered him.

Finn swooped me up into his arms and the men around us started trying to escape their bonds.

"Who the blast are you?" the guy from the tavern asked.

"Peacekeepers," Finn answered.

"Now," I ordered.

Finn obliged, running away from the docks and out onto our ship that was still docked. He took us all the way into his cabin and removed his fake beard before kissing me. "That was fun."

"Set sail!" Faxon yelled above us.

Faxon stepped into the room and scowled. "I destroyed them all."

"How many were there?"

"Counting the ones that were being delivered, seven."

"Seven! That could take out all of the Kingdoms," I gasped.

"This is bad. Way worse than I imagined it would be. We are going to have to find the creator fast," Faxon grumbled.

"Where are we headed?" Finn asked.

"Qual, the leader there is still on good terms with us, so we don't need disguises to see him, and he should give us answers. I'll be checking his place out anyway, but it helps to ask and hear what he has to say."

"And if they don't have any?" I asked.

Faxon sighed. "We'll figure it out after we talk to them." He left to his cabin looking worried.

"Let's get these awful disguises off," Finn said.

"What? You don't like me like this?" I asked with a pout.

"When we're both old? Yes. Now? No."

I laughed and we helped each other clean ourselves up and return to our beautiful, youthful selves. Finn forced me to stay with him and even though we laid there for hours and he fell fast asleep, I was wide awake. I couldn't stop thinking about *him*. He had to be behind this. If he wasn't creating them, then what? What was he doing?

"Go to sleep, Tilia," Finn ordered me.

"I thought you were asleep."

"Your fidgeting is keeping me awake."

I burrowed down deeper into the blankets and draped my leg over his hip while I snuggled up to his chest. "I love you."

"I love you, too. Now go to sleep."

"Finn," I whispered.

"Yeah?"

I pulled my shirt off and pressed my chest to his.

"Tilia," he grumbled, but it was half hearted.

"Finn," I whispered.

He didn't need any more coaxing. He covered me in kisses and playful nips and then disappeared beneath the covers. I had thought the first time was great, but this time was even better. It was amazing.

When I had finished, he slid back up to lay his head on his pillow. I slid down and in one motion removed his pants.

"Tilia," he gasped.

Afterwards, I slid up to cuddle with him. We went to sleep quickly and I began to relish naked cuddles with Finn.

6

WE ARRIVED IN QUAL AND WERE GREETED AT THE DOCKS BY warriors. They bowed to us and then escorted us to the castle. Was it courtesy to another royal or to keep an eye on us?

The docks were surprisingly quiet and unlike Crilan, there were no merchants selling their wares or their daily catch. It felt...wrong.

The castle was about half the size of Crilan's, but there were elaborate etchings all over it. I paused by one carving. It was a man, but he had horns and wings and was running towards a field of warriors while bellowing.

"Seem familiar?" A new voice asked.

"What is this?" I asked without turning around.

"That is the depiction of the Massacre of Judby and *that* is the Dragon of Crilan."

Jared! This was when he had destroyed Judby to save Esmeralda. The King of Judby had tied her up with magic ropes and almost killed her with them. Faxon had told Finn and I about this. He said that the King of Qual had been a farmer boy that had shown kindness to Esmeralda by offering water for her, which Jared repaid by giving him Qual to rule.

I turned around and one of the warriors with us said, "Presenting, the Ruler of Qual, King Jamel."

The King was young, possibly only a few years old then Finn, and wore commoners' clothes. He had dark eyes, but they sparkled with humor as he observed me. His skin was dark, no doubt from the years spent in the sun farming, and his hair was bleached by the sun as well.

"Greetings, Faxon," the King said with a smile.

Faxon bowed to him. "Your Majesty."

I curtsied and Finn bowed automatically.

King Jamel walked towards me. He had a smooth gait, not something I would have expected from a farmer. Of course, it had been a number of years since he had become the King, so he may have had training to improve his fighting skills.

He picked up my hand and kissed the back of it. "It is an honor to meet you, Princess Tilia."

"Thank you, King Jamel. It is an honor to meet you as well," I replied.

He released my hand and turned to Finn. "And you must be the pirate who stole the princess's heart."

Finn smiled proudly. "I am."

"Quite a feat. One I do not think any other pirate will be able to surpass."

Finn bowed his head in thanks.

"I am sorry to drop in unannounced," Faxon apologized.

"Nonsense!" King Jamel assured him. "You are welcome in my Kingdom and to stay in my castle whenever you desire."

A man with long grey robes hurried towards us, bowed low to King Jamel, and said, "Your supper is ready, Your Majesty."

"Perfect timing! Won't you join me?" King Jamel asked us.

"That would be wonderful," Faxon agreed.

"How have you been, my friend?" King Jamel asked Faxon.

Finn and I followed behind as the two talked and discussed

current affairs. I wasn't aware that Faxon had a relationship with the King of Qual. What else wasn't I aware of?

"There have been many dark rumors as of late," King Jamel said, catching my attention.

"What type of rumors?" Faxon probed.

"Many stories of a dark man with impressive magical powers forming an army," he said and glanced at Faxon.

Faxon waved his arms. "Don't look at me. I've got my hands full with the Princess and trying to keep Esmeralda and Jared in line. I don't have time to myself, let alone to create an army."

Jamel laughed. "Those two have always been such characters. It doesn't surprise me that their heir would be no different." He glanced at me and dipped his head, "No offense meant."

"None taken," I replied, smirking.

"Any idea who this man is or where he comes from?" Finn asked.

"That's part of the problem. The rumors indicate him being in places all over the Realm of Olanze, as well as across the waters into the other Realms."

"How could one man be in all of those places? Even with teleportation, wouldn't it alter the rumors? Or wouldn't you be able to connect them easily?" I asked.

"We are not sure," King Jamel replied. "That is one of the many problems with rumors."

"What type of army is he creating?" Faxon asked.

"Again, we are not sure."

We entered a dining room with several small tables and candles everywhere.

"It's beautiful," I whispered.

"Thank you," Jamel said and waved us towards the tables. "Please take a seat."

We sat at a table that luckily fit all of us, and we were

presented with roasted duck and steamed vegetables. Finn and I ate in silence, occasionally sneaking a touch in here and there and a few sidelong glances. Faxon and Jamel were discussing political issues and economics. If Finn hadn't been there, I might have fallen asleep.

"It seems our young lovebirds are distracted or we are boring them," Jamel told Faxon and laughed. "Cia, please show the Princess and the Chief to their rooms."

A woman stepped away from the wall, seeming to materialize from the wall itself, and bowed to me. "This way, Princess."

"Thank you for a delicious meal," I said and curtsied to Jamel.

"Thank you for sharing my meal. It is always refreshing to see young royals who don't believe they should be catered to or have every whim and desire fulfilled simply for their breeding." He looked at Finn and said, "And it is also nice to meet someone who came from dire circumstances similar to myself and proved his heart was pure enough to do more in the world."

Finn bowed. "Your kind words mean much to me. I only hope I can prove myself worthy of Crilan and their Princess."

Cia, began walking, so we followed her. I turned and waved to Faxon. "Goodnight."

"I will see you in the morning."

Cia didn't talk as we walked, but I supposed we didn't really need a grand tour. Finn linked our hands together and I took the invitation to sidle up closer to him as we walked. We made several turns, most surprising because the castle was so small, but not long after, we made it to our destination.

"I bid you both goodnight," Cia said and then her body shimmered and she disappeared.

"Whoa," Finn whispered.

"How interesting," I mumbled. I had never seen someone do

that. When you teleported, you just disappeared. Was it a cloaking spell? Even so, why would she use it in the castle?

Finn pulled me into the room and I was shocked at how beautiful the curtains were. They seemed to shimmer and shine like falling rain. The bed and dresser were dark oak with snakes carved up the legs and on the pillars of the bed.

"Snakes?" I squeaked. I really disliked snakes.

Finn laughed and pulled me into a hug. "Don't worry, I will protect you from the snakes."

"I can kill a snake just as well as you can," I growled at him.

"I know," he said as he nipped my neck. "I just like seeing that adorable scowl."

I kissed his cheek and climbed into the bed. He locked the door and climbed in with me.

"You think Faxon knows they put us in one room?" he asked and nuzzled his way through my hair, until his nose tickled my neck.

"No. He would not allow it unless it was for safety reasons."

"Exactly," Faxon said.

By the time I gasped, Finn was out of bed and had his sword pressed to Faxon's throat.

"Did I startle you?" Faxon asked Finn with a smirk.

Finn lowered his sword and exhaled loudly. "Maybe a tad."

"Why the drop in?" I asked Faxon.

"I wanted to talk to you, but without being escorted," he explained.

"It's possible that there is someone who can shimmer into existence here," I told Faxon.

He nodded. "I saw."

"Lucky for us that we have a Seer who could tell us if that person came here," I whispered.

"Things are not as they seem," he whispered. "There is

someone frightening the King. He didn't say much, but he said enough."

"You and Jamel seem close," I commented.

"I spent almost a year with him after he became King. Jared wanted to make sure that the split went well and that no one tried to assassinate Jamel. I volunteered to help him. It was a nice change of pace."

"What can we do?" Finn asked.

"I'm going to talk to him more tomorrow, but tonight we are going to sleep. I have a feeling that we are in for some rough weather ahead," Faxon informed us. "Keep your swords at the ready and stay together." He started to prepare himself to teleport, but paused and looked at Finn and then me. "Behave yourselves. I don't think I need to specify what I mean."

"We understand," I assured him. "We will behave."

He disappeared and Finn climbed back into bed. "I almost cut his head off," he grumbled.

"That would have been very upsetting," I teased him. "I'm pretty sure it is against Crilan law for the Chief to kill the Arch Mage with no reason."

"Technically I was provoked," he said with a laugh.

"Poor, Finn. He was so scared he leapt out of bed to attack the defenseless Arch Mage."

"He is far from defenseless."

"I don't know if I would have been able to tell Esmeralda or Jared!" I gasped and put a hand to my heart.

"Ha ha. Go to sleep, Princess."

"Fine. You're awfully grumpy for someone who wasn't nearly decapitated."

He started tickling my sides, which caused me to laugh loudly and struggle against him. "I give! I'm sorry!" I yelled. He stopped and I gasped, "It wasn't enough for you to attack Faxon, you needed to attack me as well!"

I waited for his impending attack, but he surprised me by kissing my cheek and said, "I love you."

We snuggled closer together and just as I had relaxed, Finn resumed his tickle assault.

"Who's the greatest?" he asked me around my laughs. "Who is the most handsome man in all of the Realms?"

"You are!" I conceded.

He stopped and pulled my head onto his chest while I repositioned my body. "Thank you."

"Do you think the 'dark man' is the same one that attacked me in Drimla?" I asked Finn softly. It seemed very likely to me.

"Possibly."

"What are we going to do?"

Finn tightened his grip on me and I found comfort in his strong arms. "We will face it together, but no matter what, I will protect you."

"I don't want to experience that spell again," I croaked. Just thinking about it made my heart speed up.

"It will be alright," Finn assured me. "Go to sleep and try not to think about it."

It was almost impossible to stop thinking about it, but eventually I fell asleep.

THERE WAS something sliding up my leg.

"Finn, stop it," I growled. While normally I would have been excited about it, I was tired.

"Huh?" he asked groggily.

The thing continued to slide up until it reached my hip. I smacked it, expecting it to be a hand, but it felt scaly.

"Ah!" I screamed and tried to kick it away.

"Tilia!" Finn yelled.

Snakes pinned our hands and legs down with their bodies.

"What is going on?" I gasped.

"It seems that you see more than you should be able to," Cia said. She appeared at the foot of the bed, a snake wound about her neck.

Finn and I struggled and tried to break free of the snakes. How could they hold us down? They were just snakes!

Two more snakes slithered their way up my legs and reared up on my chest.

"You have overstayed your welcome," Cia said. "It is time for you to leave."

"It's a bit difficult to leave when we are being held down," I growled at her.

The snakes on my chest hissed at me and bared their fangs.

"Tut tut, Princess. Speaking to me in such a manner will only anger my pets."

"Let us go now and we will spare your life," Finn ordered her.

"You will be leaving, although not in the way you wish," she told us and laughed maniacally.

"Why are you doing this?" I asked her.

"He is trying to protect us, but the stupid King cannot understand his vision," she hissed. "Your Kingdom is a threat to us all. We must prepare."

"Crilan has no desire to do anything to Qual," I informed her.

"Qual and Crilan are allies," Finn said.

"I am not speaking about Qual. I'm talking about *my* Kingdom, the one you took over!" she snapped at me.

"Trian?" I guessed.

"Yes."

"They started the fight," I reminded her.

"You are a filthy pirate wench and your Kingdom's promotion of this pirate scum to Chief is a mockery of everything."

"You're blinded by your hate and by your former King's stupidity," I snapped at her.

"You are a foolish girl who is blinded by her hormones. In time, you will see that I am right. You will understand when this man leaves you penniless to go on more adventures and find himself a new wench, that you should have never fraternized with pirates."

"What a moving speech," Faxon said and clapped slowly.

"Faxon!" I gasped.

He snapped his fingers and the snakes disintegrated. "Sadly, we do not give a second's thought to an uncultured swine's hate."

"How did you escape?" she asked him, her eyes widening in shock. She took a step back in fear.

Faxon advanced a step, but looked calm and collected. "You are not as informed as you would like to believe. First of all, I am *not* afraid of children."

"Children?" Finn asked as we joined Faxon where he stood.

"She made it seem as if I were being attacked by small children with weirdly large eyes," Faxon said. He shuddered and continued, "I may not have children or have spent much time around them, but that was not due to fear."

"You were around me a lot," I reminded him.

"You were ten when you came," Faxon said.

"Back to the point," I reminded him.

"Yes, so the next part of this fun little adventure will be you telling us who you are working for," Faxon said.

"Never," she hissed at us.

Faxon froze her in place and walked slowly towards her. "Let's see what you are afraid of." He closed his eyes and touched her forehead.

Her screams echoed in the small room, but it didn't take long for her to faint.

"Horses?" Faxon whispered in shock. "She was terrified of horses."

Odd.

"Are you okay?" Finn asked me.

I nodded. "I still do not like snakes, but they did not bite me."

"People think you're scared of children," Finn teased Faxon.

"Small children with large eyes running at you *is* rather disturbing," Faxon admitted. "But I have seen worse."

"What are we going to do with her?" I asked and pointed at the unconscious woman.

"That will be up to the King. I will take her to him now. You two should head to the ship to finish your night's sleep."

"Did you know we were going to be attacked?" Finn asked him.

Faxon shrugged. "I figured it was a high possibility, which is why I told you to be ready."

"You used us!" I gasped.

"You were never in any danger," he assured me.

I turned away from him with a, "Hmph."

"Uh oh, you made her mad," Finn whispered.

"Head to the ship. I will wake you up for breakfast," Faxon ordered us.

"I can't believe he used us for bait," I growled after he had disappeared with Cia.

"He did warn us," Finn reminded me.

"He could have given us a bit more of a warning or explicitly said what was going on."

"If we had known, we would not have gone to sleep and then she would not have attacked, which would have allowed her to continue terrorizing King Jamel for who knows how long."

"Stop making sense," I ordered Finn.

He laughed at me.

"Let's go. I need sleep."

"Grumpy Princess."

"If you don't stop, I'll show you what a grumpy Princess is really like," I threatened him.

"Stop teasing me," he whispered. "We're supposed to stay in separate rooms, but if you keep it up, I might have to break that rule."

"Now who is teasing who?"

The cold ocean breeze eased my worry and swept away the lingering fear. I really hated snakes and I really wished we would never see a snake again.

"Why didn't she give you your own fear?" I asked Finn.

He shrugged. "Maybe she figured she only needed to contain me while frightening you."

I stopped at the door to my cabin on the ship and sighed. "One fear. I have one stupid fear."

"It's important for everyone to have a fault. Perfection is impossible and those who try to attain it usually end up having a mental break."

"So, you're saying that I'm not perfect?" I asked in mock sadness.

"You are as close as is possible to perfection. Now, go to sleep. A face this handsome only comes from getting enough beauty sleep."

I laughed so hard that I was doubled over and clutched my stomach.

"She mocks my struggles," Finn said and placed a hand over his heart.

"Thank you for that laugh."

He kissed me and whispered, "I will gladly make a fool of myself anytime just to see you smile."

"You're doing a wonderful job," I assured him. "Good night, Finn. And thank you for not cutting Faxon's head off."

He groaned as he headed towards his cabin. "He startled me!"

KING JAMEL HAD BEEN SO thankful of Faxon's help, that he gave us a month's worth of food for our continued trip. I thought we would return to Crilan, but Faxon gave the Captain coordinates and we set sail.

"Where are we going?" I asked Faxon for the fiftieth time that day.

"You have to wait until Finn wakes up. I don't want to repeat the story multiple times," he reminded me.

Finn had slept through breakfast and was about to sleep through lunch. I was beginning to worry because he never slept in this late.

"Why can't I go wake him up?"

"If he is sleeping in this late, then he needs it. He has been through quite a lot this last year and he deserves to sleep in every now and then."

"Are you sure he's—"

"He is fine, Tilia. I checked on him two hours ago," Faxon assured me.

"Not even a hint about where we are headed?" I begged.

"Northeast," he answered.

Northeast? What was Northeast of Qual? Judby was northeast, but we had already been there and learned what we could. I tried to picture the map of our realm in my head, but I could not remember what else was northeast.

"Good morning," Finn greeted me as he sat next to me at the table to eat lunch with us. "Sorry for sleeping in so long."

"No problem at all," Faxon assured him. "A man needs a good rest every now and again."

"Okay, spill it," I ordered Faxon.

"What?" Finn asked.

"We are going to visit the small island of Elady," Faxon informed us. "I heard from King Jamel that his shipments depart from there. We might be able to learn some more from the dock workers there."

"Do we have to wear disguises again?" I asked with a frown. I really didn't want to wear the eyebrows again.

"No, for this mission Finn and I will be the only ones getting off the ship."

"You're making me stay on the ship?" I asked with a sigh.

"Finn can mingle among those docked and see if any of his pirate friends are about. I will be disguising myself and talking with the dock workers and investigating the patrons of the nearby taverns," Faxon said. "You will stay on the ship because we have no need of your help this time."

"Harsh," I grumbled.

"Warriors get left behind occasionally," Finn reminded me.

"Just don't have fun without me," I mumbled.

"I will try my hardest to refrain," Faxon assured me with a laugh.

Finn finished eating his food and kissed my cheek. "Stay on the ship this time," he ordered.

"Yes, Chief."

"Don't worry, Finn," Faxon whispered. "She'll not be able to leave."

"Spells are not necessary," I growled.

"Yes, they are," Finn agreed.

"Fine, I'm going to take a nap. Stay safe you two." As soon as I made it to my room, I started exercising. There would have been more room on the main deck, but I didn't want to watch

Finn and Faxon when they disembarked from the ship to do their reconnaissance or watch our ship circling around. The exercise would also help me relieve some excess energy and possibly allow me to truly nap for a bit. I had been edgy lately and I wanted to make sure that I didn't take it out on Finn or Faxon.

I began with my stretching, moved to jumping jacks, and then squats and lunges. I needed to stay in my best shape ever to continue fighting alongside my family. Jared exercised multiple times each day on top of his sparring sessions. If I ever hoped to beat him, then I needed to increase my training as well.

I pushed my body through each exercise and reminded myself that the soreness and fatigue today would be worth it when I won a round against Jared. Sweat dripped down my back as I fought an imaginary enemy and then a group of enemies.

The ship stopped, which threw me off balance and if my reflexes had been a tad slower, I would have rammed my face into the wall of my cabin. I didn't stop to ponder why we had stopped. All that mattered was defeating the invisible attackers around me and winning.

Time didn't exist in these moments while I trained. It passed, but I didn't know how quickly or slowly it moved. For all I knew time had stopped to watch me fight. I pulled daggers and threw them into the shoulders of my enemies, the tips burying into the wood behind them. I spun around and kicked one before he could stab me with his sword and then ducked another enemy's sword swinging to decapitate me. I knocked his legs out from under him and stabbed him in the chest with his own sword.

My lungs burned for oxygen and after defeating the rest of the fake attackers I sat on the ground to stretch and then meditate. I searched for that spark within me, but again came up empty. Once my breathing had returned to normal I went to the washroom and sponge washed my body and hair.

A new robe had been given to me by King Jamel and I slipped the soft silk robe on, the design matching the curtains that had been in the bedroom we had stayed in. I did a small spin and watched the design shimmer and shine. My bed welcomed me with open blankets and as the adrenaline from my practice faded, I fell into a deep, dreamless sleep.

7

Faxon and Finn returned after dark, but immediately went to speak in private. I had eaten several hours before, so I made them each a plate of food and walked through the ship to find them. Thankfully, they were in Faxon's cabin so I didn't have to search long. "Food," I advised them as I walked in and set the two plates in front of them before I sat on the ground between them.

"We're returning home," Faxon informed me.

"What did you two find out?" I asked curiously. Faxon looked ready to set someone on fire.

"We've hit the end of our mission," Finn told me. "The only ones who had been purchasing the devices were Judby and Drimla. The place that was building them had been destroyed one month ago, and the shipment we destroyed in Judby had been the final one. The maker was hanged in front of all of the citizens of Elady alongside all of the workers he had. They didn't want to incur Crilan's wrath, so they ensured that there were no survivors to continue on with building or shipping the devices."

"What about *him*?" I asked.

"He has been making his rounds, but only to collect money.

He didn't build them since he had taught the one person in Elady to do it. So, he was just making money and then returned to wherever he lives," Faxon explained morosely.

"That's good then, right?" I asked with a smile.

"Yes and no," Finn replied since Faxon was glaring at the wall in front of him. "It's good because we won't have to worry about the devices anymore. It is bad because *he* is still out there somewhere. It is highly likely that he is living in another realm and—"

"He *is* living in another realm," Faxon growled. Fire licked up his arms as his anger grew.

"Don't punch anything!" I ordered him. I didn't want to sink just because he was upset and this ship could not take a punch like he had delivered in the laboratory in Drimla.

He opened his closed fists and took a deep breath in, and then let it out slowly. The fire disappeared and he nodded at me. "Thank you."

"So, we return home to fill in Jared and Esmeralda, and then what?" I asked.

"We will see after I talk to them," Faxon said. "You two may be coming with me on one final mission, far away."

"How far away?" Finn asked.

"To another realm," Faxon answered. "I won't discuss it anymore. You two go grab some cards and meet me on the main deck. I need some distraction."

"You'll be distracted enough getting destroyed at cards," I teased him.

"You won two hands!" Finn growled. "That is hardly us getting destroyed."

"You are such a poor sport," I teased.

Finn walked out of Faxon's cabin, but I stopped at the doorway.

"Faxon, are you alright?" He worried me.

He nodded. "Yes, thank you for your concern, but I'm okay. Just trying to deal with all of this and not sink our ship."

"Keep up the good fight," I teased him and left to find Finn.

He was already on the main deck when I arrived, so I helped him arrange a few barrels for us to sit on and one to place our cards atop. The crew watched us, but none approached or tried to speak to us.

"Did you see anyone you knew?" I asked Finn as I shuffled the cards.

"A couple captains and a few others," he answered vaguely.

"Anyone I know?"

He shook his head. "No."

"Is there a reason you're being so standoffish towards me then?" I inquired.

"What are you talking about?" he asked and looked up at me from where he had been cleaning his sword.

"You seem to be avoiding me a tad."

"I'm sitting right next to you."

"I know, but you're not talking to me and giving me short answers about what you did off the ship."

"You want me to give you a step by step description of what I did?" he asked angrily. "I took exactly seven and a half steps from the ship to the dock and twenty more steps to reach the first ship—"

"You know what I meant," I snapped at him. Why was he being like this? I was just trying to get him to talk to me.

"I went and talked to a few people and then came back. That's it. Why are you hounding me like I did something wrong?"

"I'm not—"

"Just because I was a pirate does not mean I'm not trustworthy."

"I never said that!" I yelled.

"You didn't have to say it! I know that is what you meant!"

"I did not mean that at all. You should know me better than that."

"Should I? We haven't really known each other that long. For all I know, you think I'll run to the first brothel I see."

"Finn, what are you talking about? I didn't say anything like that. You're acting ridiculous."

"Ridiculous? You insult me and then tell me that I'm being ridiculous."

"I never insulted—"

"You know what? I'm done," he sheathed his sword and stomped his way to the stairs and below deck to his cabin.

What in the world had gotten into him? Why was he saying such ludicrous things? Had I done something wrong? I was just curious what had happened since I was here.

"What's wrong?" Faxon asked. "You look puzzled."

"Finn just blew up at me," I told him. "I don't even really know what happened."

"I'm sure it was nothing. He will be back to himself by morning, no doubt," Faxon assured me with a smile.

I wasn't so sure.

"Well don't just sit there shuffling all night. Let's play," Faxon said.

I dealt the cards and pushed aside the incident with Finn. Faxon was dealing with a lot right now and playing cards might help give him the distraction he needed. And me until I could figure out what was wrong with Finn.

We played for some time, but there was a tavern not far from where our ship was docked that was exceptionally loud and it continued to divert my attention from the game.

Faxon noticed it as well and after two more games he stood up and waved at me to follow him. "Come on," he whispered.

"Where are we going?" I asked in a conspiratorial whisper. I wasn't sure why we were whispering, but it felt right.

"To see what all the raucous is about. They seem to be having more fun than us and I want to see what they're up to."

"Should we..." I stopped and shook my head. No, we shouldn't wake Finn. If he wanted to be grumpy he could do it by himself.

Faxon led the way, but it was easy to find with all of the noise emanating from the establishment. A dozen or so people lingered outside smoking or talking and a man with arms that resembled tree trunks stood near the door.

"Stay with me," Faxon ordered.

I looped my arm through his and we entered the tavern. It was larger than it looked on the outside and the room was filled to near capacity. There was a bar with some stools, chairs and round tables, and a stage that had a few chairs in front of it. Some of the people were playing cards, playing for money, and others were drinking and talking. There were warriors, pirates, men in expensive suits, and women in short dresses who periodically sat with one of the men, all in this tavern.

"Quite an amalgamation of people here," Faxon commented.

I nodded in agreement. He walked up to the bar and ordered two drinks. A few people had taken notice of us and were whispering to each other, but most were focused on the stage. Who performed? Was it an animal show with performing dogs?

A woman with tan breeches, black riding boots, a black lace corset, and a white long-sleeved shirt walked towards us. She had a fancy hat on that had a peacock's feather sticking out of the top and red wavy hair that I was instantly jealous of. I had always wanted wavy hair like hers as a kid. I appreciated my hair for its unique color, but as with most women, I found that I wished for other types of hair as well.

She stopped in front of me, looked me from toes to head and said, "So, you're Princess Tilia of Crilan."

Faxon handed me my drink and looked completely at ease, so I guessed it was alright to answer truthfully.

"I am. And who might you be?" I asked pleasantly with a smile.

She stuck out here hand and said, "I'm Brigid, Finn's ex-girlfriend."

I tried to keep the surprise from my face as I shook her hand. "Nice to meet you, Brigid."

"I was beyond surprised to see the former pirate captain here in Elady," she told me. "Knowing that you are here explains it. I didn't think that he would be far from your side, especially on his own."

A few people snickered around us and I resisted the urge to punch her. "Finn is free to do as he pleases."

"Is that why he isn't here and you opted for this replacement?" she asked with a feisty grin. "I have to say, you keep mighty fine-looking men in your company."

I drank from my mug as I debated how to respond to that accusation.

"I don't think we've been introduced," Faxon said and held out his hand.

She shook hands and said, "Brigid."

"Faxon."

Those within hearing distance paused what they were doing to turn and look at us. I hadn't realized until now that he had been using a spell so that he had a slightly different face. He had released the spell and smiled at Brigid as they still held hands.

"Faxon, Arch Mage of Crilan?" she asked breathlessly.

He bowed and kissed the back of her hand. "In the flesh."

"Why is the Arch Mage of Crilan here?" she asked, her cheeks flushed now.

"I grew bored at the castle, so I opted to join Princess Tilia on her journey to continue tutoring her," he told her. "I didn't want to waste a month of perfectly good training time."

"Or to allow anything to happen to her," a man standing behind Brigid said.

Faxon's eyes sparked and he agreed. "Or to allow anything to happen to her. The King and Queen don't take kindly to those who harm their niece and heir to the throne."

"King Priam learned that lesson," someone in the room joked, which set the room off into a chorus of laughter.

Brigid whistled to get the bartender's attention. "Another round for the Princess."

"Thank you."

The table next to us mysteriously emptied and we sat down at it.

"You have quickly become legend, Princess," Brigid informed me.

"Oh? How so?" I asked.

"A royal sticking up for pirates against the King of Blith and the King of Trian is bound to get attention," she said. "And then to have your family disintegrate a castle, slaughter half of Trian's warriors, and decapitate their king to retrieve you. It's quite a story."

"I'm not sure how that makes me a legend," I said nonchalantly and gulped a huge drink of my alcohol.

"You stuck up for pirates and were almost killed because of it. You then convinced the Dragon of Crilan to pardon pirates in his water and even welcome them to Crilan," the man who sat beside Brigid said.

"King Jared decided that on his own, but I suppose I might have been part of that decision."

"Then a pirate captain defeated the Dragon in a fight,

became a Chief, and was engaged to the Princess in the same day. It's a story that will be told for ages."

"That's more of a feat of Finn's than mine."

"Word around the reef is that you defeated four chimeras and claimed Trian for your own," Brigid said.

"Well yes, but Faxon helped."

"No other Princess has done a quarter of what you have, aside from the Queen of course, but she didn't do most of her feats until she was crowned. Your name has spread across the Realm of Olanze and continues even farther," the man said.

"There's another rumor that you were the first to cut the Dragon of Crilan in over a decade and that was before Finn fought him," Brigid said.

"All true," Faxon told them. "The Princess has proven quite the fast learner and has opened my eyes alone to things I had never considered."

"And yet here you are, slumming it with us normal folks. It's truly mind boggling," she said.

"I'm not *slumming*. I'm just a person, like you or anyone else. My breeding gives me the right to rule Crilan, but that does not mean that I am better than you or better than anyone else. We are all human. There's no need to separate ourselves or choose to hate an entire group of people for a few bad apples."

"There's hope for the future yet," Brigid said with a wide smile.

A few mugs later we were swapping stories like old friends.

"You have beautiful eyes," she complimented me.

"I wish I had your hair," I told her. "It's stunning."

Someone started playing on the piano and everyone turned their focus to the stage. A tall man with no shirt on, which exposed his chiseled physique, stepped out to the center of the stage and raised his arms. The rowdy tavern quieted. He had piercing silver eyes, and was the most handsome man I had ever seen.

"Tilia," Faxon whispered.

"Shush," Brigid and I ordered him at the same time.

The man's eyes swept over the crowd until they landed on me and his smile widened. "Tonight, we have a special guest."

No one turned to look because they knew he meant me.

"Tilia, we need to go," Faxon said.

"Not yet. I want to listen," I said and pushed his hand away.

Faxon hauled me up and started to drag me outside, but the people who had been outside had come in and now it was almost impossible to move through the room without pushing them.

The man on stage began singing a story of lost love and heartache. I felt the heartache as if it were my own, pain gripped my chest, and I squatted down. Faxon stopped next to me, his hand still on my arm, but he didn't move.

The song told of the heartache turning to grief and the pain intensified. Faxon took slow steps towards the door, each one looked pained.

Grief turned into yearning and searching.

Faxon pushed me into a corner of the tavern, away from everyone else and stared into my eyes. "Tilia, he's spelling us. I can't..." Faxon's eyes widened with fear and had I not been entrapped in the spell, I would have known to be scared, too.

The searching led to finding a new person. A person who was always there. A person who was meant to protect. The person caused love to bloom anew and soon from love came lust.

I knew what this was. Faxon had taught me about this. The man was using the emotions to feed himself. He was a succubus.

The feelings filled me, no matter how hard I tried to reason with myself and as I struggled, Faxon kissed me.

He slid his hand into my hair and gripped. He gripped too hard and it hurt, making me gasp in pain. The next second we were teleported and stood in his cabin. Our breathing was erratic and he jerked away from me like I had burned him.

"I..." I tried to talk, but I didn't know what to say.

"I'm sorry," he whispered. "I was trying to leave, but he had begun the spell the instant he entered the room and I couldn't teleport."

I could still feel his lips on mine and the shock turned into embarrassment. I fled to my cabin and locked my door to keep Finn out. What had happened?

The succubus had woven a spell to cause false feelings in people. Due to our close proximity, it had caused Faxon to kiss me. It could have happened to anyone. Finn would understand. Wouldn't he? No, I couldn't tell him. He would be even angrier than he had been before.

I buried my face in my pillow and wondered if someone could die of embarrassment. I didn't view Faxon in that way, but Finn might not understand.

What if Brigid had seen Faxon kiss me? She would tell Finn!

I had to tell him. I had to tell him right now. I walked towards the door, but stopped with my hand on the doorknob. Finn was likely asleep. If I woke him up to tell him this, I had a feeling that it would not end well.

I changed clothes and climbed into bed. Tomorrow. I would tell Finn tomorrow what had happened. Or maybe Faxon would.

I exhaled and closed my eyes. Had Brigid known what that man was going to do? Was that why so many people had been there? It seemed highly likely that they would willingly go to such a thing. We should not have gone. We should have stayed on the ship.

I had to tell Finn. If he found out from Brigid or one of the others, he would be devastated.

Brigid.

She had said that she saw Finn. Was that why he was being so weird earlier? Had something happened between them?

No. I shook my head to rid it of that thought. Finn wouldn't do something like that.

⁂

MORNING CAME AND WENT. Finn tried to talk to me, but I didn't open my door. Faxon didn't stop by. My head pounded with a hangover and I needed to eat, but I was terrified to leave the room.

What would Finn say? Would Faxon act differently towards me now? How would this alter my relationships?

Someone was rattling my door knob, but before I could get up to see who it was, Finn walked in.

"Are you going to sleep all day?" he asked.

"Hungover," I whispered.

"Ah," he said with a soft laugh. He shut the door behind me and sat on my bed near my feet. "Had a late night?" he asked.

"Yeah." I swallowed nervously. How did I tell him? Did I start with meeting Brigid and tell him about the man? Or did I just say Faxon kissed me but only because of a spell?

"You look like you are going to vomit," he commented.

"No."

We sat in silence a bit. I ran through my options, but my mouth refused to open.

"I heard that you ran into your first succubus," he said and looked at me.

"It was awful," I told him. "To experience those feelings as if it were my story—"

"Have you been hiding from me?" he asked.

125

I blinked twice and said, "No. I don't feel good. I had way too much to drink."

He laughed and said, "Faxon told me what happened. He took me off of the ship and to a deserted area to tell me because he thought I might try to kill him."

"Did you?" I asked.

"No. I've fallen to a succubus's song before. I know what it does. Although the one I met used fear."

I exhaled and sat up to hug him. "I don't ever want to see a succubus again for as long as I'm alive."

He hugged me and kissed the top of my head. "I agree."

"I met Brigid last night," I whispered.

He jerked back and looked panicked. "You did?"

I nodded. "She was at the tavern."

He looked down at his hands, but didn't respond.

"So, the story you told about me being your first kiss. Not true, was it?"

"I never kissed her or slept with her," he told me softly.

"How was she your girlfriend then if—"

"I...uh...let's just say that I was on the receiving end of things." His cheeks were bright red, even the tips of his ears.

"Oh," I replied smartly. I swung my legs off of the bed and sat beside him in silence. I wasn't sure how I felt about all of this.

"Tilia, talk to me," he begged.

"I don't know what to say," I admitted. "I had assumed when I met you that you had done things with women, but then you had told me that you hadn't. Now—"

"I didn't lie," he replied quickly. "I withheld a little, but what I said was true."

"Why didn't you kiss her?" I asked.

"It's complicated, but I never viewed her as my girlfriend. She just started referring to us as a couple and I didn't argue."

"She's beautiful," I whispered

He turned my head gently with his hand and said, "There is no one more beautiful than you. I would pick you a million times over and even death would not coerce me into choosing someone else."

"Her hair is stunning," I whispered as he moved his face closer to mine.

He wound some of my hair around his finger and said, "Your hair is like gold. You and Esmeralda are the only two who have such exquisite hair."

"Her lips are fuller than mine," I whispered.

He leaned closer, our lips almost touching and said, "Yours will be the only lips that touch mine until I die."

He moved to kiss me, but I pulled back, the moment broken. "Are you angry at me for what happened?"

A frown appeared and his brow creased. "Of course not. You cannot control what happens while under that spell. Even Faxon couldn't break free until he hurt you."

"Hurt me?" I asked.

"He told me he pulled your hair so that you'd make some type of sound of pain and that allowed him to break free because he would never hurt you."

Oh.

Finn moved back in and kissed me. I expected to feel remorseful still or upset, but his understanding made me forget about it all. He deepened our kiss and I wrapped my arms around his neck as I kissed him back. I sat on his lap on the bed while we kissed and relished in the fact that he was mine and mine alone. We might have kissed all day had my stomach not chosen that moment to protest the lack of food.

"You need to eat and drink water," he ordered me.

"Yes, sir."

We headed down to the kitchen and found Faxon there. "How are you feeling?" he asked me.

"My head feels like I dropped an anvil on it," I admitted.

"You're dehydrated," he replied and went back to reading a book while eating.

"Sit. I'll go get you some water," Finn ordered me.

Finn walked away and Faxon said, "I am sorry again about last night."

"Faxon, you don't need to apologize. We were able to escape the spell and that's what is important."

He looked beyond relieved. "I'm going to figure out some way to counteract those types of spells," he told me adamantly.

"Did you kill the succubus?" I asked quietly.

His eyebrow twitched, but he didn't reply. I had a feeling that was a yes.

"Here," Finn said and set a large mug of water and a plate of scrambled eggs on the table in front of me.

"Thank you," I said and drained half of the water before eating my eggs. Faxon passed a bowl of bread rolls to me and I happily took one and buttered it. "I am so happy that King Jamel gave us all of this food," I told Finn and Faxon around a bite of bread.

"We all are," Finn agreed.

"So much better than porridge," Faxon mumbled.

"Definitely," Finn said.

8

THE ORDER OF ELDERS MET FOR THREE DAYS STRAIGHT WITH NO interruptions and I was not allowed to join them. Now that Finn was Chief, he was part of the Elders, which meant that I was left to my own devices. I continued practicing on my own, but it grew too boring. Since I couldn't spar with Jared or Finn, I went to the arena to see if there were any trainees worthy of sparring with me, but the trainees that had been there were gone.

I walked around the arena and dragged my feet through the sand as I pouted. Who could I spar with while they were all busy? I needed something to occupy my mind and time. I considered sending a message to Cristoff, but that idiot had kissed me the last time I had seen him and insulted Finn. I highly doubted Finn would be okay with me inviting him to stay in the castle for a while. I could invite Bernard, but they were all working and doing things in their new home. It wasn't fair of me to try to take them away from that just because I was bored.

"Princess," Riley said in greeting. "How are you?"

"I'm good," I replied automatically.

He leaned against the entrance to the arena as he spoke. "I heard you assisted Faxon on a few missions. How'd those go?"

"Fine," I muttered.

"You look bored," he commented.

"*So* bored!" I yelled.

He laughed softly and asked, "Would you like me to spar with you?"

"I don't want to take you away from your duties," I told him.

"The trainees left a week ago, so I've got nothing, but free time right now," he informed me.

"Then, I would love to spar with you."

He walked into the arena and asked, "What would you like to do today?"

"What's your favorite?" I asked instead of answering.

"Personally, I prefer staffs, but we could do hand to hand."

Staffs?

"Hand to hand sounds good," I told him.

We set our swords to the side and I removed my daggers. Riley stood loosely in the arena as though he didn't have a care in the world and waited.

"Ready?" I asked.

He nodded.

I lunged forward, but he was fast and avoided my punch. He tried to grab the wrist of the arm I had tried to hit him with, but I spun away and out of his reach.

"I was quite impressed with how you fought against King Jared in front of the trainees," he told me. "It's not often that you see women who are gifted fighters such as yourself."

"Thanks," I said and tried to swing my foot around to knock his legs out from under him.

He easily jumped over my leg and before I knew it, he had an arm around my throat. I elbowed him in the ribs and he relaxed his hold enough for me to break away.

"Very well done," he complimented me.

I acted as if I were going to throw sand at him, which caused him to put his arms up in front of his face, but I used his temporary blindness to advance and kicked the back of his knees at the same time I wrapped my arms around his throat.

"Give," he said immediately.

He wasn't giving me much of a fight. It felt more like he was teaching than sparring.

"I know that you aren't trying your hardest," I told him. "This isn't supposed to be like when you teach the trainees."

He bowed and I swept his legs out from under him. He used his hands to break his fall, which left his back open for me to take control by wrapping my legs around his waist and my arms back around his neck. He rolled us over so that I was on my back on the ground and somehow spun around within my hold so that he was facing me.

I released him to find a way out from under him, but he pinned me down and no matter how hard I struggled, I could not break free. "Give," I growled.

He stood up with a victorious smile on his face and brushed off his clothes.

"How did you spin around in my hold like that?" I asked him as I brushed off mine.

"You didn't lock your ankles so it gave me enough room to spin my body," he told me.

"Again," I ordered him and immediately leapt forward.

It wasn't until I had become too tired to spar anymore that I realized it was night time. "Wow, it's late," I said in shock.

"Time passes quickly when you're doing something you love," he told me.

"Thank you for today," I said and grabbed my sword.

"You are most welcome. If you ever need anything—"

I interrupted him and hugged him. "I remember everything about that night. Thank you for helping me and thank you for today." I jogged to the castle and to the dining room where I was lucky enough to find everyone eating. "I didn't miss dinner!" I said happily.

"Where were you?" Jared asked. "We looked in your room, but you weren't there and Duke was in his stall."

"I was sparring in the arena," I informed him. "I'm surprised you didn't look there first."

"Well, there aren't any trainees, so I didn't think you would be there. Especially since we were all busy," he replied.

"Who were you sparring with?" Esmeralda asked.

"Riley."

"He's a talented fighter," Jared complimented. "He never seems to lose his cool."

"That's part of what makes him a great teacher," Esmeralda said. "And why Jared isn't cut out for teaching."

"I am capable of keeping calm," he told her.

"But you rarely do. You nearly scared off an entire group of trainees one year because you were in such a mood," she told him.

"I work with the trainees every year. That group was particularly horrible."

"You threatened to banish them if they couldn't learn to hit the target with their arrow," she told him with a laugh.

"They had been practicing two days and only two could hit the target," he replied defensively.

"You're losing your cool right now," I told him.

He sighed and resumed eating.

"So, how are the Elders doing?" I probed.

Esmeralda shook her head at me. "You'll just have to wait until we come to a decision. It shouldn't be more than another day or two."

"Two!" I yelled. "I'm going crazy as it is."

"You will survive. I promise," Esmeralda teased me.

"Can't you just tell me what the decision is going to be about?" I asked and gave her my best puppy dog eyes.

"As adorable as you are, no."

"Gah!" I yelled in frustration. I wanted to know what they were all discussing behind closed doors.

We finished our food and they returned to their secret meeting while I stayed in the dining room. Whatever they were discussing, it was obviously very important and if it was taking this long to make a decision than it was most likely contentious.

I opted for a walk around the castle to keep my body busy instead of twiddling my thumbs inside. The moon shone bright above my head and the night air caressed my cheeks as I walked. I heard voices ahead and proceeded silently in case it was them discussing things where I might be able to hear. I edged around the side of the castle and to my shock and disbelief, found Eric and Natalie talking and holding hands!

I couldn't hear what they were saying, but I could tell from their expressions that it was a serious discussion. Natalie started to turn away, but Eric pulled her back and kissed her. I slid back around the side of the castle, pressed my back against the wall, and slid down until I was sitting on the ground. I should have been happy that Natalie and Eric were dating. Yet, I wasn't. What was I feeling? It wasn't jealousy. Sadness? Why was I sad? I had Finn. I didn't like Eric in that way. Natalie was happy. What was there to be sad about?

Realization hit me hard. I was sad because this meant that Natalie's spare attention would be spent elsewhere. Instead of coming to visit me at the castle when she had any extra time, she would come to visit Eric. It was possible that I had just lost my best friend.

After sulking for who knows how long, I went up to my room and wrote my father a letter. I asked how he was doing and told him about the various ports I had visited. I left out a lot of details, but I updated him as much as I could. I sealed the envelope and left it on my desk so I would remember to take it down to have it delivered the following day.

THE ORDER of Elders did not need one or two more days, they needed four. Jared found me that final day in the arena with Riley as we practiced with staffs. He had worked with me for hours each day to learn how to fight with them, and I frustratingly found that I wasn't a natural with staffs. Riley told me it was because I tried to think of the staff as a sword, but it was so much more than that.

I blocked his blows and tried to hit him, but no matter how hard I tried, his defense was unbreakable. He smacked me in the back with the staff and I stumbled forward, annoyed that he so easily defeated me for the hundredth time.

"You look better," Jared told me as he entered the arena.

"What?" I asked.

"The first day you tried to use the staff was very painful to watch. Now you are much more at ease with it and have improved significantly," he praised.

"Yet I sit here in the sand, defeated."

"How long did it take you to become good enough with the sword to hold your own?" Jared asked.

"I don't know. A few years."

"So why do you think that you should master the staff in only a few days?"

He had a point.

"I suppose that you are right," I said with a sigh.

"Come on, you've been summoned," he said and held out his hand.

I let him help me up and asked, "Summoned by who?"

"Oh, I'm not going to deny myself the fun of watching your face when you see who it is," he said and laughed maniacally.

"Wonderful," I muttered. I handed Riley the staff and thanked him for another day of learning.

Jared led me into the castle with a smug smile on his face the entire way.

"You keep that look much longer and it may become permanent," I teased him.

"I wish I could record this moment to see your face again and again," he said.

"Where's Finn?" I asked.

"On an errand," he told me and his smirk widened.

"You sent Finn away?" I asked in shock.

"Maybe."

Who could it be!

Jared stopped at the doors to the dining room and helped me brush the dirt off of my clothes. He tried to wipe the dirt from my face, but it only smeared it. "Well, this will have to do," he said and then pushed open the doors and quickly stepped inside and to the right so that he could see my face.

I glared at him and then saw who was standing with Esmeralda.

"There you are, Tilia!" Esmeralda greeted.

Prince Sebastian of Blith. He had been there when Priam kidnapped me. He had woken Eric up and allowed him to contact my family to save me. I owed him, but he had also sent me a letter admitting his feelings for me. He had even signed it "your bewitched love." Finn had told me to respond to him, to let him down, but I just never got around to it. Now he was here, in my home.

I curtsied and Sebastian took my hand to kiss the back of it. "You've grown lovelier since I last saw you," Sebastian flirted.

Now I knew why Jared had sent Finn away.

"What a surprise to see you in Crilan," I said in what I hoped was a pleasant tone.

"I was worried that you hadn't received my letter and I have never been to Crilan before, so I thought it would be fun to stop by," he said with a wide smile.

He had to know that I was engaged. There was no way that Blith hadn't heard about my engagement.

"Tilia," Esmeralda said. "Why don't you show Prince Sebastian around the grounds?" Her eyes were sparkling with mischief and her smile was more than amused.

"Of course," I said with a charming smile. "Right this way."

He walked at my side and as I passed Jared, I kicked his shin. He didn't move, but I knew it had at least stung.

"That was our dining hall where we eat our meals together," I told Sebastian. "Up those stairs are our bedrooms." I walked by the stairs and continued our tour. I was not about to take him near my room. Although, I could show him Finn's room. No.

We exited the back doors. "These are the trainees' quarters. We only have the trainees here for a brief amount of time before they take them to a different training ground. Here is the arena."

I felt like punching someone, but I tried my hardest not to take it out on Sebastian despite his unannounced visit.

"Here are the stables—"

"Which is your horse?" he asked.

It was the first time that he had talked since the dining room.

I led him to Duke's stall and my gentle giant stuck his head out over his stall door. "This is Duke."

"You have the same hair color," he commented.

"We do," I agreed.

"I've never seen a horse and its rider with the same hair color. It's cute," he said and smiled at me as he pet Duke's neck.

"Sebastian, may I be frank with you?"

"Of course, Tilia," he said and stepped around Duke's head to move closer to me.

"You have to have heard that I am engaged now."

"I was hoping they were false rumors," he said and played with Duke's halter that was hanging on the wall of his stall. "I had hoped that you received my letter and your reply was just lost in transit."

"I did receive your letter and I apologize for not responding. I was planning to, but nothing ever sounded right when I began to write it," I admitted to him.

He seemed to take that as a good thing and stepped closer to me. "Perhaps it was just meant for you to say to me in person. We could be the greatest ruling couple of our time. Our children would be—"

"Children? Whoa there, Sebastian. I think you need to back it up a bit. I am nowhere near ready for children. And—"

"And she's engaged to me," Finn said angrily.

Oh, boy.

"Exactly. The rumors were true, he and I are engaged," I said quickly. If he hadn't cut me off I was about to say just that.

"And who are you?" Sebastian asked, looking over Finn like he was a transient. His clothes were surprisingly dirty and they needed to be thrown out due to the number of holes in them.

"Finn, Chief of Crilan and Tilia's fiancé," he replied smugly.

Sebastian's eyes widened in shock and he looked at me. "You can't be serious? You're going to marry him? This will be the next King of Crilan?"

Finn began to puff up and move forward, but I stepped in front of him and said, "I am one hundred percent serious. I don't marry for power or because it would be a good political move. I marry for love."

"Love?" Sebastian asked with a bark of laughter. "Love is for fairy tales and morons."

"Then I guess we are morons," I said.

Finn hugged me from behind and then kissed the top of my head.

"I had assumed that you would be smarter than this. You have good breeding and your beauty alone would—"

"Good breeding should be reserved for horses, not people. I am the royal heir to Crilan by blood, but even if I weren't a royal, I would still be a better person than you. It seems the apple does not fall far from the tree in your case."

He bristled. "I am nothing like my father."

"How soon would it have been before you tried to make me wear dresses?" I asked him. "How long would you have waited before trying to turn me into one of your daisies and to fit into what you consider a *lady*?"

"You wear dresses," he said. "I've seen you in them."

"Very rarely. How would you feel if this is how I looked on a daily basis?" I asked.

"You are filthy on a daily basis?"

"Perhaps not dirty, but I dress as Esmeralda does. Dresses are too cumbersome for fighting and it's so hard keeping them clean," I complained.

"I see. It seems that I have made a mistake," Sebastian said.

"Thank you for traveling all this way to see me, but titles mean nothing to me when it comes to deciding who to marry. Even if you were king, I would turn you down."

"She should be thanking her family everyday for having that ability. Shouldn't she, Finn?" Lance asked as he entered the barn.

"Lance? What are you doing here?" I asked in shock. Lance was a pirate captain and Finn's half-brother. We had an unfortunate meeting during the Pirate Heist Festival and we'd barely escaped.

Finn released me so that he could stand between Lance and me. "What do you want?" he asked him.

"Captain Lance is my ride," Sebastian said. "And it seems he too had a desire to visit your home."

"Leave!" Finn ordered them.

"Not until I've come for what I want," Sebastian growled.

I began to draw my sword, but Sebastian snapped his fingers and I froze in place. I hadn't known he was a mage. I should have known.

"Don't touch her!" Finn growled and moved towards Sebastian.

Lance cut him off, using the same speed that Finn had and wagged his finger at Finn. "No touching the royalty. Your fight is with me, brother."

"I thought you said that she had magic?" Sebastian asked Lance.

"She did," he assured him. "She buried me in sand by controlling it."

"She should have been able to escape by now if she had magic."

"Just take her and go," Lance ordered him. "I'll keep this idiot busy and meet you at the rendezvous point."

Finn drew his sword and as Sebastian carried me over his shoulder, all I could hear was a whirlwind of steel clashing against steel.

"Don't you fret, Tilia. We'll be a very happy couple. You can wear your silly pants whenever you want and sooner than you think, you'll learn to love me."

"Never love you," I growled.

"Oh, but you will. My Arch Mage developed a new spell for subduing prisoners that works surprisingly well to alter someone's personality."

"It won't be me," I told him. "You want me, but that will make me into someone I'm not."

"I don't want you. I want your good looks."

"My family will save me. They'll burn Blith to the ground—"

"Or we could stop you right now," Faxon said.

He leaned against the side of the castle with his hands in his pockets as if he hadn't a care in the world. As if I wasn't being kidnapped.

Sebastian set me down and faced Faxon. "I've always wanted to fight you," he said smugly.

Esmeralda stepped around the castle and snapped her fingers. Sebastian froze in place. "Too bad for you, that you won't have that opportunity."

"How?" he asked.

"You may have shields, boy, but we have much more magic than you. Faxon broke your shields and I was able to freeze you and suppress your magic. Do you feel that? You feel that empty core of yours? That's what it's like not to have magic. Now, I suggest that if you would like to keep your magic, you take your captain here..."

Finn dropped Lance, whom he had bound, on the ground next to Sebastian's feet.

"...and leave my Kingdom. We'll let this childish mistake go and Crilan and Blith will continue to be allies."

"Faxon," I whispered.

He held up his finger to tell me to wait.

"What will it be, Prince Sebastian?" Esmeralda asked.

"I will leave. You people really are insane," he said.

"You tried to steal our princess to turn her into a living zombie despite knowing that we best you and your entire Kingdom in magic and fighting power, but you think *we* are insane? You clearly have a few years left to figure things out before you become King," Jared told him.

"Faxon," I called again.

Esmeralda released Sebastian from her spell and he grabbed Lance and hauled him to his feet. He walked away from the castle, towards the docks without another word or glance back.

"Well, that was fun."

"Faxon!" I yelled angrily.

"What?" he asked in shock.

"Release his damn spell," I ordered him.

Esmeralda and Faxon looked at me and then started laughing.

"Not funny," I growled.

Finn poked my arm. "You can't move?"

"No," I growled.

"We could leave her like this," Jared suggested.

"I will put scorpions in your beds," I threatened them.

"Where are you going to find scorpions?" Esmeralda asked.

"I can have them shipped here."

"Alright, I will let you go," Faxon said. He waved his hand at me and I could move again.

"I am *really* tired of people trying to kidnap me. What the hell is it about me that screams *please steal me away*?"

"You're just too beautiful," Finn told me and kissed my cheek.

"I was kidnapped four times by the time I was fourteen," Esmeralda told me.

"Four?" I asked in shock.

She nodded. "Jared and I weren't an item yet and I was often off on adventures around Crilan."

"Who got you back?" I asked.

"Once, your mom caught up to my kidnappers on her horse and froze them with a spell and then left them there for the guards to go back and get. One time my father personally came to take me back from a man who was holding me for ransom."

"The two other times were me," Jared said.

"It was quite a while between that and the next time I was kidnapped. It seemed Jared had scared them enough to make the others rethink their plan."

"And then came the Massacre of Judby," Faxon said.

"Yes, well no one tried to kidnap me again after that," Esmeralda said.

Jared hugged her and kissed her cheek. "I would do it all over again."

"Why didn't Faxon ever rescue you?" I asked.

"He was always at another Kingdom when it happened," Esmeralda explained. "Which we believe was part of their plan. They knew that they couldn't defeat both of us, but defeating me by myself wasn't so difficult back then."

"Is that why you spent so much time learning so many spells?" I asked.

She nodded. "Exactly. I didn't want to be vulnerable if there was a way to avoid it."

"It seems I keep running into magic users now that I don't have my magic," I complained.

"Well, how about we move on to a topic that you've been begging us to discuss for a week?" Jared asked.

"You finally made a decision?" I asked.

Jared nodded. "Let's go into the dining room and discuss it."

We started to follow them, but Finn held me back and brushed his hand down my cheek. "Are you okay?"

"Yes," I answered right away.

"I came as fast as I could. Lucky for me, Lance wasn't feeling well today so he was a tad slower than usual. I would have defeated him no matter what, but it made it easier."

"I know. And I was about to tell Sebastian exactly what you said, but you beat me to it."

He smiled. "I know."

I leaned my head against his chest and exhaled. "He would have made me wear dresses every day," I muttered.

Finn laughed and hugged me tightly. "If it were up to me, you wouldn't have to wear clothes at all."

I smacked his chest while I backed away from him. "Finn!"

He kissed one of my red cheeks and linked hands with me as we went to meet my family.

We sat down and I asked, "So, what is this all about?"

"I received a request for help from an acquaintance of mine," Faxon told me.

"So, we're going to help him?" I guessed.

"That's what we were discussing. Their Kingdom is part of another Realm and is quite far from here," he told me. "And, it's regarding *him*."

Oh.

"So, what are we going to do?" I asked.

"We have agreed that I must go help them. He is my problem and I cannot leave them to defend themselves against him without my assistance," Faxon informed me.

"I'm going to go as well," Finn said. "They are being attacked by a large group of fighters ranging from woodsmen to trained warriors and even though they have a strong fighting force, they cannot handle the vast number of his army and him at the same time."

"So, the rumors were true. He was gathering a huge army," I whispered in shock.

"Yes."

"I'm going," I said adamantly.

"Are you sure that you can handle seeing him?" Esmeralda asked me.

"Faxon will be there. If there are that many people in his army, then I should be there to help them fight."

Jared nodded. "Good. I want to go, but with all of the unrest in Olanze lately, I feel it is best if I stay here."

"And I will stay here as well. If something happens to Faxon, I will be able to teleport to you and bring you home," she said. "Or, at least that is the plan."

"When do we leave?"

"Dawn," Faxon said. "You'll need to pack heavy."

"Are we teleporting?" I asked hopefully.

He shook his head. "I was only there once and I don't want to teleport us right into a battle. We are going to sail as close as we can and then I will try to communicate with him so that we can teleport."

"Another realm," I murmured. I had never been outside of Olanze.

"There's something else we should tell you, so that you can prepare," Esmeralda said.

"What?"

"Part of the group that is fighting against *him* are elves," Jared said.

Elves? Elves!

"I didn't know they actually existed," I whispered in shock.

"They do and they have quite a few creatures that we do not have here," Esmeralda informed me.

"Do we get to meet the elves?" I asked hopefully.

Faxon nodded. "You'll get to meet their entire royal family. Apparently one of the princes was visiting one of the other royal families when the attack began and that prompted the entire elvish army to join the fight."

"How long will we be gone?" I asked.

Esmeralda sighed. "That's the problem. We have no idea how long you will be gone."

"Which means that the wedding may have to be postponed," Jared explained.

"Oh." I hadn't really thought about our wedding much lately. "Well, that's okay. If we can save their people, then we can get married afterwards."

I looked at Finn and he nodded his agreement.

"Good," Esmeralda said. "I was hoping you would say something like that."

"What's going on?" Eric asked as he entered the dining room.

I quickly turned away from him and stared down at my hands.

"They're going on another mission," Jared explained. "We were just going over the details."

"Oh," he replied. "Am I—"

"No," Jared said, interrupting him, "you won't be part of this mission."

"Okay." He didn't seem upset by that.

"We wouldn't want to take you away from Natalie," I said bitterly and shoved my chair back.

"Tilia," Eric said in shock. "We were going to tell you and—"

"It's fine Eric. I'm glad that she found you. Now, if you will excuse me, I have packing to do." I left before I said anything rude or admitted how I felt. I knew that I should tell him how worried I was that he would take her from me, but I didn't want to. I didn't want to admit that I was afraid. There had been too much fear lately as it was.

I had begun sorting my clothes into piles to determine what I was going to bring when Finn walked in. "Are you okay?" he asked and leaned against the inside wall of my room.

"Yes."

"Tilia, talk to me," he whispered.

"I don't want to talk about it," I told him honestly.

"Are you jealous?" he asked.

"Jealous of who?" I asked him.

"Natalie and Eric."

"No."

"You seemed pretty upset. You didn't even tell me that you found out they were a couple."

"You've been busy," I reminded him.

"If you aren't jealous, then why are you upset? You seemed to think the idea of them dating would be a good thing before."

"It was good in the abstract sense," I mumbled.

"So, what changed?"

"Everything."

"Care to be a little more specific?"

"No."

"I don't understand. If you were fine about it before why aren't you now?"

"Because that was before and this is now."

"Tilia," he begged.

"I don't want to lose her. She's going to spend all of her time with him and she won't have time for me. I hardly have time for her as it is, which makes me a terrible friend, but now when she does have free time it won't be to come see me or hang out with me and watch the trainees. She will go off with him somewhere and I'll only get to hang out with her when Eric is busy."

"Ah," he said. "I see."

"Can you leave now?" I asked.

"No."

I groaned and tossed another shirt on the pile to pack. "Fine."

"You need to learn to talk to me more," he whispered. "You are bottling too much up. There have been a lot of changes for us both and it is important that we are able to discuss them and get them off our chests."

"Why were you so angry that night in Elady?" I asked.

"Tilia—"

I set down the shirt I had been trying to make a decision on and faced him. "No, you answer me. If you want us to be open and honest then you need to answer me."

"I was upset because I saw Brigid and she tried to kiss me. She didn't, but I was worried that you would be mad at me and that it would cause us to fight. So instead I was a raging jerk and we got into a fight anyway."

"She tried to kiss you?" I asked in shock.

"Yes, but I moved out of the way and told her that I was engaged so she couldn't do that."

And to think that I had complimented her hair!

"What are you thinking now?" he asked.

"That I shouldn't have complimented her," I grumbled.

He laughed and hugged me. "I heard that you have been spending a lot of time with Riley."

"Yes, he has been teaching me to use a staff and keeping me sane while you were all shut in at your super secret meeting," I told him and picked up a pair of breeches.

"You two seem pretty close," he commented.

"It's not really that. There's just something about him, it's that power he has. It makes him easy to be around and helps me relax. After everything that has happened, it's been nice to have that."

"So, you enjoy being around Riley when I'm not there?" he asked.

I turned to say something, but he was smirking and teasing me. "If I said yes, what would happen?"

"I'd most likely become angry and—"

"Would you try to decapitate me?" I asked with a smirk.

"He startled me!" he yelled.

"Who did?" Jared asked.

"Faxon," Finn responded.

"How?" Jared asked.

"He teleported to our room and we didn't know he was there,

so it scared Finn. He almost cut off his head," I told Jared. "I don't know if I would have been able to tell you."

"I didn't cut his head off. I stopped the blade in front of his neck and he is perfectly safe."

"I don't know. You might have caused psychological damage. A psychologically damaged Arch Mage is a loose bomb," I commented.

Jared said, "Maybe we will have to have him tested."

"Who?" Esmeralda asked.

"Faxon," I told her.

"For what?"

"Finn almost decapitated him and now he might have damaged him psychologically," Jared told her.

"Finn!" she yelled. "Why would you try to kill Faxon?"

"He startled me!" he told her.

"That's no reason to kill someone," she chastised.

"I didn't! I stopped. It's not my fault that he just poofed into the room and scared us," Finn grumbled.

"Poofed?" Jared asked.

"Yeah, poof here he is. Poof there he went," Finn said.

"Ha. Next time he teleports into a room where I am, I'm going to say that," Jared said.

"We should all start doing it," Esmeralda agreed.

"Jared," Faxon said after he teleported to where we were.

"Poof!" we all yelled at him.

He blinked slowly twice and asked, "What?"

We all laughed and he rubbed his temples. "I've missed something again, haven't I?"

"We were just discussing how Finn almost cut your head off in Qual," I updated him.

"Yes, that was terribly frightening. I had nightmares for two days," Faxon lied.

"See, you did psychologically damage him!" I told Finn.

"He's obviously lying," Finn muttered.

"Could you imagine the headlines? 'Chief decapitates Arch Mage because he was startled,'" Faxon said.

"Maybe next time you should let us know before you teleport in," Finn said.

"Now where is the fun in that?" Faxon asked him.

"You need to talk to me?" Jared asked Faxon.

"Ah, yes. Let's go to your room and leave Tilia to sort through that mountain of clothing," Faxon said.

"Maybe you should help her," Finn suggested to Esmeralda.

"I suppose I can do that," she said with an exaggerated sigh.

"Well if you have more exciting plans, please don't let me stop you," I teased her.

"I had very exciting plans. I was going to change and go to bed. Very cutting edge."

"Someday I hope to be just like you," I teased her.

"You're pretty close already," Finn commented.

We both turned to him and he smiled.

"What is that supposed to mean?" I asked him.

One moment he was there and the next he was gone.

"Coward!" I yelled after him.

"I love you!" he yelled from his room.

"Men!" I grumbled.

"So, how's the sorting going?" Esmeralda asked.

"I don't know what to bring," I admitted.

"I can be of service," she told me. She cracked her knuckles and then whispered something too soft for me to hear. She clapped her hands and clothes began resorting themselves into different piles.

She pulled me away from the piles and I watched as her magic did the work for us.

"What type of spell is that?"

"That is one I came up with myself," she told me. "It sorts

clothes by type of mission and possible meetings."

"Handy," I commented.

"Incredibly."

We stood by as the clothes finished and then she helped me put the clothes away that were not going, and we sorted through the maybe pile.

"So, do you want to talk about why you bit Eric's head off?" she asked.

"No."

"Tilia."

"I talked to Finn about it," I told her. "I don't want to talk about it anymore."

"Well, at least you talked to someone about it," she agreed.

"Thanks," I mumbled.

"A guard reported that Lance and Sebastian sailed away," she told me.

"Good. Those idiots."

"You know, this will be something that you can hold over Sebastian's head the rest of your lives? Next time you're trying to get the Kingdoms to agree on something and he isn't doing as you ask, you just remind him of this incident and how bad it would look should it get out to the public."

"You are such a devious woman," I told her.

"Thank you."

"Have you ever experienced a succubus's spell?" I asked her softly.

She flinched. "Twice." She looked at me and her eyes widened. "What happened?"

"Well, nothing too bad," I mumbled.

"Tilia, what happened?"

"Faxon kissed me."

She paused, one of my shirts in her hands, held up in the air in front of her. She stood perfectly still, and then she burst into a fit of laughter that had her rolling on the ground and kicking her feet.

"It's not that funny," I grumbled and tossed another pair of breeches into the pile of to go clothes. She continued to laugh and I wondered if she would ever stop. Seven clothing choices later, I sighed and stared at her with my hands on my hips. "Are you done yet?"

She wiped her eyes and stood up. "I'm sorry. It's just so funny. I'm sure Faxon was incredibly embarrassed and I wish I had seen his face when he finally broke free of the spell." She started laughing again.

"He felt awful."

"How did he break the spell?" she asked.

I blushed and looked at my hands. "Pulled my hair so that I gasped in pain."

She stopped laughing, her face growing serious, and said, "That's genius. Since he would never hurt you intentionally, he broke the hold of the succubus's spell."

"Right," I said.

"Well, what did you learn from this experience?" she asked.

"Avoid incredibly attractive men because they are likely a succubus."

She laughed again and I said, "I didn't know what I was going to say to Finn so I hid in my room."

"How did you break it to him?" she asked curiously.

"Faxon did. He took Finn to a deserted area away from the ship in case Finn tried to attack him."

"How did Finn react?"

"Apparently, he has had a run in with a succubus, too. He said the one he ran into used fear instead of lust."

"Yes, that was what the first one I ran into used," she told me. "It took me a long time to recuperate after that experience."

"How old were you?"

"Nineteen."

"So, where was Jared?" I asked.

"He was the one who rescued me."

"He killed the succubus, didn't he?" I didn't doubt it. Jared did not take kindly to people hurting Esmeralda.

"Actually, no. The succubus tried to use fear on Jared, but it wouldn't work, so he used more of his magic and more until he died of exhaustion."

"So, Jared made him die because he wasn't afraid of anything?"

"Oh no, Jared was scared, but he used that fear to increase his anger and the succubus does not feed on anger so he continued to try to make him afraid. He would get a bit of fear from Jared and then he would grow even angrier. By the time the succubus had died, Jared was ready to take on the entire Realm of Olanze singlehandedly. It took a few days for him to calm down."

"Wow," I whispered. Jared continued to impress me. I needed to find a way to channel my fear into anger like Jared did.

"He is quite a man," she said with a deep sigh.

"Ew."

"Oh please. I have to watch you and Finn fawn over each other constantly. I am allowed to fawn over Jared occasionally." I opened my mouth and she growled, "If the word *old* leaves your mouth I will turn you into a toad."

"Wow, you're so crabby. Is it nap time?" I teased.

She waved her hands and I held up the shirt in my hands. "You can't hit me behind this protective shirt."

"Well, I can't argue with that logic," she said and laughed.

"Are you and Jared going to be okay while we are gone?" I asked.

She put her arms around me and said, "It is going to be very quiet and boring. However, it will give me time to catch up on all of the things that I have been putting off. Are you going to be able to handle so much time with Finn and Faxon?"

"It is rather frustrating and often times psychologically damaging, but I will suffer through it to meet elves."

"I am jealous of that. I would love to finally meet the elves," she said and spaced off, no doubt daydreaming about them.

"Well, maybe after we defeat the evil man, you and Jared can transport where we are to meet them," I suggested.

"Maybe," she said, but I could see the light in her eyes at the prospect. Who wouldn't want to meet elves though?

"Well, I will plan for it and have Faxon contact you after we defeat this army and save the elves. Do you think they'll give me a Pegasus after saving them?"

She shook her head. "From what Faxon says, the Pegasus are highly intelligent and respected by the elves."

I sighed loudly. "Well, there goes that awesome plan."

"Perhaps I can trade Jared in for an elf. I hear they live for a very long time and are incredibly talented fighters," she said a bit louder than she had been talking.

"Excuse me!" Jared bellowed and entered my room. "I will kill any elf you even glance at if I have to."

She stepped into his chest and he hugged her tightly. "You know just what I want to hear."

"Okay, go to your room. I do not want to see you two getting smooshy and lovey," I ordered them. "Plus, I have a ton of packing to finish before dawn."

"Pack for warm weather," Jared told me.

"Okay."

"And you definitely need to take the Dragon's Tooth," he said.

"I wouldn't dream of leaving it behind," I assured him.

"Oh, and dress to impress with all of your daggers. Rumor is that the elven Princess loves daggers too."

"Oh! Competition!" I said excitedly.

"Exactly what I was thinking," he beamed proudly.

"Jared, I have such an amazing story to tell you," Esmeralda said with a wicked smile.

"Really?" I asked in embarrassment.

"Oh, don't worry. He will think it is as funny as I did."

"Well go tell him in your room so I don't have to witness it," I requested.

"Tell me what?" Jared asked.

"Wait," I stopped them. "Jared, can you teach me how to use my fear and transform it to become anger?"

"It is not really something that I can teach," he admitted. "I just focus on the thing that is scaring me and tell myself that if I get away or get out of it, I will kill anyone who witnessed it and save myself from embarrassment. Or I just tell myself over and over again that I am the Dragon and the Dragon fears nothing, but is angry about everything."

"Well, I'm not the Dragon," I whispered.

"No, but you're my protégé," he said. "And you did cut me. So, you're the first to make the Dragon bleed. That should help you a little bit."

"Thank you."

He pulled Esmeralda's arm and said, "Now hurry so you can tell me the story."

She began whispering to him as they walked away and just as their door closed, Jared began laughing maniacally. His laughter turned into huge booming laughter and seemed to last hours longer.

I finally finished packing, and climbed into bed. We were setting off on another journey, one that could lead to amazing discoveries for us. What were elves like? Were they similar to us? Or were they more like a tribal group?

9

IT WAS HARDER THAN I WOULD HAVE THOUGHT TO SAY GOODBYE TO Jared and Esmeralda. We took the same ship that we had used on our most recent mission and set sail, northeast. Faxon brought a bunch of books and other things to continue my education, since we were unsure of how long this journey would last. I was not too thrilled about that, but he told Finn that he had to participate as well. The look on Finn's face made it infinitely better.

I had just finished the third novel Faxon had assigned me to read when Finn yelled from below deck. I ran as fast as I could and found him in Faxon's cabin.

"What happened?" I asked breathlessly.

Finn looked at me in shock and glanced at Faxon, "Uh…"

"I told Finn he didn't have to read one of the novels I had assigned him because he had already read it," Faxon said quickly.

Finn smiled at me, but it wasn't a true smile. "Yeah."

"Liars," I accused them.

"Okay," Finn said with a sigh and ran his hand through his

hair. "Faxon has been helping me with my magic," Finn admitted. "I finally learned to make a protective shield."

Finn was learning magic? I knew he had a bit of magic, but he had said it was barely anything, just enough to light a candle. And why hadn't he told me? Why was he hiding it from me?

"Oh," I said as understanding hit me like a brick. He didn't want me to know because I did not have magic anymore and he had basically taken my place as Faxon's apprentice.

"I was going to tell you, but—"

I raised my hand and tried to smile. "It's fine. It is a good idea for you to see if you can increase the amount of magic you have and even better to learn how to protect yourself with it."

The words I said were how I should have felt. Instead, I felt sad, and the emptiness in my core that I had successfully shoved from my mind, now felt even larger. I walked away from them and went to my cabin. My breathing had become erratic and I knew I was close to crying. No. I had cried enough. It was okay to be upset that Finn was working with Faxon on his magic instead of me. It was fine to be sad and miss my magic. I would *not* cry. I should be happy for Finn. He had not been fortunate enough to be surrounded by people who wanted to provide guidance and nurture him like I had. He had a rough childhood and early teen years with that abusive captain. He deserved this. I was being selfish and it was time for me to stop being so childish.

Finally sorted out, I went back to the main deck to finish reading my novel. The day flew by as I read and submersed myself in the story.

"Dinner time," Finn whispered from beside me.

I turned and found him sitting next to me. "When did you get here?"

"About an hour ago."

"Why didn't you say anything?"

"You were so absorbed in the book that I didn't want to interrupt you, but your stomach was growling so I figured I should interrupt on its behalf."

I put the bookmark in place and kissed his cheek. "Sorry for not noticing you. I wasn't ignoring you."

We stood and headed down to meet Faxon.

"I was going to tell you about the lessons," Finn assured me.

I slipped my arm around his waist and hugged him with one arm. "I know. You were trying to protect my feelings and I appreciate it. I am glad that you are learning magic and have these opportunities now."

He kissed the top of my head and squeezed me. "Thank you."

There were three plates of food at the table with Faxon when we arrived. "Good evening," he greeted me.

"Evening."

"How is the book?" he asked and tilted his head in the direction of the book I was holding.

"Really good," I admitted. "At first it was slow, but now it's so intense and I can't figure out what will happen next."

"I'm glad that you are enjoying it," he said with a wide smile.

"So, were you able to contact the person who sent the request for assistance?" I asked. The food was good and I hadn't realized how hungry I was until I started eating. I finished my plate of food and asked for seconds.

"I was able to contact them. They are expecting us," he said and stared at me with an amused glint in his eyes. "Next time, you wouldn't be so hungry if you ate all of your daily meals."

"Well it is your fault," I accused him.

"Mine?" he asked in disbelief.

"Yes, you are the one who gave me this book and ordered me to read it. If it had not been so interesting, I would not have missed lunch."

Finn laughed and Faxon shook his head. "Just like a woman to try to blame a man even when it is her fault," Faxon said. "You're just like your aunt."

"I am so going to tell her that you said that," I warned him with a glare.

"One more thing won't make any difference," he told me and brushed some dust off his sleeve.

"You know, if you keep doing things to upset her, she will hold more and more things from you," I warned him.

"Wait, what things? You know things that she has kept from me? What things? What things!" he asked with wild eyes.

"The sea dragon told me that it was only able to communicate with royalty," I told him.

"What! Why didn't you tell me that?" he asked and then made his notebook and pen appear out of thin air, so he could make a note about it.

"She told me not to. I cannot disobey an order from the Queen."

"Finn," he admonished. "You should have told me."

"I can't disobey the Queen either," he said and shrugged. "Sorry, Faxon."

"What else is she keeping from me?" he asked, pen poised to take more notes.

I shrugged. "Not sure."

"You do too!" he accused.

"I really don't know," I told him truthfully. "If there are more things I cannot remember them right now."

He looked skeptical, but he sent his notebook back to wherever he kept it and turned to Finn. "Tomorrow we will continue with your training. I think by the time we reach our destination, you will be able to create and sustain a field that will protect you and whoever is within the battlefield and keep enemies away."

"That's awesome," I told Finn with a genuine smile.

"Let's hope I can learn that in time. It would be very useful in a battlefield, especially one against magic users."

"Speaking of the battlefield," Faxon said. "I suppose I should tell you a bit more of what I know about our allies."

I pushed my empty plate to the middle of the table and crossed my arms on top of the table.

"Most of the humans there do not have magic," he explained. "The elves have magic, but it is not like mine. They can heal and perform a few spells, but they do not use that in battle. They are faster, stronger, and live longer lives than humans. I have heard a rumor that the King of the Elves is over five hundred years old, but I have not been able to confirm it."

"So, they are likely much harder to defeat in battle," I said.

"Yes, but the women do not usually fight, only the men," he continued.

"Wonderful," I mumbled.

Faxon laughed and said, "Don't worry, they know that I am bringing you and that you are a fighter."

"How far from the docks will we have to travel to reach the fight?" Finn asked.

"Instead of docking and walking to our destination, we will teleport once we are close enough and the ship will head to the harbor where some of their people will unload our stuff and transport it to the castle where we will be staying," Faxon explained.

"Are you sure that you can teleport us safely?" I asked. "Originally, you said we had to sail because you could not teleport us safely and might inadvertently send us to the battlefield."

"I'm going to communicate to one of the people there and they will go to a clear space for me to teleport to them."

"Have you done this before?" I asked nervously.

He looked insulted. "Of course, I have."

I raised my hands into the air. "I was just checking."

"As if I would put you in such a dangerous situation without having tested it first. Do you have such little faith in me?"

I rolled my eyes. "Drama queen."

"So, how long until we reach our destination?" Finn asked.

"I can't remember," Faxon answered. "I'm hoping it will not be much longer because I want to make sure we get there in enough time to help them."

"Arriving after they have been defeated would be pretty embarrassing," I agreed.

"Alright, I'm heading to bed. Tomorrow we will continue with your math lessons," he told us.

Finn and I groaned at the same time, Faxon left with a laugh.

"Can we outlaw math when we become King and Queen?" Finn asked me.

"Sadly, that is a decision that must be passed by the Order of Elders, and I have a feeling that math will not be outlawed as long as Faxon is alive."

"Did you hear him rambling about equations and letters in math? What was he talking about? Why would you have letters in math?" he asked and rubbed his temples. "I already have a headache just thinking about it."

"Let's hope we make it before we get to that stuff," I whispered.

❦

OUR MATH LESSONS were even more torturous than we had anticipated. For four hours, Faxon instructed us, made us practice, and then even forced us to take a test. Finn and I hid once Faxon dismissed us and we didn't come out until the next day. Finn used his speed to sneak food out of the kitchen for us to eat and we were discussing hiding for another day when Faxon found us.

"Here you are! I looked everywhere for you!" he exclaimed.

"We've been had!" I exclaimed.

"We are almost close enough to teleport," he informed us. "So, go get dressed and take the bags you want to keep with you for immediate use. Meet me on the main deck when you are ready."

Finn kissed my cheek and disappeared. I hurried to my cabin, changed into fresh battle-ready clothes, and took the bag that had my essentials and weapons in it. When I made it to the main deck, Finn and Faxon were already there.

"Sorry to keep you waiting," I said and hoisted my bag over my shoulder.

"I want you both to place one hand on each of my shoulders and then hold hands," Faxon ordered us.

We did as he asked, and he closed his eyes. His lips moved, but I could not hear what he was saying. His lips stilled and then we entered the vortex of the teleportation spell. It lasted longer than when we had teleported home from Trian, and just as my lunch threatened to make a reappearance, we stopped.

I opened my eyes and Finn and I released Faxon. He turned and greeted someone behind us.

"You okay?" Finn asked.

"Yeah, that spinning is not something I think I will ever get used to," I admitted. We were inside a room of stone walls with candle chandeliers. It seemed likely that this was the castle, but this room had nothing inside of it, not even a table or chair.

"Macon, I would like to present Princess Tilia of the Realm of Olanze, heir to the Kingdom of Crilan," Faxon said.

I turned and curtsied to the rough looking human.

He bowed and said, "It is an honor to meet you. Faxon has told me much about you."

"Don't believe everything he says," I grumbled.

"Oh, I assure you that it was all good things," Macon said.

"And this is Finn, Chief of Crilan and fiancé of Princess Tilia," Faxon introduced.

Finn and Macon shook hands and I could tell that they were testing each other a bit. "Nice to meet you, Macon." Finn greeted him with a smile.

"Nice to meet you as well," Macon said and they released their handshake.

"What is the current situation?" Faxon asked Macon.

"Well, you've arrived in the middle of night so everyone is asleep. The Kings would like to meet you and go over everything in the morning, if that's alright with you?" Macon asked.

Faxon nodded. "Sounds good. If you will just show us to our rooms, we will settle in for the night."

Macon opened a door and poked his head outside, summoning someone out there. The new man led the way and Macon walked behind Finn and I, beside Faxon.

"It's nice to see another female with a sword at her hip," Macon said to me.

"You don't have many of those here?" I asked.

"We have a couple, but really only one who is noteworthy," he told me. "I believe you two will either be the best of friends or hate each other. It's often hard to tell with Marin."

"These three doors will serve as your quarters while here," the new man, who's name I hadn't caught, said.

"Thank you," I whispered.

He left and Macon said, "This isn't a castle that I am familiar with, so I won't be much help in telling you where everything is, but there will be someone to take you to breakfast tomorrow morning."

Macon left and Faxon turned to us. "Do *not* leave your rooms. I mean it. I don't want to find out that you wandered around and got into a fight with people who are supposed to be our allies due to a misunderstanding."

"We will stay in our rooms," I promised.

"Good." He opened his door and paused. "Your *own* rooms," he added.

"Yes, sir," I agreed.

Finn kissed me goodnight and I went to my room. This place felt *different*. I couldn't single out what it was or how, but it just did not feel the same as Crilan. The room was rather large, but sparsely furnished with a bed and dresser. I set my bags on the floor next to the bed and lay on the bed with my clothes, boots, and weapons on. You never knew when the enemy would attack, so it was best to be prepared.

The bed was incredibly soft and it didn't take me long to fall asleep. It also didn't seem like it was long before knocking at my door woke me. "Breakfast is ready," a strange voice called through my door.

"Coming," I called back. I ran a brush through my hair, braided it, and then opened the door.

The man bowed to me and when I stepped out, I found Faxon and Finn waiting as well. "Please follow me this way," he said.

We did and after a few turns, a staircase down, and a second set of turns, we were led into a dining hall. It was empty, shockingly, and we were the only ones who ate. After we had finished we were led to a war room where we encountered our first elf.

He was handsome and looked incredibly fit. His hair was silver and his ears were indeed pointed as the stories told.

Faxon bowed low to him so Finn and I mimicked him.

Macon said, "This is the King of the Elves, Cesar."

"It is a great honor to meet you, Your Majesty," Faxon said humbly.

"Please rise," King Cesar requested. He had a kind voice, almost fatherly.

"King Cesar this is Princess Tilia, Chief Finn, and Arch Mage Faxon of the Kingdom of Crilan," Macon introduced.

King Cesar bowed low to us and smiled at me. "It is an honor to meet you all."

I was surprised that we were the only ones present. "Where are the others?" I asked.

"On their way," Macon assured us.

Finn stood against the far wall so that he could see anyone who entered and keep his back guarded at the same time. I stood beside Finn and adjusted the daggers on my wrists.

A human man walked in, an air of confidence around him that suggested he was important. "This is King Trenton, ruler of the human realm," Macon introduced.

We were all introduced to him and I wished that we had been the last ones to come so we didn't have to be introduced so many times.

A female elf with long silver hair and delicate pointed ears entered. She was beyond graceful and the most beautiful female I had ever seen. I felt inferior to her in every way and all she had done was enter the room. "Queen Amadis of the Elves," Macon introduced.

She walked over to me and curtsied low before me. "It is nice to meet you, Princess Tilia."

I curtsied back and said, "Thank you, Queen Amadis."

I couldn't help staring at her. She was so lovely. "First time meeting elves?" she asked in a whisper.

I blushed and looked down. "I don't mean to be rude."

"Nonsense," she told me with a kind smile. "I'm sure this is quite a shock for you."

"You are so lovely," I told her finally.

She smiled wide and said, "Thank you. You are quite lovely as well." She turned and faced Faxon. "You vibrate with power," she told him softly. "It's alarming how powerful you are."

He bowed and said, "I assure you that we mean you and your people absolutely no harm. We are here to take care of something that should have never reached your shores."

She returned to her husband's side and said, "The Princesses and Princes will not be joining us this morning. Princess Marin had a run in with Malavar late last night that has left them all shaken and in need of a bit more sleep than usual."

"What happened?" Faxon asked, full of concern.

Who was Malavar? Was that the name of the man?

"He summoned her from her bed, called her so that she could only answer it and had no power to stop. He offered her a compromise of her joining him or he would kill all of us," King Cesar said.

"How awful," I whispered and gripped my sword's hilt.

"It seems you may have some experience with him as well," Macon commented.

"Princess Tilia was a victim of a cruel spell that he placed on her to upset me," Faxon explained.

"To get at you?" King Cesar asked.

Faxon explained further, "Princess Tilia is one of a handful of people whom I treasure. He figured out that I was fond of her and hurt her and used a spell to make her terrified of me."

"What a horrid spell," Queen Amadis gasped.

"How do you know this man?" King Cesar asked. "We were told that he came from your Realm, but it seems that he may hold a vendetta against you, if he hurt the Princess that way."

"He is my brother," Faxon said.

The shock I felt was shared by everyone around us.

"Your brother?" Macon asked.

"Yes," Faxon answered, though the disdain in his voice was obvious.

"And you have no issue defeating him?" King Cesar asked.

"My brother has been taunting me for a long time. I had

thought he was dead, but it seems that he was here, hiding. I failed to kill him and it is my duty to end his life before he can cause any more pain."

"How likely are you to be able to defeat him?" Macon asked.

"He is not strong enough to defeat me," Faxon assured them. "I will be able to defeat him as long as I can see him face to face."

"Faxon is the strongest mage in our Realm," I told them. "He is capable of incredible feats and I do not doubt that he can defeat him."

"Very well. What is the plan?" Macon asked Faxon.

"When his troops attack, I will use one of his men to send him a call of a sort and when he shows his face, I will end his life."

"He doesn't always come with his troops," King Cesar explained.

He nodded at Finn and me, "That is why they are here."

"What can two teenagers do against an army?" the human King asked.

"Finn is the fastest man in all of the Realms, which I have no doubt of, and Tilia is a skilled fighter."

"Women fighting our battles," the human King said with a sigh. "I never thought I would see the day."

"Our Realm allows women to fight," I explained. "And our King and Queen are terrifying in battle. I was trained by them and I promise that I will be more than capable of defeating the army."

"How fast are you?" Queen Amadis asked Finn.

"Very fast," he said with a smirk.

"Can you take this from my hand?" King Cesar asked and held an apple in the palm of his hand.

Finn shrugged and then disappeared from beside me, only

to reappear a moment later tossing the apple in the air and catching it. "Yes."

King Cesar beamed like a proud father. "Impressive."

Finn bowed and said, "Thank you."

"Well, I guess we will just wait until he attacks again and go from there," Macon said.

We all agreed and headed out of the room. Queen Amadis walked next to Finn and I and inquired about my sword. I drew it to show her, holding it out.

A woman ran down the hall towards us with her sword drawn. I blocked her incredibly fast strike with my sword and was shocked to find Finn with his sword between ours and a male elf with his sword between the woman's and Finn's. I hadn't seen Finn or the male elf move. Was he as fast as Finn?

"Enough!" Queen Amadis ordered.

Finn and I stepped back, but kept our swords drawn. The human girl looked at me curiously just as I looked at her. The male elf glared at Finn and gripped his sword hilt tightly.

"Favian," the Queen snapped. "Sheath your sword."

"I will once they do," he growled.

"After you," Finn snarled.

"Boys," I said softly. "If we are all in this castle together, then perhaps that means that we are allies."

"Then why haven't you sheathed your sword?" the human girl asked, moving her black hair behind her shoulder as she watched me.

"Because you have yet to sheath yours," I commented.

"Finn. Tilia. Stand down," Faxon ordered us.

"Who are they?" the male elf asked.

"I thought they were attacking you," the human girl said to the Elf Queen.

She smiled and said, "I asked about her sword. She was simply drawing it for me to inspect."

"Oh," the human girl said and lowered her sword a bit.

Queen Amadis turned to us and bowed. "Please forgive my children. They are protective to a fault. I am pleased to introduce my son, Prince Favian and his fiancée, Princess Marin of the Elves."

She was a princess of the Elves? She didn't look like an elf.

"This is Princess Tilia and her fiancé Chief Finn," she continued with the introductions.

"A double set of engaged Princes and Princesses," Faxon commented.

We all sheathed our weapons and bowed or curtsied to each other.

"It's nice to meet one of my cousins," Finn said to Princess Marin.

I looked at him in shock and then at Marin. She didn't look like him. How did he know they were related? He said he had never been here or heard of anything from here?

She squinted her eyes a moment and then they widened as she gasped. "Is that what this feeling means?" she asked him.

He nodded.

"Father!" she called.

A man materialized beside her and Faxon immediately dropped into a bow.

"What?" I asked Faxon, but he hadn't looked up yet.

"You called?" the man asked her. He turned and looked at us and after taking us in, he looked back at Finn. "Nephew," he greeted. "It has been a very long time since I met a nephew."

"Tilia, bow," Faxon ordered me.

Finn bowed to the man, so I bowed as well.

"Who is he?" I asked curiously. "How are you related to her?"

"She doesn't know?" Marin asked Finn.

"It is not common over there," he mumbled.

Faxon stood up and glared at Finn. "You withheld this from me?"

"I didn't want to be tested by you anymore," he admitted.

"I don't mean to be rude, but what the hell is going on!" I asked loudly.

"Do you remember when I told you that I was a descendant of Aquinn?" Finn asked.

"The sea god, yes?" I asked cautiously.

"Well, I am his son. My mother was human."

"You said your father was a soldier—"

"That was my stepfather," he explained.

"That's why Lance is your half brother," I realized.

"Yes."

"So, you're half god?" I asked in disbelief.

"Yes."

I turned and looked at the man next to Princess Marin. "And he's—"

"A god as well," Marin said with a smile.

"Whoa."

"You are a fascinating woman," the god said with a smile. "You and my daughter will be fast friends."

"Thank you for showing," Princess Marin said. "I just wanted to be sure what Finn and I thought was true."

He turned to Faxon and said, "Thank you for coming. It is difficult not to involve myself where my daughter is concerned, and if you had not come today, I was likely to step in."

"I will fix this issue. I promise," Faxon said and bowed again.

"I am sure that you will," he said.

"Okay. Now that we are all on the same page, why don't you get to know each other better," Queen Amadis suggested.

"Princess Tilia, would you like to join us for breakfast?" Princess Marin asked.

"Please, call me Tilia, and we ate recently, but I could eat more."

She laughed and said, "You sound like my type of woman. I apologize for attacking you."

"You have no need to apologize. I most likely would have reacted the same way if our roles were reversed," I said.

"I apologize as well," Finn said to Prince Favian. "I was only trying to block Princess Marin's strike."

"It seems we were all pretty much on the same thinking," Prince Favian said. We walked a bit and he asked, "How did you move so fast?"

Finn smirked. "Speed is my best ability."

"I didn't even see you move," Princess Marin praised.

"Oh, you haven't seen anything yet," I told her. "Just wait until we get on the battlefield. You weren't exactly slow yourself," I said to Prince Favian. "Had Finn not intercepted, I might not have won that battle."

"Have you seen elves before?" Princess Marin asked.

"No. King Cesar was my first," I admitted.

"You don't have elves in your Realm?" Prince Favian asked.

"No."

"Are they all human?" he asked.

"Yes. According to Faxon, we have quite a few more humans with magic than you do."

"Do you have magic?" Princess Marin asked.

I flinched and Finn immediately linked our hands together to provide emotional support. Princess Marin and Prince Favian seemed to see it all.

"I had magic," I told them, "but a Prince attempted to attack my Kingdom with a magic expunger, a device that takes away your magic. I was able to get him away from my Kingdom, but he used the device on me."

Prince Favian looked shocked and Princess Marin looked sad. "That's terrible. I am so sorry."

"I knew the risks when I set out to confront him," I replied with a sad smile.

"A device that steals your magic," she whispered and looked at Favian. "It's terrifying."

"We spent the last few months tracking and destroying the rest of the devices in our Realm," Finn told them. "It seems that our Kingdom has become a bit too terrifying to them and they wanted a device capable of defeating us."

"Would that defeat you?" Prince Favian asked.

Finn laughed. "No. We have warriors who do not use magic. Our King is a terrifying monster of a fighter and he has no magic at all. If they stole our magic they would only anger him and seal their death warrants."

"I wish I could meet him," Princess Marin said with a glint in her eye.

"Perhaps after we defeat this enemy, we can spar," I suggested.

"That would be wonderful," she replied.

We entered the dining room and there was another male elf who was completely identical to Prince Favian.

"Twins?" I questioned.

"Yes," Princess Marin said. "This is Prince Sebastian of the Elves and Princess Deana of the humans."

Finn and I bowed and Princess Marin introduced us.

We went to sit down when Finn froze and looked slowly up into Princess Deana's eyes. "You're a—"

"Quiet," she ordered nervously.

"How did you know?" Princess Marin asked.

"The scent," he whispered.

"What's going on?" I asked.

"This is a secret to even my people," Princess Deana said to Finn. "Please, do not spread this information."

"Your secret is safe with me," he assured her.

I looked at them expectantly and Princess Marin said, "I think it will be more fun for you to find out when we go into battle."

"Fine," I said and shrugged my shoulders.

"So, how are you liking our Realm so far?" Prince Sebastian asked.

It was strange to see identical twins together, but his voice was much different. "We haven't seen much of it to be honest. We were taken to our rooms and only a few other rooms in the castle," I admitted.

"Would you like a tour of our grounds?" Princess Deana asked with a smile.

"Sure," I replied with a return smile.

"What are you ladies hungry for?" a man with an apron asked.

"Ribs," Princess Deana and Princess Marin requested at the same time.

He turned to me. "You, milady?"

"Ribs sound great."

"You, milord?" he asked Finn.

"Ribs as well."

He didn't ask the elves what they wanted, but when he returned he set a plate of vegetables and fruits in front of them before bringing out our ribs. I lifted my first rib up to eat it and found the princesses staring at me.

"What?" I asked.

They looked at each other and then Princess Marin said, "We're waiting to see what type of eater you are."

I took a bite and moaned. "This is delicious!"

"Oh good, she's not a weirdo," Princess Marin said and started eating.

We ate in silence and I was shocked that both princesses finished their ribs around the same time that I did.

"It's not often that we can find women who eat food or enjoy it as much as we do," Princess Deana told me.

"Well, I can see how it would be awkward when your Princes don't eat the same types of food as you," I commented.

"Elves don't kill animals for food," Prince Sebastian explained.

"Makes sense," Finn replied.

"So, what's your favorite weapon?" Princess Marin asked me.

"Daggers and swords," I replied right away. "What about you?"

"Same," she said happily.

"I prefer a bow and arrow, but swords are my secondary," Prince Favian said.

"I'm awful with a bow and arrow," I admitted.

"Me too!" Princess Deana said.

"I'm more of an ax user," Finn commented.

"Axes are fun," Prince Sebastian said, "but swords are my favorite."

"So, why don't you tell us something about yourselves?" Prince Favian asked.

Finn glanced at me and I smirked. "Go on, tell them how we met."

"Tilia," he groaned.

"Oh, come on," I urged him.

"I would love to hear that," Princess Marin said while Princess Deana nodded.

"I suppose I should start by saying that I wasn't always a Chief in Crilan," he began.

"What were you?" Prince Sebastian asked.

"A pirate."

Everyone stilled and Princess Marin asked, "A pirate?"

"A pirate captain to be exact. I found Tilia outside of a party in a dress wearing jewels and I stole her necklace," he admitted.

"You stole her necklace?" Princess Deana asked in shock. "Why didn't you cut him or something?"

"He is too fast," I told her. "You'll see. I tried, but I went that night and stole them back."

"How did you steal them back?" Prince Sebastian asked.

"Well, I suppose I should backtrack. My mother was the Princess of Crilan, sister to the current Queen. My father was royalty of another nature. My father was the King of Pirates."

"A pirate king?" Princess Marin asked. "You guys are very interesting."

"Thank you. Yes, my father was the King of Pirates and I was raised on his pirate ship until I was ten, and then I was taken to live with my Aunt and Uncle in Crilan to learn to become Princess. However, I was also doing pirate things without them knowing and that's how I stole the necklace back from Finn."

"How did a pirate become Chief of a Kingdom?" Prince Favian asked.

"I retired as captain so that I could live with Tilia on land. King Jared held a tournament, which I won by defeating him, something that hadn't ever happened before. As part of his bet with Tilia, he appointed me Chief."

"Pirate royals," Princess Marin said. "That makes a demigod human as Elf Queen seem less strange."

"I was wondering about that," I admitted.

"I was raised by Amadis and Cesar after they found me. My parents had been murdered by ogres—"

"Ogres!" I exclaimed.

"You don't have ogres either?" Princess Deana asked.

I shook my head.

"Well, I'm working on obliterating them," Princess Marin said. "You will likely face some when they attack again."

"How exciting!" I said and looked at Finn who was also smiling.

"Dad was right, we are going to be fast friends," Princess Marin said and laughed.

"So, you were raised by the elves, but then you fell for their prince, and now you'll become their queen?" Finn asked.

She nodded. "Exactly."

"We were best friends and went on all of our missions together," Prince Favian said.

"Missions for the King and Queen?" I asked.

"No, we were mercenaries," Princess Marin explained. "Macon trained us at his mercenary training school."

"Mercenary royalty!" I exclaimed. "Together we could make every old King sputter himself to death."

They all laughed and we relaxed at the table.

"Are you certain that your Arch Mage can defeat Malavar?" Prince Favian asked.

I nodded. "One hundred percent."

"He's a terrifying man," Princess Marin whispered and her entire body tensed.

"They told us what happened. I am sorry that you had to experience that. He attacked me a few months ago, causing me incredible pain and made me fear my own family until they altered my memory and later removed something from my brain," I whispered.

"He's terrifying," Princess Deana whispered.

"Faxon is worse," I told them and then laughed. "Or better since he is on our side. His abilities are terrifying, but he is a wonderful man."

"Tilia," Faxon said from behind me.

In the space of a matter of seconds, everyone at the table

sprang into action. Swords were drawn, chairs were shoved away, and Finn had almost decapitated Faxon again. Faxon luckily used a shield, which kept everyone an arm's length from him and then he froze us all.

"I apologize for startling you," he said to us.

He released us and I sighed. "You should really find a way to make a chime sound or something to warn us when you're tele-porting. Finn tried to decapitate you again."

"How did you get here?" Prince Favian asked angrily.

"Simple teleportation spell," Faxon explained.

"How did you freeze us?" Princess Marin asked and rubbed at her arm.

"That's more of a reflex spell, but I'm sure that I could teach it to you," he offered.

"Did you use your Sight on them?" I asked curiously.

He smirked. "A Seer always observes his allies and enemies."

"What are you talking about?" Prince Sebastian asked.

"May I sit?" Faxon asked. Everyone nodded, so he took the seat to my right and explained, "I am a Seer, I can look at you and am able to figure out how much magical power you have, what type, and there are many other abilities, but that's the one Princess Tilia was referring to."

"How fascinating," Prince Sebastian whispered.

"What did you need?" I asked Faxon.

"To give you this," he whispered and held out his open palm, which had a ring.

"I thought you didn't want to give me something because then people would know that you had given it to me and that I might be important to you?" I asked softly.

"He already knows that you're important to me," he reminded me, "and it's time to stop trying to hide."

"What does this one do?" I asked him.

"It does as the last one did, allows you to contact me and hear what you're thinking," he said.

"I don't have magic, remember? The last one didn't work because I couldn't activate it," I reminded him.

"This one does not need the wearer to have magic because it is imbued with mine."

"Your what?" I asked.

"My magic."

"You put your magic in the ring?" I asked in shock.

He nodded.

"But—"

He set his hand on my shoulder and said, "I have plenty of magic to spare. This is a very small amount and it is stored in the crystal ball here in the center." He indicated the small pinkish stone in the middle of the ring.

"It's very common for magic users to imbue crystals with their magic so that if they are low during a fight, they can take the magic from that crystal and use it," Prince Favian told me.

"Although it will need to be recharged once it is used, won't it?" Princess Marin asked.

Faxon nodded. "Very true."

"Are you sure?" I asked him. "I don't want you to do something that you will regret or blame yourself for if I—"

He took my hand and slipped the ring on. "The only thing that I care about is your safety. With this ring, you will be able to contact me when you need help. I thought about this for a long time. You remember when the magic expunger activated and you almost died on that island?" he asked.

How could I forget?

"Yes."

"If you hadn't been able to contact me with your last bit of magic, using that ring, you would have died and we would have never found you. We would still be searching for you, having torn apart Drimla and sunk the Kingdom to the bottom of the ocean floor when we couldn't find you," he told me.

"I like these people," Princess Marin commented softly.

"With the ring, I will know that you are safe, or will be as soon as I arrive," he said.

"Let's hope that I won't have need to use it anytime soon. I'm personally tired of being kidnapped and attacked to the point that I need to be saved," I told him grumpily.

"See!" Princess Marin shouted at Prince Favian. "It's not just me!"

"Excuse me?" I asked.

"We've had a bad couple of years with kidnapping and attacks," Princess Marin told me. "And I'm supposed to be strong and yet I keep needing him to save me," she said and jerked her thumb at Prince Favian.

"Perhaps it is a curse of being a princess," I suggested.

"I've never been kidnapped," Princess Deana said.

"You'd better knock on wood," Princess Marin told her.

"Have you been able to See him or sense him?" I asked Faxon.

He nodded. "He's moving closer to us, but slowly. I believe he is moving with his warriors."

"Can you tell how long until they get here?" Prince Favian asked.

"If they continue at the pace that they are, most likely tomorrow morning," Faxon said, "but I think they will likely stop to rest tonight."

"Are you certain that you will be okay?" I asked him softly.

He glared at me. "Do not forget who I am, Tilia."

I raised my hands in the air. "I know. You're the strongest mage in the world. I was just making sure."

His frown relaxed into one of concern and he whispered,

"Stay safe. I'll see you for dinner." He kissed my cheek and then disappeared.

"That is amazing," Prince Sebastian whispered. "Our mages can teleport, but he doesn't even chant or anything."

"Most things are second nature to him now," I explained. "That spell to freeze us was done by his eyes blinking shut."

"So, you and the mage seem pretty close," Prince Sebastian commented.

"I was dumped, uh, delivered to my aunt when I was ten years old and Faxon had been a silent part of my life up until just before my seventeenth birthday when he began tutoring me in magic," I explained. "We grew pretty close quickly after that, with me becoming his apprentice of sorts and I got into a lot of trouble the next year and a half. He doesn't usually let anyone in, so it's been rough on him. I am the only child any of them has had."

' "Are you certain that there is no cure for this device stealing your magic?" Princess Deana asked. "From what it seems like, your land has a lot of magic and must have something—"

"Faxon said that he knows of nothing and that the ones it had been used on before never recovered," I replied sadly. "If Faxon doesn't know of a way, then that usually means that there isn't one."

"Would you like the tour of the castle now?" Princess Marin asked.

I nodded and we all headed out of the dining room and around the castle. It wasn't as large as home, and it was not ornate, but it was still a decent castle. The garden outside was very lovely and I smelled each of the strange flowers they had growing.

"You could take a couple home with you to grow in your Kingdom if you would like," Princess Deana offered.

"Really?" I asked happily.

She nodded. "Of course."

"That would be wonderful. These flowers smell so exquisite."

"It sort of reminds me of the rainforest on the island in the Fire Ring," Finn commented.

"Oh yeah, the one where we almost fell into the volcano after the giant crab and squid were fighting."

"Whoa, back up," Princess Marin said. "What happened?"

We sat on the cool grass in the garden and I asked, "How about we swap a story for a story?"

"Marin, can I talk to you?" Prince Favian asked her.

They walked away and spoke quietly for a couple minutes and Prince Favian's brow furrowed. What was he upset about? Did he not want her to tell us stories? Was he worried we might somehow use the information against them?

The two hugged and then they came back.

"Okay, you go first," Princess Marin requested.

"I had just joined Finn's crew and we were sailing—"

"His crew?" Princess Deana asked.

"Pirate crew," I explained.

"You weren't joking about being pirates?" Prince Favian asked with a scowl.

I turned and tugged down my shirt so that they could see the tattoo, my father's mark with Finn's mark, on my shoulder. "This is my father's pirate mark and Finn's pirate mark," I explained.

Finn showed them his tattoo and they quieted again.

"Anyway, we were sailing and he took me to the Fire Ring, a group of four islands that make a ring shape and each have a volcano on them. First, we ran into a sea dragon who decided to let us pass and then while we were on the volcano looking at it, a huge crab and a huge squid started fighting and they slammed into the island."

"How huge?" Princess Deana asked with wide, sparkling eyes.

"Twice the size of my ship at least," Finn replied.

"The squid's eye was larger than my body," I told them.

"You saw its eye?" Finn asked me.

"It swam under me," I said, "right before the mermaid grabbed me."

"A mermaid!" Marin and Deana exclaimed.

I nodded. "She was trying to kill me, but I cut her with my dagger and then had to cut my hair because she was pulling me down to drown me by it."

Finn touched my hair and sighed. "She had beautiful, long hair."

"It's growing back," I reminded him.

"Wow, I wonder why the crab and squid were fighting?" Princess Deana asked.

"I didn't stop to ask," I told her and everyone laughed. "Your turn."

"Which story to tell..." Princess Marin whispered and tapped her finger against her chin.

"Tell her about the ogres attacking the Elven Kingdom," Prince Sebastian suggested.

"I can't really tell it," she admitted. "I don't remember all of that day."

"I do," Prince Favian said. "First, I should tell you that Marin is supposed to get rid of all of the ogres in existence," he told Finn and me.

"Why?" I asked.

"They've turned evil," she said. "My father has given me the task of destroying them."

"One day at the Elven Kingdom, a horde of ogres was sent to attack us, but they were targeting Marin specifically," Prince Favian continued. "There were over two thousand of them. The elves are great fighters, but that was still a large number of ogres to deal with and we don't keep our army in one spot and we had no idea how long it would take to get everyone there. It turned out we didn't need any of them."

"Why not?" Finn asked.

"Because we had Marin," he said with a proud smile. "She flew into action and killed them."

"Wow," I whispered.

"You're up," Prince Favian said.

"Tell them about the chimeras," Finn suggested.

"Chimeras? You have chimeras, too?" Princess Deana asked.

I nodded. "Yes, we don't have many of them, but they show up occasionally."

"So, what happened?" Princess Marin asked.

"Well I suppose you need back story..." I started.

"A crazy King who wanted to kill all pirates kidnapped Tilia to hang her as a warning to the pirates," Finn summarized. "And her family turned the castle to ash, beheaded the King, and told them that they were lucky because her family felt merciful that day."

"That was merciful?" Princess Deana asked in a whisper followed by a gulp.

"I wouldn't have let them off so easy," Prince Favian said and folded his arms across his chest.

"To get back at me for that happening, the Queen sent me a letter, which was spelled to reverse teleport a chimera to us."

"They sent a chimera to you?" Princess Deana asked in shock. "What did you do?"

"Well, initially I froze because they'd also sent mist that made you feel fear and the last time I had faced a chimera I was almost killed, so my track record with them wasn't the best."

"Mist that makes you afraid? I really don't like the sounds of these things," Deana whispered.

"It didn't effect my Aunt or Faxon because they have shields that protect them from spells like that. And my Uncle uses fear to make himself angry, so it didn't really matter to him."

"How did you break free?" Marin asked.

"Faxon broke it," I answered honestly.

"He broke the spell?" Sebastian asked.

I nodded. "He broke the spell and I became enraged because this had happened in front of a large crowd of our citizens and I sort of went a bit crazy and killed the chimera."

"They locked her and the chimera in a containment bubble," Finn told them. "I almost killed Faxon for that."

"She was perfectly safe," Faxon said behind Finn where he had appeared, sitting on the grass.

"It's very disconcerting when you do that," Finn told him.

"Maybe I should put a bell on you, like a cat," I suggested.

"I won't wear it," he told me.

"Why would you lock your princess in a containment spell with a chimera?" Prince Sebastian asked Faxon.

"She needed to face her fear and the stupid thing spit fire, so we had to use the containment spell to protect our citizens," Faxon explained.

"What if she had gotten hurt?" Deana asked.

"The spell was created with the terms that King Jared or Queen Esmeralda could enter at will. If she were in danger, Jared would have leapt in and cut the beast to shreds before it could severely harm her."

"You have a lot of faith in your King," Favian noted.

"You should see him fight," Finn said and shook his head. "If I didn't have my speed, he would murder me in a breath."

"Finish your story," Faxon urged me. "It's getting to the best part."

"You mean because you were there and helped?" I guessed.

"Partly."

"Fine. After I killed the chimera, the spell on the letter activated and Faxon noticed somehow. He grabbed me just before we were both teleported to the castle dungeons of Drimla."

"Why did you grab on to her?" Favian asked.

"Because I could teleport us back from wherever we were going and I am a decent healing mage, so if she was injured I could treat her," he explained.

"And?" I probed.

"And I wanted to have some fun," he admitted. "It gets so boring in peaceful times."

"When we arrived, there were three more chimeras waiting for us and a shadowy figure above our heads. It was the Queen! She wanted me to die and thought this would ensure my death."

"What did you do?" Sebastian asked.

"Faxon froze the chimeras in place and I cut all of their heads off."

"Do their heads fall when they're frozen?" Marin asked.

I shook my head. "No, that's part of why we did it. It's so much more fun to see people's reactions when you release the spell and all of the body parts fell into a heap."

"What did the Queen do?" Deana asked.

"She tried to flee, but I wasn't done showing off. Faxon made a piece of the floor shoot up under me really fast, which tossed me into the air. I did a flip in the air and landed next to her and then killed her."

"Then we killed the Prince who was going to attack us and Tilia claimed their Kingdom for ours. Then I teleported us back home," Faxon finished.

"Your Kingdom sounds amazing and terrifying all at the same time," Princess Deana whispered.

"Did you come to talk to me?" I asked Faxon.

"I actually came to ask Prince Favian a question," he replied.

"Me?" Favian asked.

Faxon nodded. "Would you step away from the group for a minute so I can ask you something?"

"Why do you have to take him away?" I asked.

"Because I don't want you to hear our discussion," he admitted.

Favian stood and followed Faxon across the gardens. Faxon talked quickly, his lips moving faster than usual and his arms moving animatedly. After a moment Favian replied and made strange movements with his hands.

"Any idea what they're talking about, Princess Marin?" I asked.

"Please, let's drop the titles. And sadly, no I do not," she said.

"Tilia," Finn whispered, "what's that on your hand?"

I looked down and found a strange red bug with black dots on my hand.

I prepared to kill it, but Deana grabbed my wrist. "It's just a ladybug. They're not dangerous."

She released me and I raised the hand with the bug on it closer to my face. It was cute looking. I blew on it and the shell split to let out wings which it used to fly away.

"What's the Elven Kingdom like?" I asked curiously.

Marin smiled and said, "It's beautiful. There are trees everywhere, tall grass, and we have a fighting arena right behind the castle."

"That comment just sealed your friendship with Tilia," Finn said and chuckled.

"I really wish we could spar now," I told her.

"Me too, but knowing my luck we would wear ourselves out and then we would get attacked," she said with a longing sigh.

"After we defeat them," I assured her.

She nodded, smiling.

"Alright, I've taken up enough of the Prince's time," Faxon said when they returned.

"Have a nice chat?" I asked him.

"I know you don't like being kept in the dark, but it's for your own good," Faxon told me. "Have I ever done anything to warrant your distrust?"

"No," I mumbled while looking at the blade of grass I held in my hand.

"Finn, don't let her pester the Prince," Faxon ordered.

Finn nodded and then Faxon disappeared. "Tilia," Finn warned.

"I'm not going to ask," I promised and pouted at him.

"Oh, that's a good pout," Marin praised.

"Indeed," Deana agreed with a nod.

"Finn," I begged.

"Your pouting does not effect me," he said and folded his arms across his chest.

I thought about something sad and let a few tears well up in my eyes.

"She's really good," Marin whispered.

"I can't even cry on demand," Deana said in awe.

"She can't full cry," Finn told them. "She can just muster up a few tears to make Faxon feel bad and then he usually gives in to her."

I sighed and wiped my eyes. "It has yet to work on Finn."

"Why do they insist on pouting?" Favian asked Finn.

"They think it will make us feel bad for them," Finn replied.

"Like a kicked puppy," Sebastian said.

"Men," I grumbled and Deana and Marin nodded in agreement.

"You're grumpy," Finn commented. "Do you want to spar?" he asked.

"A short match," I said happily.

"What? You're going to spar with a fight coming at any moment?" Sebastian asked.

"Finn won't even raise his heart rate," I said, "and I'll just exert enough energy to calm down."

"I've got to see this," Deana said.

"I thought we were going to surprise them on the field?" Finn asked me.

"You'll hold back," I assured him with a smile.

"Of course, I'll be holding back," he said with a smirk.

"Is there an area we can use?" I asked Deana.

"Yeah, this way," she said and waved at us to follow her. She led the way to a circle of dirt that looked well worn down. "This is where the guards train," she explained.

"It's perfect," I said in thanks. I went to the middle and drew two daggers, holding one in each hand.

"Ready?" Finn asked. He held his sword down at his side and waited for me to start.

"Ready," I said and launched myself at Finn. This was the best way for me to unwind. With Finn, I could be sure that I would not hurt him and he would not hurt me. I attacked again and again while Finn blocked each attack. Much too soon, I felt my heart beating faster and my breathing increase. I raised my hand and Finn stopped.

"Done?" he asked.

I nodded. "Yes, I got my excess energy out."

"That was incredible," Deana said. "You two looked so in sync."

Favian shook his head. "They weren't in sync, he was just moving faster than her."

"If that was you holding back, which judging by your relaxed breathing pattern it was, how fast can you go?" Marin asked.

"That will be a surprise for you at the battle," I told her. I put my daggers away and Finn sheathed his sword. "Thank you."

He bowed and said, "I live, but to serve you, milady."

"If only he meant it," I said dreamily.

"They always misinterpret what that means," Favian said to Finn.

"Why is that?" Finn asked him. "Why are they so stubborn that they refuse to even try to understand?"

"Well, they are stubborn in general," Favian commented. Finn and he laughed together and I found myself enjoying this. It was good for Finn to be around someone his own age who could make him laugh and who he could joke about things to.

"What is it supposed to mean?" I asked.

"Yes, please *enlighten* our stubborn minds," Marin said.

"It means that I am here to ensure you are happy and safe. That does not mean falling to your every whim and desire," Favian informed us.

"We would be happier if you did what we asked," I said.

"It's almost terrifying how similar those four are," Sebastian whispered to Deana behind us.

"What are you talking about?" Marin and I asked at the same time. We looked at each other and burst into a fit of laughter.

Everyone joined in and I found myself hoping that we could stay longer. I had Natalie back in Crilan, but she didn't love fighting like Marin did.

We made our way to the dining room where we would be having dinner and my mood began to sour. Not only would we be facing the battle soon, but we would leave soon thereafter.

"I wish we knew how to teleport," I told Finn.

"Why is that?" he asked.

"So, we could visit places like this more than once or twice in our lifetime," I said.

"It is nice here," he commented.

"How was your day?" Faxon asked when we entered.

"It was lovely," I answered and then turned to the King of Humans and King of Elves and bowed. "Your Highnesses."

"Have my children been behaving?" King Cesar asked.

"They've been very kind," I assured him.

"Wonderful," he said.

"Tilia," Marin called, "come sit with us."

"Coming," I called to her.

"It warms my heart to see my daughter find another woman her age that also loves fighting. She's so very often an abnormality in that sense. I only wish you lived closer," King Cesar said.

"Tilia and I were just discussing that," Finn admitted to him.

"Dinner is ready," a man announced at the back of the room.

We took our seats at the table with the Elven Princes, Marin, and Deana. Marin tossed me a round piece of fruit that was bumpy and green and just looked odd.

"What is this?" I asked.

"A delicious treat only grown in the Elven Kingdom," she told me.

I took a bite and the fruit seemed to melt in my mouth. "This is amazing," I told her and then handed it to Finn.

He took a bite and asked, "Can we take one of these plants home?"

Everyone at our table laughed, which caused the adults to look at us.

"We'll quiet down," Marin assured them.

"No," King Cesar said. "It's nice to hear all of you laugh."

"What's one creature you wish you could miniaturize and keep?" Deana asked me.

"Would it stay miniature forever?" I asked.

She nodded.

"That's a tough decision," I admitted.

"Finn?" she inquired.

"Either a dragon or a panther," he replied immediately.

"A panther would be fun," I said.

"Is that your answer?" Deana asked.

I shook my head. "No. I'm still thinking."

"I would want a dragon," Marin said.

"I want a chimera," Sebastian answered.

"I would want a hyena," I finally answered.

"A hyena?" Finn asked in disbelief.

"Yes, that way it could use its creepy laugh howl to scare my enemies and would be easily transportable," I explained.

"If you had a full sized one, it could just run next to your horse," Favian said.

"Yeah, but what fun is that? My enemies would see it and know where the noise was coming from. I could hide the miniature one and they would think that it was me and it would freak them out."

"That does sound like fun," Marin admitted.

"What about you Deana?" I asked.

"Oh, I wouldn't want one," she said. "I was just wondering what your answers would be. I'm shocked that you didn't say a tiger or lion."

"They're too beautiful in their normal state that miniaturizing them would make me feel bad. I love watching them as they are," I told her.

"She tamed a panther once," Finn told them.

"I didn't tame it. I just calmed it down."

"What happened?"

"This huge panther jumps into her path and what do you think she did?" Finn asked them.

"Stabbed it?" Sebastian guessed.

"Nope," Finn replied.

"Yelled at it?" Marin guessed next.

"Nope."

"Ran?" Favian guessed.

"I've been insulted," I pretended.

"She put her sword on the ground and talked to it."

"It could have hurt you," Sebastian said.

"Oh, he didn't want to hurt me. He was just angry because we scared him and encroached on his territory. I explained that I was not tasty and that I wouldn't hurt him, and he left us alone."

We continued talking happily to one another and told jokes one after another, when suddenly Faxon sat up rigid in his seat.

"What is it?" I asked him.

Everyone stilled and all eyes turned to Faxon.

He stood up and turned slowly into a circle and then stopped and stared for a full minute in silence. "They're speeding up," he told us. "They'll be here by dawn if they maintain that speed."

"Dawn? Can't he at least let us sleep in," I complained.

"What made you sit up like that?" King Cesar asked.

"He used a large amount of magic to give his troops energy. I can feel him all the time, because I'm focused on his magical signature, or scent if you will, but when his level spiked like that, it made me worry he was going to teleport troops here," Faxon explained.

"Could he do that?" Marin asked.

"He could teleport about one hundred of his people, but he knows that would be suicide," he answered.

"Does he know you're here?" I asked Faxon.

"No," he said with a sly smirk.

"You've altered your signature," I said in shock. "Who does he think is here?"

"I'm using one that he doesn't know," he answered vaguely. "One that he will assume is from someone who is from here."

"Faxon," I ordered.

"Your mother's," he whispered and took his seat.

My mother's? I had no idea that he knew my mother well enough to be able to do something like that.

"Tilia," Finn whispered and slipped his hand beneath mine to hold it. "You okay?"

I nodded, but despite rarely thinking about her, it opened the hole I felt from her death. I never knew my mother. I had no idea what she had been like, aside from stories. I didn't know what she smelled like. I didn't know what she looked like. I had pictures, but pictures never did anyone justice. I wished that I had known my mother.

"Sorry," I whispered and then quickly left the room before I started crying. I would not cry in front of the others.

I walked down the hallway, but I did not remember how we had gotten there, so I turned down a second hallway and then sat against the wall. I closed my eyes and took deep breaths to let the pain pass. She was gone and there was nothing that I could do about it.

Someone walked towards me, but I didn't bother opening my eyes.

"I never knew my mother," Marin told me in a whisper.

"Me neither," Deana said.

"How old were you when she died?" Marin asked me.

"Two," I answered.

"I was three," she said. "My mother and my stepfather were murdered by ogres."

"How did you survive?" I asked and opened my eyes to look at her.

"I killed the ogres. King Cesar found me after I had just killed the last ogre and he took me home and they adopted me."

"My mother had an illness and we were too far out to sea to make it to a doctor in time," I whispered. "We had a doctor onboard of course, but it was beyond his abilities. To this day my father blames himself for her death," I told them. I wasn't sure why I trusted these strangers so quickly. I should not have. I should have kept my distance and secrets.

"Mine died during childbirth," Deana told us.

"I was lucky to have Amadis," Marin said. "She was a wonderful mother to me, but..."

"But she isn't your mother," I answered for her.

She nodded.

"I wish it would ease up," I told them. "I am nineteen now and I thought the pain would be easier, yet just hearing mention of her opens that hole in my heart."

"Oh good, it's not only me," Marin said. "I thought I was falling prey to female emotions."

"Perhaps we both are," I told her.

"That would make three of us," Deana said.

"Can I ask you two something?" I requested.

They nodded.

"Why do I feel so comfortable around you? I don't know you. I should be wary of you. Yet, I feel..."

"Connected," Deana offered.

"Yes."

"Perhaps this was in our destinies. It could be a sign that we are meant to become friends and become allies for some greater purpose," Marin whispered.

"You believe in destiny?" I asked in shock.

"I didn't use to," she admitted, "but my father, my true one, told me about my destiny to destroy the ogres and I realized that I was constantly involved in situations with ogres, even when I shouldn't have been. It makes sense."

"Do you believe in destiny?" I asked Deana.

She shrugged. "I don't believe in much these days," she admitted softly.

"You seem unhappy here, except when you're with Sebastian," I commented.

She blushed. "Life here isn't exciting, not like your lives. And I'm always stuck inside these walls."

"You sneak out occasionally, don't you?" Marin asked hopefully.

"Of course, but it's not enough," she told us. "I feel caged."

"Are you the only heir?" I asked her.

She nodded.

"I'm too different and the people aren't likely to want me crowned," she told me.

"Why not?" I asked.

Deana looked at Marin and then she said, "I'm a shapeshifter."

I stared at her in disbelief. A shapeshifter? "Wow. I would *not* have guessed that about you."

"Because I'm not bloodthirsty?" she asked.

"No, because you haven't changed all day," I answered honestly. "I only knew a couple of them, but they switched forms at least every couple of hours."

"The people don't know that she is a shapeshifter," Marin explained. "She's supposed to be the Queen of the Humans, but that's not likely to go well when she's technically not human herself."

"You are human," I said in shock.

"Not if you ask the humans," Deana responded.

"That's absurd," I told them.

"Welcome to my land," Deana mumbled.

"What will you do?" Marin asked her.

"I don't know. If I don't take the throne there is no one else here to take it."

"Don't you have cousins or someone next in line?" I asked curiously.

"No, they all died in one of the previous wars, which brought a terrible sickness with it," she told me.

"Couldn't your father name someone as heir?" I asked.

"Name someone as heir?" Deana asked me, unsure.

"In times where there is no suitable heir, a King can name his apprentice or advisor or someone else as his heir. It's a designated heir," I explained.

"You mean I could be free of becoming Queen if I can find someone for my father to name as his designated heir?" Deana asked excitedly.

"Yes."

She took my hands, pulled me to my feet and made me dance around in a circle. "You've just given me the best news!"

"Glad I could help," I said with a happy laugh.

"We should get back in the dining room or the men will likely come searching for us," Marin said.

"Thank you for coming to talk to me," I said appreciatively.

"That's what friends are for," Deana told me.

"I really hope that mage of yours is wrong about how fast they're moving," Marin said with a sigh. "It would be nice to sleep in."

"Agreed," Deana and I responded at the same time.

The three of us laughed and entered the dining room.

Finn set his hand on my leg and I squeezed it reassuringly. We didn't stay much longer since the fight was likely to start so early in the morning, but the rest of the evening was fun. Finn and I walked to my room and we lay together in silence on my bed. I liked to think that Marin was right about us being drawn together by destiny; I just hoped our destinies did not end any time soon.

"I love you," Finn whispered as we fell asleep.

"Forever," I whispered in response.

He nodded and we fell asleep in each other's arms.

10

"Oh, someone is going to be in trouble," Marin whispered.

"Why?" I asked as I rubbed my eyes and sat up in bed.

She pointed behind me to where Finn was sleeping.

"Like you and Favian weren't sleeping together last night," I accused her.

"Did you both sleep in the clothes you wore yesterday?" Deana asked.

"What are you two doing in here? What time is it?" I asked grumpily.

"You're not a morning person either," Marin said happily.

"It's about an hour past dawn," Deana answered. "We came to get you for breakfast."

"Food?" Finn mumbled.

"What are you two doing in here?" Favian asked and peeked inside with just his head entering my room.

"They're dressed," Marin informed him.

"Did someone mention food?" Finn asked as he stretched and sat up.

"You slept in your clothes?" Favian asked.

"During battle, it's better to sleep in your clothes, so that you don't have to fight naked," I told him.

"You just have to learn to dress quickly," he replied.

"What if they attack you in your room? Are you going to get dressed while fighting them?" I asked with a smirk.

"No, I'll fight them as I am, and once they're defeated, then I will get dressed," Favian answered as if that was obvious.

"Food?" Finn asked again.

"Yes, Captain, food this way," I said.

He stood up and walked around the bed with his eyes closed. Once he reached me, he threw his arms around my neck and leaned heavily on me. "Food."

"Is he still asleep?" Deana asked.

"Yep," I replied.

"Well, let's get our breakfast before we get attacked," Marin said lightheartedly.

"Yes, if she doesn't eat before a battle she'll be very cranky," Favian said and smiled at Marin.

We made our way and I realized that we were missing someone. "Where's Sebastian?"

"He's already in the dining room," Deana answered. "He was very hungry when he woke up."

"Oh, did he do something to work up an appetite?" Marin asked with a smirk.

Deana instantly blushed. "No!"

We laughed at her uncomfortable reaction and entered the room to find Sebastian sitting at a table filled with food. The smells wafted over and Finn jerked awake.

"Food," he said happily and walked quickly to the table.

"Reminds me of someone else I know," Favian teased as Marin sat just after Finn had.

I laughed and we all took our seats and ate.

"Where are the adults?" I asked.

"Still in bed most likely," Deana answered. "They were up late going over strategies and plans."

"Did they settle on one?" I asked around a bite of sweet bread.

"They deferred to Faxon's plan to have us attack the warriors, while he fights that evil man whose name we can't say," she explained.

"Yay fighting!" I said excitedly.

"No getting hurt," Finn ordered me.

"That's why I have you," I told him with a smirk.

"Good morning," Faxon greeted us.

"Morning," we all replied.

Faxon leaned over me to grab some food and then leaned on the back of my chair while he ate.

"How much longer?" I asked Faxon.

"An hour," he replied as he gobbled down his food.

"Oh man, I'm glad that I woke up when I did," Marin said.

We finished our meals and the other adults came in to eat.

"We should go warm up," I told Finn.

He nodded and we followed as Deana led us outside. We stood in a loose circle, stretched our muscles, and then took a short jog to loosen ourselves up.

"What's the game plan?" I asked Marin.

"I guess we didn't really talk about our—" she began, but was interrupted by a trumpet blaring from atop the castle wall.

"Enemies!" one of the men standing on top of the wall yelled.

We all drew our weapons and charged out of the side door.

"Stay safe!" Faxon ordered me from behind.

The army in front of us consisted of large beasts with tusks, men in leather hides, and warriors in full armor. It was the strangest combination of an army that I had ever seen.

"We call the ogres!" Marin yelled as she and Favian jogged towards the group of tusked beasts.

"Save some for me to fight," I ordered Finn.

He kissed me lightly and winked. "As the Princess wishes."

"We call middle!" I yelled to Sebastian and Deana who were off to the right, closest to the castle.

They waved and then Deana shimmered before turning into a lioness. She was beautiful and incredibly large.

"Ready?" Finn asked me.

I nodded and spun my sword. "Time to party," I said with a smile.

The enemy charged forward, weapons raised overhead, and we all moved to meet them. Finn was no more than a blur as he cut down man after man and used his speed to kill them before they even saw him. Marin and Favian spun and twirled with their swords as extensions of their arms and the two moved as one flawless unit. It was a dance of death and love, and it was beautiful. Deana and Sebastian kept close together as they killed those that came close to them and then moved forward due to the bodies piling up and limiting their movement behind them. I watched in shock as Deana turned into a beautiful lioness and tore into the army. She was gorgeous, ferocious, and amazing.

I wasn't one to be left behind and I leapt into the fray, stabbing, slicing, ducking, and dodging. A man tried to slam a mace into the side of my head, but I ducked in time and stabbed his open side with my sword. The sounds of battle filled the previously quiet field and the sun rose slowly to warm us and dry the sweat on our skin.

"Hello, Princess," Malavar whispered behind me.

I gasped in shock and spun around, ready to decapitate him, but he froze me in place with a spell.

Faxon! I screamed in my head, but knew he probably hadn't heard me since I hadn't been able to touch my ring.

Malavar grunted in pain and I saw blood spray from his shoulder where a cut had opened. Finn appeared next to me and then we were running away from where Malavar had been. He stopped in the middle of the enemy army and we resumed fighting.

"Are you hurt?" Finn asked over the noise of the battle.

"No," I answered, "he just froze me."

We didn't talk again as we fought, focused on the task at hand. My blood pumped fast and my joy grew as I lost myself to the fight.

I was so focused, that I didn't see when Malavar teleported behind me and touched my head. I gasped, but it was too late. He took control of my body and when Faxon teleported to him, I ran towards Faxon with my sword ready to attack.

"Tilia," Faxon yelled. "What are you doing?"

"Don't you love these children?" Malavar asked him. "They're so much fun to play with."

I sliced at Faxon's stomach and he jumped back in time to avoid it. "Release her," Faxon ordered Malavar as he continued to avoid my attacks.

"Do you really think that you can defeat me?" Malavar asked him.

"If you don't, you are more delusional than I believed," Faxon growled at him.

I pulled a dagger and was about to stab Faxon's shoulder with it, but he grabbed my face with his hand and released the spell Malavar had used on me. I dropped to my knees and Faxon began attacking Malavar with spell after spell. Fire. Ice. And some things I had no idea what they were.

"Finn!" Faxon yelled. Finn appeared beside him. "Watch her."

"Tut tut," Malavar said and tried to use a spell on Finn. Finn created a shield around us both, which prevented Malavar from using his magic. "Took a new apprentice, did you? Such a shame that your first one was defeated by the device that I created."

"I knew it was you creating them. Why? What were you hoping to accomplish?" Faxon asked.

"Annihilation of magic users, aside from myself of course."

"Making yourself the most powerful man in the world," Faxon finished.

"Precisely."

"Sadly, that won't work," Faxon told him.

Malavar whispered straight into my head, "*I can restore your magic, but not if I'm dead.*"

"Liar!" I screamed as I fought off more of his warriors.

"Tilia?" Faxon asked.

"*It's true. It would take me but a moment to return your magic to you. Lower your sword and join me. If you do, I will restore your magic.*"

It was a trap. It had to be. Why give me my magic when he knew I would use it against him?

My sword lowered as I warred with myself over what to do. Should I give him a chance to prove it?

Malavar and Faxon battled against each other with spells I had never seen or heard of before. I wanted my magic, but it was not worth the cost of what he asked of me.

Malavar attempted to grab me again, but Finn shielded me from him. The shield was weak, his training not yet complete and his attention wavering. His spell wavered and Malavar took advantage of the lapse to move me away from Finn and right in front of a group of Malavar's warriors.

"Tilia!" Faxon yelled. He teleported to me, but one of the warriors cut his face deeply, right over his eye, and blood began to spill out of the wound.

"Faxon," I whispered in shock and attacked the warriors to keep him safe.

Malavar placed his hand on Faxon's head and whispered, "It's over. You kept people at arm's length your entire life and it made you impossible to defeat. By allowing this girl in, you solidified your own defeat."

I stabbed Malavar between the shoulder blades and he yelled in pain, and then backhanded me. I flew across the field and landed on my butt, the impact making me gasp and shooting pain from my tailbone all the way to my head.

Faxon grabbed Malavar and Malavar began to scream. "Love does not weaken you," Faxon told him. "Love is the strongest thing in the world. It motivates you to become better. It gives you hope when you have none. It has allowed me to learn that I am worth more than my power and that I can defeat you and remain a good person. Goodbye, Brother."

Malavar burst into flames and burned white hot for a moment before turning into ash. Faxon scooped the ashes up into a glass jar that he had and sent the jar to one of his containment rooms, using a spell.

The enemy stopped fighting and stared at the spot their leader had fallen.

"You have five minutes to vacate the premises," Faxon ordered them. "Or you will share your leader's fate."

They retreated immediately.

Faxon slid to his knees and clutched at his face, over the large wound on his eye.

"Faxon!" I yelled and ran to him. "I'm so sorry."

"Don't apologize," he told me and smiled as he sat down.

"I shouldn't have come with you," I said angrily. "I'm nothing, but trouble for you."

"Tilia," he whispered.

"Stop talking," I ordered him.

Marin and Favian came over.

"I can't heal him," I told them.

"I can," Queen Amadis said. She patted my shoulder. "Fear not, Tilia. I will restore your mage to full health."

Finn and Favian carried Faxon inside the castle, but I stayed where I was.

"That was a fun fight," Marin told me. I looked at her and she smiled broadly. "Amadis is the best healer I know. I promise that she will heal him."

"Is it really over?" Deana asked as she walked towards us.

"Yes," I whispered. "He's dead."

"I've never seen someone disintegrate before," Marin whispered.

"I made a ship and its crew disintegrate when I had my power," I told them. "My aunt made an entire castle disintegrate."

"Scary," Deana said.

"Come on, let's go get changed and get some water," Marin said and put her arm around my shoulders. "Then we can check on your mage."

It took longer than it should have to wash up and change clothes, but when I stepped out of my room, Marin was waiting with a mug of water and led me to Faxon's room. He was lying in his bed and resting when I entered.

Amadis walked over to us and whispered, "He's doing fine, he is just tired from using a lot of magic and taking such a severe injury."

"Thank you," I whispered.

"I'm sure that you want to talk to him, but you should let him rest for now," Amadis told me.

I nodded and followed them to the dining room where everyone was gathered.

"I can't believe how easily he defeated Malavar," Macon said to the others.

"I can't believe how fast you moved," Favian said to Finn.

"You and Marin were amazing," Finn told him.

"That was developed from years of time together," Marin explained.

"You were amazing, too," Deana told me.

"Right back at you," I told her. "When are you and Favian getting married?" I asked Marin curiously.

"We were supposed to get married in a month, but it depends on how long things take here. We might have to postpone it," she admitted.

"You don't look disappointed," I commented.

She laughed. "I just hate wedding planning."

"Me too!" I told her. "I don't care what the flowers are or what color silk is hung from the walls."

"Or what is served," she continued.

"As long as there is meat, I'm happy," I said.

"Exactly," she agreed.

"What are you two agreeing about now?" Favian asked.

"She hates wedding planning, too," Marin explained.

"When are you supposed to get married?" Favian asked.

"We didn't set a specific date yet," I admitted, "but within the next six months."

"It's too bad you two couldn't just have a joint wedding," Deana commented.

Marin and I looked at each other and the same devious smirk slid across our faces.

"We could," I said. "We would just have to make my aunt teleport here."

"We have seamstresses who could make you a beautiful dress," Marin offered.

"I don't think you will be able to convince the others of this," Finn said. "I mean, what about the crews?"

"They wouldn't have been able to come anyway," I reminded him. "They're all working full time to keep the town running. Though, I supposed Cristoff would come if I asked."

"No," he growled.

"Oh, jealousy. Who's Cristoff?" Marin asked curiously.

"A jerk who thinks he can steal Tilia from me," he said.

"He knows he doesn't have a chance. He just enjoys jerking your chain," I said with a roll of my eyes.

"He's going to end up with a sword to the gut if he doesn't stop," he told me.

"Oh, he'd just come back to life," I reminded him.

"What? Come back to life?" Marin asked.

"Yeah, he has some weird ability that lets him heal faster," I said. "I'm not really sure how it works, but I saw him get killed and then he was alive again."

"We're going to have to come to your Realm for a visit," Marin said.

"We would love to have you visit," I told her honestly.

"So, back to the wedding," Marin said. "I think I can convince my family to do it. What about yours?"

"I'll have to talk to Faxon, but I am sure they would be fine with it."

"What's for dinner?" Faxon asked as he shuffled into the room.

"Faxon!" I yelled at him. "You're supposed to be resting."

He pulled a chair over next to me and plopped down into it. "I needed to check on you." His eye was back to normal, but he did bear a scar on either side of it. It made him more intimidating, which I was sure he would be fine with.

"I'm fine, Faxon," I assured him.

He shook his head. "You're not." He set his hand on my face and something burned inside of my head.

"What are you doing!" Finn yelled at him, but Favian held him back.

"Removing the final shred of Malavar from her," Faxon whispered. He let me go and I gasped for breath. "How do you feel?" he asked.

I cocked my head to the side, searching inside for the wrongness that had been there, but it was gone. I felt happier than I had since the attack. It felt like something had been lifted from my shoulders.

"Really good," I whispered in shock.

"I don't," Marin whispered.

Favian walked to her and hugged her.

"What do you mean?" Faxon asked.

"Nothing," she replied quickly.

"Faxon, could Esmerald and Jared teleport here if you found a space for them to do so safely?" I asked.

"Yes," he replied cautiously.

"What would you say about the idea of Finn and I and Marin and Favian having a joint wedding here?" I asked him hopefully.

"I think that's a great idea," he said with a smile, but then turned to Marin and Favian. "Wait? You aren't married yet?"

They shook their heads.

"But you're joined," he said and waved his hand in the air, indicating something between them.

"You can see it?" Marin asked.

He nodded. "It's a bit dark where it is connected to you," he told Marin.

"Malavar did something when he called me. I haven't been able to feel Favian since then," she admitted.

"We had hoped it would fix once he was dead," Favian told us.

"I can repair it," Faxon said and sat up. He lifted his arm towards them.

"Are you sure you can?" Favian asked.

"Just hold still," he ordered them. He closed his eyes and his hand began to glow. The glow spread from his hand to Favian's body and then it lit up a small golden rope that went from Favian's chest to Marin's. The glow covered Marin and then it disappeared, but the rope between them glowed brightly.

"It's fixed!" Marin said happily, lunging forward to hug Favian and kiss him.

"What is that?" I asked.

"They're tied together and can feel what the other feels, see past memories of the other, and can even communicate tele-pathically," Faxon told me and then slumped forward.

"That's it! To bed with you!" I ordered him.

"But—"

"No!" I snapped. "I am your Princess and I order you to go to bed!"

He smirked and bowed his head slightly. "Very well." He snapped his fingers and disappeared.

"He's quite a character," Deana said with a smile.

"You don't know the half of it," I told her with a sigh. Truth-fully, I was incredibly worried for Faxon. My back muscles were tense and I couldn't get them to stop flexing. He was so impor-tant to Crilan, and me. If he died... I shook my head to stop that thought process.

"Eat," Finn ordered me.

I did as he ordered and everyone ate while recounting events of the battle. I didn't join in, but only because I was tired. Faxon had done so much for me and I had put him in danger. I needed to find a way to become better. Finn and I needed to learn to work like Marin and Favian did.

We finished eating and Finn took me back to his room so that he could change. He changed and then pulled me into a standing hug. "I'm sorry that my shield fell," he whispered into my hair.

"You did your best, Finn," I said. "We all have our limits."

He pulled me onto the bed with him and held me in his arms. "I need to learn more," he whispered.

"Me too."

"I need to find a way to increase the magic that I have."

"We need to learn to fight like Marin and Favian," I told him.

"They were pretty spectacular," he admitted and ran his fingers through my hair.

"You were amazing," I whispered and rolled over to lay my head on his chest.

"As were you," he said.

"I have so much to learn," I told him. "I just wish I had a tenth of the magic I had before."

He kissed my forehead and said, "I know. I wish I could help you."

"There's no use wishing. I need to work with Jared and find a way to become better."

"You need to rest," he told me. "You have time to learn and we have time to become stronger."

"We never know when an enemy will attack again," I reminded him. "There could be another like Malavar."

"Let's hope it won't be for a while."

We lay in silence for a while.

He asked, "Do you think Esmeralda will agree to the joint wedding?"

"I think so. I think she will agree that it is a good way to solidify a bond with this Realm and the future rulers." Maybe I should have my dad come too? I would ask Faxon later.

"Soon you will be mine and you'll never be able to escape me," he whispered happily.

"I believe things will be the other way around," I told him and kissed his neck. "You will be stuck with me for the rest of your life. I hope you are ready."

"Readier than I have ever been about anything in my life before," he assured me.

Someone knocked on our door.

"Who is it?" I called.

"Favian," he answered.

"I wonder what he could want," Finn whispered. He went and opened the door. "Hi."

"May I come in?" he asked.

"Sure," Finn stepped back so that Favian could enter.

I sat up and smiled at him. "To what do we owe the honor of your visit?" I asked.

"I came to see if I could help you," he told me.

"Help me?" I asked. "With what?"

"Come with me," he requested.

Finn shrugged, so we followed Favian out to the garden where he sat down.

"Sit, please."

I sat and he motioned at Finn. "You might want to sit over there with Marin." He pointed to where Marin sat about fifty feet away. I hadn't seen her when we entered.

"What is this about?" I asked nervously.

"After some discussions with my family and me, Faxon believes he may have found a way to help you, but it is only a guess right now on what he thinks."

"Thank you for being so specific," I mumbled at him.

He smiled. "Close your eyes. Focus on your core, the center of your being. What do you see there?"

"A hole," I replied a bit angrier than I meant to.

"Imagine that hole not as a hole, but as a ball with a shield around the ball," he instructed.

I tried.

"Imagine the shields breaking and revealing a source of light within it, a light like fire."

What was he trying to do?

"Visualize it," he instructed.

I took a deep breath and visualized the ball cracking and light spilling out of those cracks, like a sun caught in a shell.

"Imagine that shell breaking apart completely exposing that light and freeing it."

"Why?" I asked.

"Just do it," he ordered me with a soft laugh.

"Fine."

I sighed loudly and focused again. I pictured the shell falling away from the light source and it shining brightly, a sun within my core. Warmth filled me and I gasped as it exploded once released from the shell. My eyes flew open as I yelled in shock.

"Tilia!" Finn yelled, but Marin held him back.

I stood up and looked at my self in surprise. I was glowing. "What? How?" The warmth continued to fill me and spread to every inch of my body.

"It worked!" Faxon yelled happily from behind me.

I turned and found him with tears in his eyes.

"What is this?" I asked him.

"Remember how you frightened me when you were meditating and I couldn't see your magic?" he asked as he slowly walked towards me.

"Yes."

"The day that the device was used and you thought you lost

your magic," he whispered. "You remember that when I touched you, there was a shock?"

I nodded.

"You didn't lose your magic," he said happily.

"But I haven't been able to do anything and—"

"Somehow you sealed your magic inside of yourself using whatever method you do when meditating. You sealed it to protect yourself and it was so tightly sealed, that I could not even see it," he explained.

"So, I have my magic?" I asked softly.

"You felt like it was missing because you shielded it so well that even you couldn't see it. You may have even convinced yourself that it was gone when you were out of reserves and had protected it."

"I have my magic back?" I asked softly.

"Yes," Favian said with a nod.

"Try something," Faxon ordered.

"What?" I asked.

"Light this on fire," he said and set an apple on the ground between us.

I focused as hard as I could and pictured the apple stem lighting on fire and burning down until it set the entire apple on fire. Time passed and then suddenly the stem lit and the entire apple began to burn.

I screamed in shock and joy and threw my arms around Faxon's neck. He hugged me back and I went and hugged Favian. "Thank you!"

"I didn't do anything," he said, but accepted my hug.

"It's back!" I yelled and teleported from where I was to Finn. I kissed his cheek and then teleported to Faxon and then to Marin who danced with me.

"Try getting Titania," Faxon suggested.

Titania was a giant sword, as long as I was tall, that was

exceptionally light due to being made out of some weird material that was also incredibly strong. I traced the symbol in the air and spoke the words to summon the sword, "I summon thee, Titania."

The symbol glowed in the air and then the sword's hilt slid out of the portal I had created. I gripped it tightly as I pulled it out.

Marin's eyes were so wide, I worried they might pop.

"You pulled a sword out of thin air," she whispered.

"It's more of a summoning spell," I explained. "Titania is actually in a room in my Kingdom, but I can use this spell to grab her from wherever I am."

"It's a rather large sword," Favian commented.

I twirled it and smiled. "She's lighter than she looks."

"May I?" Marin asked with outstretched hands.

I set Titania in her palms and her mouth formed a little o of shock. "It is light." She lifted the sword, twirled it, and pretended to stab an enemy.

We were all smiling like fools when Esmeralda appeared next to Faxon. "Where's Tilia?" she asked him urgently.

"Here," I called to her and jogged to where she was. "What's going on?"

She gripped my shoulders and whispered, "It's your father."

I gasped and my hand went to my mouth. My father? "Is he hurt? What happened?" I asked with shaking hands.

"Faxon, I'm taking her," Esmeralda told him. "Finn, stay with Faxon," she ordered.

They both nodded and their solemn expressions were the last things I saw before we entered the swirling vortex of teleportation. It seemed to last an unbearable amount of time and when we stopped I had to drop to my hands and knees to catch my breath.

"I'm sorry," Esmeralda told me. "The longer the travel time, the worse it feels."

I took deep breaths and soon everything became clear again. "Okay," I told her and stood up.

She took my hand and rushed me into my father's office where Sedgwick immediately grabbed me and hugged me against his chest. "I'm sorry, Tilia. I did all that I could."

"No," I whispered. I refused to acknowledge his words. I ripped myself out of his hold and rushed to the desk where he lay. "Dad," I whispered. "Dad, I'm here." There was blood all over him, on the desk, and pooled under it. It was too much blood for one man.

"One of the stacks had started to fall," Bernard whispered. "He yelled for everyone to move, but Cristoff's foot was stuck under another box that had fallen. Cap' lifted the box up and then shoved Cristoff out of the way just as the stack fell. We rushed to help, but there was just too much damage to him."

I shook my head vigorously and clenched my eyes shut. No! No, he couldn't be dead! I was going to get married. I was going to have his grandchildren! He wouldn't get to see any of that now. We had just reunited. I should have spent more time with him. I should not have gone on so many missions with Faxon. I barely got to spend any time with him.

Warm hands gripped my shoulders and turned me around. I opened them and found myself looking into Jared's eyes which gleamed with unshed tears. "Don't bottle this up," he ordered me. "This was a terrible accident and there was nothing that you could have done to change this outcome."

My legs shook and I gripped his arms tightly. "He's gone?"

"He's gone," he whispered gently.

I opened my mouth again to say something, but all that came out was a sorrowful wail. My knees buckled and Jared eased me down to sit on the floor. He hugged me and I cried my despair, not caring who was there to witness it. Esmeralda dropped to the ground beside me and hugged me from the side as well. Sedgwick knelt in front of me and I threw myself into his arms, burying my head into his chest. He clutched me tightly and we cried together. I had known that any day could be his last when he was sailing on the sea and that anything could happen, a hurricane, a pirate desiring his title, a battle that he lost. I never thought about him dying on land.

I didn't know how long I cried for, but when my tears were spent I pulled back from Sedgwick and asked, "Did Cristoff—"

"He's alive. Cap' saved him," he whispered.

I looked around the room. "Where is he?"

"We aren't sure," Bernard whispered. "After Sedgwick announced it, he took off out of the town."

I wiped my face on the sleeve of my shirt and stood up on wobbly legs. My head was pounding from all of the crying and I stumbled a step forward. "I have to find him."

"It might be best if you let him be," Jared said.

I shook my head. "He's blaming himself. I know Cristoff, he's going to blame himself for this." I gripped the back of the nearest chair and closed my eyes. I had my magic back, so I could locate his magic signature.

I could hear the others talking quietly, discussing his funeral, but I pushed them away as I focused on finding Cristoff. There! "I'll be back," I told whoever was listening and then teleported to Cristoff. When I arrived, I found myself at the edge of a cliff and started to fall forward. I screamed in fear, but Cristoff grabbed my arm and pulled me back to solid ground.

"What are you doing?" he asked me in shock.

I turned and looked at his sullen face. It was dirty, streaked with tear tracks, and his eyes were red and swollen.

"I came to find you," I whispered.

He cringed away from me. "I didn't hear him," he told me. "I wasn't paying attention and—"

"He saved your life," I told him.

"He would still be here if I hadn't been such an airhead," he snapped.

I shook my head. "You were like a son to him. He was protecting you just like he would have me."

He backed away from me and whispered, "I'm sorry, Tilia. I'm so sorry. You must hate me now, and I don't blame you."

"I don't hate you," I told him.

"I was wrong to think for a second that I was good enough for you," he whispered.

He was dangerously close to the edge of the cliff now.

"Cristoff, stop," I ordered him.

He shook his head and said, "It's my fault he's dead."

I raced forward and grabbed his hand. I pulled him forward, ducked, and caused him to fall over my body and land on his back. I sat on his stomach and he stared at me with wide eyes. "What are you doing, you idiot!" I screamed at him. "Are you trying to kill yourself? You almost walked off the edge of that cliff!"

"I—"

"No!" I interrupted him. "Dad saved you because he loved you and that's final. You will weep for his death, but you will not blame yourself. Do you understand me?"

Fresh tears fell from his eyes and he pulled me down into a bone crunching hug. "What am I going to do without him?" he cried.

We sat up and I repositioned us so that I sat on the ground and he leaned into me sideways. "We will continue on with our lives. You will become the best man you can, marry a pretty woman, and have beautifully annoying kids. I will become Queen and be just as annoying as I am now," I assured him.

I had no idea why I was acting so calm when I felt like my heart had been shredded into tiny pieces. I knew my crying was not done, but as I held Cristoff's head as he sobbed, I also knew that I needed to be strong. I could not let my father's death be in vain and I could not let Cristoff believe it was his fault.

We sat together as the ocean pounded into the cliff below us until Cristoff was ready to return to the town.

"Thank you," he whispered, "for coming to find me."

I lightly punched his arm and said, "You would have done the same for me."

We walked to the office and several of the crew pulled Cristoff away. As he walked away, he turned and looked at me once more. I hoped he wouldn't continue to hold himself responsible for what happened.

I couldn't go back into the office. I couldn't see his body again, so I sat on the porch steps and faced the docks. The normally boisterous town was quiet now. The death of the King of Pirates was a heavy weight on us all.

"They're going to give him an official Captain's funeral," Esmeralda told me.

I twisted my neck to find her sitting beside me. "How long have you been there?"

She smiled tenderly. "A few minutes."

"When are they doing it?" I asked her softly.

"Tonight."

"Finn should be here," I told her.

"I can get him," she offered.

"I need to go back to at least say goodbye to our allies," I said as I struggled to keep the lid on my emotions. I had managed it while with Cristoff, but now they threatened to overtake me again.

"Tilia, did you teleport?" she asked me. "Out of the office when you went after Cristoff?"

I whispered, "My magic is back."

"That's wonderful," she told me joyously. I nodded, but now I didn't particularly feel like celebrating. "Your Father would be very happy for you," she assured me.

I took a deep breath to keep the tears at bay and stood. "Let's get Finn."

"We're fetching Finn," Esmeralda called to Jared.

"Stay safe," he called back.

"He has become worrisome in his old age," she whispered. "He never worried about things before."

"It's been a bad year for us," I reminded her.

She sighed and squeezed my hand. "It will get better."

We teleported back to the castle grounds and ended up teleporting into the dining hall where everyone was eating. Most pulled their weapons at our sudden appearance, but thankfully none tried to attack.

"Oh," Esmeralda said in shock. "Pardon my intrusion."

"Tilia," Finn called as he rushed to me. His arms wrapped around me in a warmth that I would need that night, but for now I had to stay strong so I gently pushed him back.

"Later," I whispered and cleared my throat to rid it of the tightness. I turned to the Queen and Kings and said, "May I introduce, the Queen of Crilan, my Aunt Esmeralda."

Esmeralda curtsied low and bowed her head. In her dress, it was a beautifully executed curtsy, but in her fighting attire it was a little odd.

"Esmeralda this is King Cesar and Queen Amadis of the Elves," I introduced.

They stood and instead of bowing, they shook hands.

"It is an honor to meet the Elven Royals," she said.

"The honor is ours," Queen Amadis told her.

"I see where your niece gets her beauty from," King Cesar complimented her.

She smiled. "Thank you. I'm rather proud of my niece."

"She's a fighter, too?" Marin asked a bit louder than she had intended to judging by the pink that tinged her cheeks after she said it.

Esmeralda turned and walked to their table. "Princess Marin and Prince Favian of the Elves. Prince Sebastian of the Elves and Princess Deana of the Humans," I introduced.

The Princes bowed to Esmeralda while Deana curtsied.

Marin seemed too stunned to move. "Your power is astonishing," she whispered.

"Oh my, I forgot to reign that in after I teleported. How rude of me!" Esmeralda said with a gasp.

"You're out of sorts," Faxon whispered to her. "Are you well?"

"Emotional," she informed him.

"I regret that we must leave earlier than we had anticipated," I told everyone.

"What happened?" Faxon asked me with concern.

I started to answer, but I couldn't find the words.

"The Pirate King has died," Esmeralda whispered.

Faxon started to move towards me, but I held up a hand. "If you touch me, I will cry," I told him a bit louder and harsher than I meant to.

He stopped and nodded. "I understand."

"Who is the Pirate King?" the Human King asked.

I should have remembered his name, but I couldn't. "My father," I informed them.

"Your father was a pirate?" he asked in disbelief.

"Yes."

"He was a great man who protected everyone that he could right up until his last breath," the god who was Marin's father said. He turned to me with a tear in his eye and said, "I am truly sorry for your loss."

"You," Esmeralda whispered, eyes wide and mouth agape. "You're real."

He turned and smiled at her as she stood before him with an open mouth. "Hello, Esmeralda."

"I didn't think you were real," she told him softly. "I thought I hallucinated that."

"What are you talking about?" I asked her.

"Jared was dying," she whispered. "I didn't have enough magic left to heal him. I prayed for help. He came. He offered me Jared's life, but to keep Jared alive I would never be allowed children."

"The two of you combined would make a terrifyingly powerful child," he told her. "It was the only option."

That's why they never had kids! I had assumed they were never ready or that Esmeralda wasn't capable of having kids.

"Wait, when was Jared dying?" Faxon asked angrily.

"Later," she ordered him.

"Will you come back?" Marin asked me. I hadn't realized that she and Deana had come to stand behind me. I had been focused on Esmeralda.

"I don't know," I admitted.

"We could still have a joint wedding," Marin offered. "We can postpone it until you're ready."

"You don't have to do that for me," I told her despite how happy her offer made me.

"It wouldn't feel right," she told me.

"I agree," Favian said as he came to stand beside Marin. "Our destinies are intertwined now and a wedding without you and Finn wouldn't be right."

"A joint wedding?" Esmeralda asked in shock. "What are you talking about? I'm so out of the loop."

"How does it feel?" Faxon sneered at her.

She glared at him and his jacket caught fire. He removed it and stamped on it until the flame went out.

"Don't start this battle again," he warned her, "or you'll wake up to a bed full of toads."

"Jared will be the one to seek revenge if that happens," she reminded him.

"Children," I chastised them, "you are making a bad impression on our allies."

"Sorry," Faxon and Esmeralda muttered.

Marin lifted Titania from the table. I couldn't believe that I hadn't seen the giant sword sitting there. "You probably want your sword back," she said.

I set my hand on it and said, "Why don't you hold on to her? I can pick her up next time I come to visit."

"We could have the wedding at our place," Esmeralda offered. "Completely up to you four, but the invitation is there."

"I want to see the Elf Kingdom," I told her with a pout.

"You are welcome to visit us anytime that you wish," Queen Amadis told me.

"You can teleport now," Finn reminded me.

"It's going to take me a bit of time to learn to do long distance teleportation," I explained, "but I will work on it."

Deana hugged me and I whispered into her ear, "Don't forget about the designated heir option."

She squeezed me tighter and said, "I won't."

Sebastian shook my hand and Marin pulled me into a tight hug. "Don't stay away too long."

Favian and Finn were gripping each other's forearms in the man equivalent of a hug.

"Try and keep her safe," Favian told Finn.

He laughed and looked at Marin. "I think you'll have your hands full as well."

"We are standing right here," Marin reminded them.

"And we can choose to make it more difficult on you," I added.

Finn walked to Marin and she hugged him. Finn's shocked face was priceless.

Favian gripped my forearm and said, "We're going to miss you two."

I yanked his arm and pulled him into a hug. "I'll miss you as well, grumpy elf."

"Do you need to get anything?" Esmeralda asked me.

"One second," I told her. I teleported to my room and then Finn's to grab our stuff and then teleported back to her. "Ready."

"I have *got* to learn that," Marin whispered.

Faxon and Favian were standing across the room whispering to each other.

"That's a scary sight," I whispered to Esmeralda.

"He's just teaching him a quick spell. Nothing to worry about," she assured me. "Faxon, we're leaving. Meet us at the docks of the Lost Port."

He nodded and waved his hand at her.

Finn took my right hand and Esmeralda took my left. I curtsied to the royals and Macon, who I realized I had not introduced Esmeralda to. "Until we meet again."

They bowed or curtsied in return and then Esmeralda teleported us away. We stood at the edge of the town and I took a deep breath. The temporary distraction was gone and now I had to face my father's funeral. I wasn't ready. I couldn't do this.

"Deep breath," Esmeralda whispered.

I obeyed and we headed towards the waterfront where Dad's ship was docked. Part of me wished that I could keep the ship for myself, but I knew that he would want to go out with it. I teleported onto the ship, for one last time on the vessel I had called home for the first half of my life. I walked into my Dad's room and ran my fingertips over his bookcase, looked at the pictures on the walls, and then faced his treasure case where he kept his most valued items. Inside was a picture of my mother and her crown. I opened the case and took them out, sure that my father would have wanted me to have them. I did not believe in an afterlife, but if there was one, I was sure that he and my mom would be together.

He had a few other treasures, some were things I had owned as a child, but I left those to drift to the ocean floor with him. There was a drawer in his desk that he had never let me open as a child, but now that he was gone, it was time to open it. I set the crown and picture on the desk and tried to open the drawer, but it was locked. I used my magic to unlock it and slid it open. The sight of its contents instantly filled my eyes with tears. My drawings, colorings, and letters filled the drawer. He must have kept every single item I had made for him. I shuffled through them to the bottom where I found a diary with my mother's name on the outside. I didn't dare read it now, but I placed it on the desk with her other items. I was about to leave when I noticed something shiny underneath his pillow.

Unlike the others, Dad had continued to sleep in his cabin on the ship. He said that the land was too still for him to properly sleep on. I sat on his bed and pulled out a picture frame with a picture of my father, mother, and me as an infant in their arms. They looked positively joyous and I could see the love they held for me and each other plainly. Tears began to pour out of my eyes and great sobs shook my body as I clutched the picture to my chest. I wished that I had known my mother. I wished that she hadn't died when I was young and that my father could have kept her by his side. I wished that my father hadn't died so soon. We were becoming closer and I was finally able to have him in my life. I didn't want to even think about my wedding when I had to walk down the aisle without him by my side.

He had done plenty of terrible things in his life, but he had kept order among the pirates and disciplined those who got too out of line. Without him the pirates would have taken over every port in the Realm and farther.

He had taught me to fight with a sword. He had been the first to teach me to throw a dagger. No matter how tired he was after a fight or battle, he always gave me a bright smile and spun me around when he returned to me. I was proud to be his daughter and I knew the hole that his death left would not heal any time soon.

Warm hands slid around my body and pulled me against a warm body. I opened my eyes and Finn kissed my forehead. I sobbed in his arms and he held me silently, letting me know with his presence that he was here for me.

Once I was empty of tears, Finn wiped my face dry and kissed each of my eyes. I kissed his cheek and walked to the desk to retrieve the items I claimed.

"Is that all?" he asked softly.

I nodded and then saw the chest filled with seashells that we had collected before he gave me to Esmeralda to raise. I lifted the lid and took the most beautiful shell from the full chest. I surveyed the room one final time and whispered, "Goodbye, Dad."

Finn slipped his arm around my waist and we walked off the ship and joined my extended family on the dock.

"Is there anything else that you want from the ship?" Sedgwick asked me.

I shook my head. "This is all I will take from him."

"We could use another ship," Sedgwick offered.

"No, it is only right that he and the ship go together," I said adamantly. I would miss the ship, but I knew it is what Dad would have wanted.

He nodded in understanding and whistled loudly. Crew

members carried my father's body on a wooden board down the dock towards the ship. They paused next to me and allowed me to touch his face one last time. "All hail the Pirate King," I whispered.

"All hail the Pirate King!" everyone yelled.

They carried his body onto the ship's main deck where they had set up a pyre. Sedgwick started to walk towards the ship to set sail, but I grabbed his arm and stopped him.

After handing Finn my items I said, "I'll set course. I can teleport back."

He nodded and began preparing the arrow that he would shoot to light the pyre.

"You sure?" Finn asked me softly.

"Yes." I teleported on board and the crew disembarked the ship and removed the plank. I steered the ship out to sea and whistled the tune Dad always did when we began a new journey. Once we were far enough from shore, I tied the steering wheel to keep course and teleported back to the docks.

Sedgwick drew the bow, knocked the arrow, which was on fire, and let it fly. It hit the side of the pyre and the kindling began to burn. Finn held me against his chest and Sedgwick gripped one of my hands in his.

"Captain Rocco was the best Pirate King in all of history," an unfamiliar deep male voice said over the weeping crew. "His memory will live on for generations to come." The speaker walked out from behind us, towards the end of the dock and lifted his hand. A small wave sped from beneath the dock under his feet and pushed the ship deeper out to sea. Wind picked up, filling the sails and the ship sailed faster. "One last voyage for the great Captain Rocco," he said.

"Who are you?" I asked him softly.

He turned and I instantly saw the resemblance between him and Finn. He had dark hair that hung just below his shoulders, a beard that was at least four inches long, and stormy grey eyes that reminded me of the sea during a hurricane.

He bowed to me. "Tilia Swanson, you are your father's most prized treasure, and my son's as well. I am deeply sorry for your loss."

"Father, what are you doing here?" Finn asked softly.

"I came to pay my respects to Rocco. He was a friend of mine," he answered mournfully. I didn't think that gods felt anything, but I could see the pain on his face.

"You were on the ship several times," I remembered suddenly.

He smiled. "You do remember."

"Aquinn," Sedgwick said with a bow. "He would be honored to know you were here."

"Two gods in one week," I whispered in disbelief.

"Two?" Aquinn asked.

"We met Marin of the Elves and her father was there," Finn explained.

"Marin is a feisty one. Not unlike our Tilia here," Aquinn said with a grin. "Seeing you two together makes me very happy." He turned to Esmeralda and Jared. "I will attend their wedding ceremony. No need for anything special due to my attendance. I just wish to see my final son married."

"We may be having a joint wedding," Finn told him.

Aquinn nodded. "I approve of this as well."

"Is there anything you want?" I asked Aquinn softly.

He turned his full attention on me and for a brief moment I felt the staggering amount of power that he had. "I would request that the two of you be bound, as Marin and Favian already are."

"Bound?" I asked. "What is that?"

"You can't be serious?" Faxon asked angrily.

I was more shocked at Faxon's tone towards a god than his reason, but I stayed quiet to let them talk it out.

"Of course I'm serious," Aquinn said. "They will be bound to allow a complete marriage."

"That is the elven way, not our way," Faxon argued. "They are young and while I accept their marriage, a binding is permanent."

"What does being bound entail?" I asked.

"You two will be connected for the rest of your lives. You will be able to sense where the other is, as well as feel what the other is feeling. You can also communicate to each other just by thinking," Aquinn explained.

"You will share memories with each other. You will know when the other is mad or jealous or angry. You will know everything about the other. When one of you dies, the other will feel it completely," Faxon continued for Aquinn.

"Why are you against this?" I asked Faxon.

"What happens if you decide five or ten years from now that Finn isn't right for you? What if he decides you're not right for him? You will still be bound. Even if you chose to separate physically, you would feel the other's every emotion."

"We can discuss this later," Finn said in a stern tone. "Tilia and I will make a decision together after we have discussed everything."

Aquinn bowed his head. "As you wish, Finley."

"Tilia," Faxon started.

Finn interrupted him. "Your advice is appreciated, Faxon, but this is a decision that we will make for ourselves."

Without a word, Faxon disappeared. I felt bad that Finn had shut him down like that, but it was our decision, not Faxon's.

"Can we talk?" Finn asked Aquinn.

His father smiled warmly. "Of course, my son." He held out his arm and Finn released my hand to step next to Aquinn who laid his arm across Finn's shoulders as they walked away and talked quietly to each other.

What were they going to discuss? Finn was in a rather strange mood. I was in a strange mood too, when I thought about it. Things continued to happen to distract me from my father's death, but no matter how terrible of me it was, I welcomed them. Dad was on his final journey out to sea and the only thing left to do was go home.

"Is that your mother's crown?" Esmeralda asked.

I picked up the items I had taken from Dad's cabin and Finn had set on the ground. "Yes."

"I'm glad that you have it now," she said with a smile and tears glistening in her eyes.

"We should head home," Jared said quietly.

"Who is going to become the new King?" Bernard asked some of the other former-pirates still gathered.

"It's hard to say who is still out there. There might be a whole new crop of captains, after the King Priam fiasco," Lawrence said.

"I hope it's not someone like that Lance idiot," Sedgwick added.

Who would become King? That decision could possibly change everything about the sea and sailing. Without dad to keep order, what would happen out there?

"Don't fret," Sedgwick said when he noticed me frowning. "We will keep our ears to the wind to find out what's going on."

"Where's Cristoff?" I asked suddenly. He had disappeared sometime after Aquinn showed up.

"I think he went back to his house," someone in the back said.

"Can you take this for me?" I asked Esmeralda. "I need to talk to Cristoff before I go home."

She took the items and nodded. "Of course. We will have dinner ready when you arrive."

Jared set his hand on her shoulder and they disappeared. I turned and walked down the streets towards his house, or at least the area his house was at. I hadn't actually been inside his house or seen where it was, so I only knew the direction. I could have teleported to him, but I didn't want to do that if he was not decent. That would be a hell of a fun conversation with Finn.

Cristoff's magic signature grew stronger and I followed it to a small, one-bedroom house in the center of town. I took a deep breath for courage and knocked twice. There was some shuffling and he asked, "Who is it?"

"Tilia."

More shuffling, like he was moving things around in the house and then he opened the door. "Hi."

"Hi," I returned the greeting.

He shifted nervously. "I was going to come see you tomorrow."

"Oh?" I asked curiously. "Why is that?"

"Can you come in?" he asked.

I stepped into the house and saw the large duffel bag under his bed and that some of his dresser drawers were empty. "Are you leaving?" I asked softly.

"Yes."

"Were you going to tell me or just disappear?" I asked angrily. We would never be a couple, but after all that had happened, I thought we were friends.

"I was going to say bye," he swore as he walked around to stand in front of me. "I swear. I just couldn't find the courage today."

"Why are you leaving?" I asked. "If it's because of me, you don't have to worry about that. I don't blame you and I'll be at the Capitol and—"

He reached out towards me slowly and I stopped talking as he pulled me against his chest. "You are the most forgiving woman on all the seas. You are the most beautiful and the sweetest."

While I appreciated the compliments, this wasn't exactly what I asked about. "Cristoff—"

"When you told me that I would marry a woman and have kids there was only one woman's face that I saw. Yours. I know I can't have you and I know that I don't deserve you. I also know that living on land just isn't for me."

"These are your crew members," I reminded him. "I will stay away and you won't see me. You'll be able to move on and find a woman—"

He shook his head. "I would never find another woman half as perfect as you." I tried to pull away, but he held me tighter and leaned his forehead against mine. "I'm not saying this to make you feel bad or insinuate that my leaving is your fault. I just want you to know how amazing you are. If Finn doesn't show you that every day, then it is a travesty. I am going to find a crew and I am going to become the new Pirate King. I won't let the peace and prosperity that Captain Rocco created, and worked so hard for, disappear with his death. I will take up his mantle and I will make the Captain and you proud."

"There will be many more seeking the title," I warned him. "You will have a constant target on your back." I felt more fear for him than I wanted to admit. I didn't want him to die trying to achieve something he wasn't ready for.

He smiled and said, "May I come see you during the next Treasure Heist Festival?"

"You must visit me in Markleville," I whispered as a few tears slid down my cheeks. "It's an order from the Pirate Princess."

He wiped my tears away and beamed happily. "I will see you next year," he promised.

"Thank you, for all that you've done for me," I said as I tried to shove my sadness down.

"Thank you, for treating a lowly pirate the same as you treat a prince," he said in return.

"One year," I confirmed.

He brushed his lips across mine and promised, "One year."

"If you die, I'll hunt down your soul and kick your arse," I threatened.

"As the Pirate Princess orders, I will stay alive to see her again in one year's time," he said and bowed to me.

"I have to go," I whispered. I shouldn't have let him kiss me again. I should have just let him go, but despite not holding my heart, he had a place in it next to Segwick and Faxon.

He hugged me once more and whispered, "Keep that boy on his toes and don't back down on anything you believe in."

We separated and I smirked at him. "The Pirate Princess never backs down," I said with a laugh.

I left his house and wrapped my arms around myself. I had to have faith in him or I would never stop worrying and waiting for the news of his death. Cristoff was trained by my father and his unique abilities would help him secure my father's title. I wiped my face and nodded. Cristoff would be the next King. I was certain. He had to be.

"Where have you been?" Finn asked me with worry as I rounded the corner at the end of the street towards the docks.

"Are you ready to go?" I asked him. "Where's your father?"

"He left. He'll be back to talk to us once we've made a decision about the binding," he explained.

I leaned into him and he wrapped his arms around me. "Let's go home."

"Home," he agreed.

11

WE SPENT TWO DAYS DISCUSSING WHETHER WE SHOULD BE BOUND or not. We made lists of pros and cons. We discussed different hypothetical situations. We then took a full day apart to think on our own. As we sat on the arena wall the fourth day, Finn dropped a bomb on me that I hadn't seen coming.

"Because my father is a god, I have a longer lifespan," he whispered. "So, in the end you won't have to worry about me dying before you. Unless there are some crazy circumstances that are totally out of our control."

"You live longer? How much longer?" I questioned.

"I'm not certain," he admitted.

"Can't we ask your father?" I requested.

"Ask me what?" Aquinn asked from the center of the arena where he was spinning a spear.

"How long will Finn live? What's his lifespan compared to mine?" I asked and jumped down from the wall. I walked towards him and was mesmerized by the graceful way he twirled the spear around and around from in front of his body to behind and back and even over his head.

"Well, that depends on Finn. If he keeps rushing headlong

into things and focusing more on you than himself, it may not be much longer," Aquinn said and looked pointedly at Finn who was still sitting on the wall.

"You're avoiding answering my question," I accused him.

He smiled. "What will happen if you don't like the answer? Will you leave Finn?"

"Of course not!" I snapped angrily.

"Then why does the answer matter in making your decision of being bound to him or not?" he asked.

"If he is going to age slower than me or live twice as long as me, I can't bind myself to him and force him to deal with my death for what could be another lifetime."

"What if there was a way to ensure that both of your lifespans matched?" Aquinn asked, halting the spear's spin to stand beside him.

"Father," Finn warned. "What are you talking about?"

"What do you mean?" I asked nervously.

"What is the difference in our lifespans?" Finn asked. "Tell us that first before we discuss anything else."

"To be one hundred percent honest, I am not sure. It has been a very long time since I've had a child. I remember my last son lived to be two hundred and four, but I don't remember how long the others lived."

"Would your brother know?" I asked.

"Possibly," he murmured as he stroked his beard and looked over our heads.

Two hundred and four years old? Finn would live two or three lifetimes longer than me.

"Tilia, are you alright? You look sick," Aquinn said and took a step closer to me.

Finn rushed to my side. "You should sit down," he suggested.

I sat and put my face in my hands. This was too much.

"What is the way to make our lifespans match?" I asked quietly. "Please don't say you cut his life short."

"I can extend your lifespan, Tilia, but all things come with a price," he told me.

"What price?" Finn asked in a growl.

"Don't look at your father that way," Aquinn ordered him. "I mean no ill will towards you or your mate."

"Mate?" I questioned and looked up at him.

He waved his hand dismissively. "I spend a lot of time around those who use that term. It's not an insult."

What would it be like to live to two hundred years old? To rule as Queen for more than one hundred years? I would be the longest reigning monarch in history.

"What's the price?" Finn asked him again.

"You're rather surly today," Aquinn commented.

"You've upset her," Finn informed Aquinn. "And now she's going to think about me living without her, and how devastated I will be, and that she doesn't want that for me."

That was what I had been thinking. Darn him. "I don't know if you'd be devastated," I commented and made swirling designs in the sand.

"The price, Father."

"Well, I haven't decided on the price yet. I had to see if you were interested first," he admitted.

"I thought gods would be more organized than this," I whispered to Finn.

"He's not good with change." Finn whispered back. "The sea doesn't change. Sure, the day to day sea might change, but if you look at it from one hundred years to the next hundred years, it's rather constant."

"I am fine with change," Aquinn said angrily, "and I can hear you two."

"I see the family resemblance," I muttered.

A woman laughed and I felt peace settle over me. "You've always had a temper, Aquinn," she said as she materialized beside him.

She was gorgeous, beyond gorgeous, and there was no doubt in my mind that she was a goddess.

"Don't mesmerize my son," Aquinn ordered her.

"I'm fine, Father," Finn told him and sat down beside me. He took my hand and held it as we looked up at the divine beings expectantly.

"I like her," she told Aquinn. "She's a good balance for the world."

"Goddess, do you have a name?" I asked her politely.

"No, we used to have names the humans called us, but we gave them up long ago." She paused. "Well, all of us but Aquinn."

"Doesn't that get confusing when you all talk to each other?" I asked.

"No, we can sense who the other is speaking to."

"Handy," I commented.

"Is there a reason for your presence other than to try to pester me, Beautiful One?" Aquinn asked her.

"I want to talk to you before you decide on the price for Tilia," she said. "My information may help you."

"How can they not have names?" I asked Finn in a whisper from the side of my mouth.

"It's strange," he agreed.

"Children, no gossiping," the Goddess chastised.

"Sorry."

"Sorry."

We waited silently and then I heard an odd bell.

"What was that?" I asked softly.

"What?" Finn asked.

It sounded again.

"The bell," I whispered.

"Someone is trying to contact you," Aquinn told me.

"What?" I asked smartly.

"Make a bowl with your hands," he instructed.

I obeyed.

He wiggled his fingers over my hands and they filled with water. "Now, just say, 'hello' as you look in the water."

"Hello?" I asked as I looked at the water.

"There you are," Favian said with a scowl.

"Whoa," I whispered, my eyes widening as his image appeared in the water. "How'd you do this?"

"Faxon taught me," he said.

"What's up?" I asked since he clearly wasn't in a happy mood.

"Marin is being stubborn. Please, talk sense into her," he requested. I could hear worry and pain in his voice. What was happening?

"Where is she?" I asked.

"Here," she said in a labored breath.

Favian moved and I saw Marin. She was pale and sweaty. "What's wrong?" I asked with concern.

"She's dying," Favian growled. "She won't take her Father's blessing to increase her lifespan. It's the only way to save her."

"What's the price?" I asked her and glanced up at Aquinn who was examining his fingernails.

"No children," Marin whispered and then sobbed. "No children, ever."

"Marin, your life is the most important thing to Favian. He loves you. He doesn't love you because you're going to make him babies."

"But—"

"Would you leave her if she was infertile by birth?" I asked Favian.

"Of course not."

"Marin, you can't die. We haven't even had our weddings yet. You can't die," I told her urgently. My tears dripped into the bowl, temporarily disrupting the view.

"I will have to watch the others die," she said. "I'll have to watch you die."

"Not necessarily," I said.

"What?" she asked.

"What's happened?" Favian asked me.

"Finn's got the long lifespan like Marin. I don't. His father has suggested the possibility of extending my lifespan."

"Marin's lifespan isn't as long as Favian's," Aquinn told me. "The elves live to almost a thousand years old."

"See!" She burst out. "I'll still have to watch you die."

"Children," the Goddess said softly, her voice calming and slightly chastising at the same time. "We can solve all of this with your compliance and agreement on the price."

"No children for me?" I asked her.

"One male heir for Tilia and one female child for Marin. Sebastian will carry on the elves' lineage for the throne," she explained.

"What kind of lifespan are we talking about?" I asked.

"All four of you will live long, happy lives together and I assure you that your deaths will not be separated by more than five years, unless you do something foolish like jumping from one moving ship to another," Aquinn said with an arched eyebrow.

"I made it safe and sound," I reminded him. "Marin, I'm going to agree," I told her.

Her breathing was shallower and I could see that she was closer to death than before. She took one big breath and then nodded. "Me, too."

"The deal has been sealed," the Goddess said with a wide

smile. "Boys, you can finish up here. Tilia, you and I will talk later."

She disappeared and Aquinn muttered, "She's letting you off easy. My price would have been higher."

"I'm beginning," Marin's father told Aquinn.

Aquinn nodded and set a hand on Finn and me. "You'll have to end your communication," he told me.

"Favian, contact me tomorrow," I instructed him.

"Thank you," he whispered. I could see Marin's father with a hand on each of them and then the water returned to water.

I dropped my hands, letting the water fall to the sand and Aquinn said, "If we do this, you must be bound as well."

Finn looked at me and I said, "If you try to leave me for a pirate wench, I'll hunt you down for the rest of your life."

He smiled and kissed my cheek. "The only woman in the world for me, is you."

"Good," I said with a nod.

"We won't bind you until the wedding," Aquinn told us. "This is going to hurt a lot as it is."

"Hurt?" I asked.

I didn't get a verbal answer. Instead, Aquinn began to glow and then power unlike anything I had ever felt before slammed into my body, shattered my defenses, and burned me from the inside out.

I knew I was screaming, but I couldn't control myself. Finn was screaming too, I could hear him, but I was blind to anything except the pain.

I wasn't sure when it ended or what happened afterwards. I woke in my bed feeling as though I'd been thrown into a volcano. I tried to sit up, but my body hurt too much.

"Don't move," Faxon ordered me angrily.

"Water," I requested.

Faxon lifted my head up and then I felt a mug pressed

against my lips. I parted them to drink and was beyond thankful for Faxon. Most of the water ended up spilling down the front of my throat and soaking my shirt, but the water eased the burn in my throat.

"Thanks," I whispered as he helped me lay down again.

"Are you in pain?" he asked.

"Yes."

"Would you like me to help you sleep more?" he asked and I felt a cold cloth brush across my forehead.

"How long has it been?" I asked him as my brain became foggier.

"Two days."

"Is Finn—"

"He's sleeping still."

"Have you helped him?"

"Esmeralda is with him," he explained.

"How long will I hurt?"

The cloth disappeared and something broke across the room. "I don't know," he said, sounding choked up.

"You're mad at me," I guessed.

"Not at you, no."

"You're mad about my decision," I amended.

"You are young, Tilia. This decision will be with you no matter what you decide in the future."

"Faxon," I whispered.

"Yes?"

"Thank you for worrying about me."

"I'm putting you to sleep," he told me, "but I will stay by your side."

"You're the best grumpy mage ever," I thanked him.

"YOU'RE STILL SLEEPING? What a lazy girl!" the Goddess chastised me.

I opened my eyes and blinked several times to clear the haze sleep still had over them. "Huh?"

"Are you still in pain?" she asked me.

I stretched my body and while I was still sore, I wasn't in pain anymore. "Just sore," I told her and sat up.

Faxon was asleep in the corner of my room in a chair.

"He will not wake up while we speak," she assured me.

"You wanted to talk to me?" I asked. It was still surreal that I was speaking to a Goddess. She was gorgeous, flowing hair, perfect curves, and eyes that saw into your soul and through you at the same time.

She sat on the edge of my bed and said, "Your life has been rather volatile recently and yet, through it all, you remain strong and as pure as one who enjoys battle can be."

I knew I wasn't pure. Killing tended to remove that from you.

"You will continue to face adversity and strife, but I have faith in you to keep moving forward and to protect your Kingdom and allies. However, you are not ready for what is coming."

"What's coming?" I asked. If I wasn't ready, then it must be terrifying.

"I'm meddling more than I should already," she told me softly, "but those two meddled more than their fair share with their children, so I will tell you this. A battle will come, one that will be waged in stages across the Realm and into your allies' realm as well. They will be unlike any enemy you have faced and in order to win you must become stronger! You and the Prince and Princess of the Elves must train together and learn to work together as one unit. Only then will you be able to win."

"You want Marin and Favian to train with us? I can't leave Crilan and—"

"They must come to you. After you've wed and returned from your wedding trip, you will all move to Avlin where you will train and prepare."

Avlin?

"The small island East of the Lost Port?" I asked.

"It is uninhabited save for a few animals and is far enough away from Crilan that you will not endanger your people, but close enough to reach in a time of need."

"I can teleport," I reminded her. "I could get there from farther away."

"You must learn not to rely on your magic alone and you must push yourself beyond the point of exhaustion."

"How will I know when I'm ready?" I asked.

"You won't," she said and then patted my hand. "You will have help along the way. We will not forsake you four as you train."

"It's not Malavar again, is it?" I asked nervously.

"No, he is dead and will remain that way," she assured me.

"This is crazy," I whispered.

"I will leave you for now. The others are being informed by their fathers about the plan. I will see you at the wedding." She kissed my forehead and then disappeared.

Faxon opened his eyes and frowned angrily. "I don't like it."

"What?" I asked him.

"What she told you. I don't like the idea of you going off to train on Avlin."

"I thought you were sleeping."

"I woke up partway through your discussion," he advised me. He walked over and held his hand in front of my face. "You look better."

"Just sore now," I said.

"I'm not going to let you fight some battle by yourself," he told me and folded his arms across his chest.

"I'll have the other three," I reminded him.

"At the very least I will teach all of you more magic."

"Faxon," I argued. "She said that the four of us need to learn to work as a group and—"

"And if I teach you how to do spells like the containment spell and how to shield each other, it will help," he interrupted.

"You're not going to back down on this, are you?"

"Nope."

"Why are you so stubborn?" I asked.

"Because he's unsatisfied with his life and is still striving to find something to make him feel worthy," Jared said from my doorway.

"Your rude comments are neither helpful nor correct," Faxon informed him.

"Finn's awake and eating downstairs. You ready to head down there, too?" Jared asked and ignored Faxon.

I nodded. "I'll get dressed and meet you down."

Jared put his arm around Faxon's shoulders and dragged him out my door. I took my time, brushed my hair, chose comfortable clothes, and walked down to the dining room. I did not expect to find Natalie and Eric there as well.

"Tilia!" Natalie yelled and rushed over to me. I hugged her and she said, "I was so worried about you."

"I'm fine. Thank you."

Finn pulled out my chair and kissed my cheek as I sat down. "Did you have a nice nap?"

"Yes, did your father speak to you?" I asked.

"Yes."

"Do you feel different?" Faxon asked us.

"No," Finn and I answered at the same time.

I piled my plate high with food and didn't waste time shoveling it into my mouth. I noticed halfway through my plate of food that Natalie and Esmeralda were talking, laughing, and smiling at each other.

"What are you two conspiring about?" I demanded a bit grumpier than I intended.

"We're discussing your wedding," Natalie replied happily.

"I need to contact Marin to discuss it," I said and wiped my mouth with my napkin.

"Someone's grumpy," Eric commented.

"You get zapped by a god and see how pleasant you are after being in pain and sleeping for three days," I snapped at him.

"Five days," Finn said as he cut a piece of his meat to eat.

"What?" I asked.

"We slept for five days total," he explained.

"Oh."

"Which is why you're so hungry," Jared told me.

I resumed eating and when I was done, I stood up and left the room.

Finn found me at Duke's stall and hugged me gently. "You okay?" he asked.

"Just grumpy," I whispered and pet Duke's muzzle.

"Are you regretting our decision?" he asked softly.

I spun around and stared at him in shock. "No! Are you?"

"Of course not," he told me with a smirk. "But, you're acting very angry."

"Faxon was really mad when I woke up the first time," I whispered.

"He'll get over it in time," Finn assured me.

"He's determined to come with us and teach us magic," I informed him.

"That's a good idea," Finn said. "What's the real reason you're mad?"

I sighed dramatically. "I just have a lot of emotional crap going on inside right now."

"About your dad?" he guessed.

"My dad and Cristoff."

"Cristoff? Why are you upset about Cristoff?" he asked angrily. "Did something happen? Did he kiss you? I'll go cut his—"

"He's gone," I told him. "He left Crilan."

Finn stilled and then turned me around to face him. "What are you talking about? Why would he leave?"

"It's all my fault," I told him. Hot tears slipped down my cheeks. "He told me that there was no other girl for him, that I was the only one he would ever want. He blames himself for Dad's death and to try to make it right, he's going to try to become the new King of Pirates. He left to go find a crew and he could die or—"

"He's a big boy," Finn told me gently. "He made the decision on his own and he is more than capable of being King."

"He kissed me again before he left," I told him.

Finn's jaw clenched, but he relaxed and exhaled loudly after a moment. "I'll give him a pass since he left."

"You really think he will be okay?"

He wiped my tears away and said, "If I know anything about Cristoff, it's that he survives more often than he should. He's a decent man and your dad was the one who taught him everything. I think he will be fine."

"Okay." If Finn thought he would be okay, then I believed him.

"I'm glad he took on the task," Finn told me. "I was considering whether I would have to do it."

I stepped back from him and asked, "How would you be King and Crilan's Prince at the same time?"

"That's why I hadn't made a decision," he said.

"You were considering leaving?" I asked in shock. "If you

were considering leaving why did you agree to our binding and—"

"I was never going to leave you," he told me and smiled. "You really are grumpy today."

I walked away from him and headed towards the castle.

"Come back," he called and caught up to me. "Tilia, I'm sorry. I would never have made a decision without talking to you first."

"Really? How do I know? You might have just left me alone in Crilan again while you sailed away!" I snapped at him.

"Tilia," he said and cringed. "I thought we were past that?"

"I don't want to talk anymore." I started walking faster, but he kept pace with me with his stupid speed.

"Hey, don't be mad. I promise I wasn't going to leave you."

I teleported to my room and sat down with my head in my hands. I couldn't believe him! One minute everything is great and we're never going to be apart and the next he's considering leaving to be a pirate again!

"Stop running from me," he ordered me as he appeared by my bed.

"Leave me alone," I ordered him. "I need some space."

"No. We need to talk this out."

I teleported to the arena and had to duck to avoid Jared's sword.

"Tilia!" Esmeralda yelled in shock from behind me. "You know you can't teleport somewhere like this!"

"Tilia," Finn said from beside me. "Stop."

"Sorry," I told Jared and then teleported to my room in Markleville. The castle was silent and I flopped back onto my bed with a sigh. I was overreacting and I knew it, but I was too mad to be able to talk to him. I just needed some time alone to digest everything.

I could not believe he was considering becoming King!

I screamed my anger and threw a pillow across the room.

"Feel better?" Faxon asked me.

"What are you doing here?" I growled at him.

"You teleported across Crilan. I had to make sure that you were okay," he told me.

"I don't want to talk about it," I told him. Especially since he would try to use this to prove that his concerns were valid. Finn and I weren't going to separate, but I could be mad at him for a while.

"There's a festival in the town, if you want to do something for a distraction," Faxon offered.

"Okay," I agreed. He teleported us and I almost threw up. "Why don't I feel sick when I teleport myself?" I asked him.

"Because you're in control. It's like riding in a carriage that someone else is driving," he said.

"I've never ridden in a carriage," I said softly.

"I'll take you sometime," he said. "All young ladies should experience it at least once."

The town was bustling with activity and there were vendors everywhere.

"I don't have money," I said sadly as I eyed a pretty shawl. It was white silk with red swirl designs.

Faxon picked it up, paid for it, and then wrapped it around my shoulders. "What good am I if I can't indulge in a shopping trip for you every now and then?" he asked.

"You don't have to buy me anything," I told him. "You've saved my life and Finn's and done more for me than I could ever hope to repay you for."

"You have done far more for me than you will ever know," he told me softly.

"What do you mean?" I asked him.

He shook his head and replied, "Not tonight. We don't need any more serious discussions today."

I could agree with that.

"Your Highness!" a vendor to my right said loudly.

I turned and found the woman bowing. "No, please stand. You don't need to bow to me," I told her with a smile.

She stood and asked, "What are you doing here? We hadn't heard that you would be coming?"

"We needed a day away from the Capitol," Faxon told her. "So, I brought Princess Tilia here to enjoy the festival."

"Arch Mage," the woman said and dipped her head in respect. "Please, take a lantern," she told us and handed Faxon a paper lantern.

"Oh! I've heard of this festival!" I said with excitement. "I've always wanted to see it, but never got the chance!"

"There's still some time before they light the lanterns," she told us. "You still have time to shop more."

Faxon set some coins on her table. "No, please," she tried to give them back, but Faxon shook his head and walked away from her.

"Oh, what's that!" I asked and drug Faxon by the arm towards another vendor who had a display of pastries.

He bought us each a pastry and followed behind me as I talked to each of the vendors and examined their items. I hadn't found anything else I really wanted until I came to a young girl selling knitted mittens. She was no older than ten and her face was smudged with dirt.

"What's your name?" I asked her.

"Cilia," she responded proudly.

"Where are you parents?" I asked.

"Dad's back at the farm. He has to make sure nothing hurts the animals," she said.

"Do you know who that is?" a little boy who I hadn't seen was sitting behind her asked.

"No," she said and looked at him. "Do you?"

"That's the Princess. Princess Tilia," he told her.

She turned and her eyes were as wide as the moon. "I'm sorry! I didn't know and—"

"It's okay," I told her and smiled. "Can I try on a mitten?"

"Of course!" she said. She asked, "What's your favorite color?"

"Teal, like the ocean," Finn's voice said from behind me.

I gritted my teeth and then smiled politely at the girl, "I think this purple is very pretty."

She lifted the mittens and I slipped them on. Her work was very good. "Did you make all of these yourself?" I asked.

"Yes ma'am, uh, Princess."

"Tilia," I told her. "You can call me Tilia."

"Yes, Tilia," she beamed.

"They're very warm and beautiful," I praised. "How much?"

"Oh, I couldn't charge you," she said and blushed slightly.

"Faxon," I called since he was talking angrily with Finn off to the side.

He handed me a handful of coins and resumed talking with Finn who I ignored completely.

"Now, I think I also need a pair for my friend Princess Marin," I told Cilia.

"What about these?" she asked and held up a pair of dark grey ones.

"Those are perfect," I said. She had about five pairs left and I decided to buy them all. "What do you sell these for usually?"

"Five," she responded.

"Do you have a bag?" I asked.

She held up a small knitted bag that she no doubt had made. "This should work."

"It most certainly will," I said. I picked up the rest of the mittens, put them in the bag, and gave her the rest of the coins Faxon had given me.

"This is too much," she whispered as she examined the coins.

"Faxon," I whispered. "Do you have any more?"

"No, that was the last," he whispered back.

"Here," Finn said and handed me some coins.

If it wasn't for Cilia, I wouldn't have taken them. I did though, and handed the coins to her. "Why don't you and your brother get a pastry and enjoy the festival now that you've sold everything?" I suggested with a smile.

"Thank you, Princess," the boy said with a wide smile.

"Thank you," Cilia said and hugged me before running towards the pastry vendor.

"That was very nice of you," Faxon told me.

I held up my hands and said, "These are really good mittens. Very warm and soft."

"Tilia," Finn pleaded. "Please talk to me."

"We better make our way to the docks so that we can have a good view," I told Faxon, grabbed his arm, and drug him through the crowd.

I was having trouble squirming my way through until the boy I had met at my party here in Markleville saw me. "Make way for the Princess!" he yelled over the noise of the crowd.

I cringed, but it was too late. Everyone parted and we walked down towards the docks. "Thank you!" I called to everyone.

"The Princess?"

"I didn't know the royals were here."

"When did they get here?"

"The Arch Mage is here, too! He's so handsome!"

"Would you like to begin the festival for us?" an older gentleman with a gray beard asked me.

"Yes please!" I said happily. I turned to take the lantern from Faxon, but he had disappeared and Finn was in his place.

"Together?" he asked as he held the lantern out towards me.

"I'm still mad at you," I told him.

"I know," he said softly.

I lightly gripped the edges of the lantern and light the ring in the center with fire.

"Focus on your wish," the older man instructed everyone.

"What's our wish going to be?" Finn asked me quietly.

"Not to get ditched again," I muttered.

"Tilia," he whispered.

"What do you suggest?" I asked.

"A relaxing wedding journey," he whispered. "Where we aren't attacked or interrupted by family."

I was blushing and I knew it. "Okay," I whispered back.

"Ready?" the older man asked me.

Finn and I nodded.

"Release!" he yelled.

Finn and I gently pushed our lantern up into the sky and we watched as thousands more joined it up in the sky and out towards the sea.

"Hopefully my father heard our wish," he told me and slipped his arm around my waist.

"Hopefully," I agreed.

"Can we go home?" he asked me and kissed my cheek. "You can be mad at me there too."

"In a little bit," I told him as I leaned against his upper body. I watched the lanterns in Finn's arms and hoped our wish would come true.

12

I<small>T TOOK ME ONE WEEK TO LEARN HOW TO TELEPORT TO</small> M<small>ARIN IN</small> her Kingdom and three days beyond that to learn to teleport the four of us at the same time over that distance.

Finn and Favian were with King Cesar in his study discussing things that Marin assured me were not interesting. She took me on a grand tour of the castle grounds and introduced me to her horse Fire.

"She's beautiful," I told her as I pet the mare's muzzle.

Marin beamed proudly. "Thank you. She and I have been through quite a lot together." I walked to the next stall and Marin said, "That's Ice, Favian's horse."

A male elf entered the barn and stopped when he saw us. "Oh, I didn't expect to find anyone here," he said.

He was handsome, though I hadn't found an elf who wasn't yet, but unlike Favian who exuded power, this male seemed much more relaxed and unimposing.

"I was just giving Princess Tilia a tour of the castle and I brought her to meet Fire," Marin explained. "Tilia, this is Alex, our Horse Master. He is the youngest in Elven history and personally, I think the best."

"Nice to meet you, Alex." I said and dipped my head.

"You're the one who fought against the magic user, aren't you?" he asked quietly.

"Yes."

"Marin told me that you tamed a leopard," he said curiously.

"I didn't tame it. I just showed it that I wasn't a threat and not a meal either so it left. I encroached on it's territory so I didn't want to hurt it," I explained.

"It's refreshing to meet someone who thinks like that," he told me.

"Would you like to go for a ride?" Marin asked.

"I considered teleporting Duke, my horse, here, but I didn't want to risk something happening to him," I told them.

"You can take my horse," Alex offered. "He's very well trained and has a smooth gait."

"That's very kind of you," I thanked him.

Marin saddled her mare and despite my attempts to help, Alex saddled his gelding, Traveler. Traveler had a gorgeous black coat with silver hairs sparkled throughout, looking like the night sky. I mounted and Alex whispered something to Traveler.

"What are you telling him?" I asked.

"To behave and take care of you," he said.

I pet Traveler's neck and said, "I'm sure we'll get along perfectly."

"Ready?" Marin asked from atop Fire.

I nodded and she said something loudly in Elvish. Both horses began walking and then leapt forward, racing out of the front gates and down the road. Alex was right, Traveler had a very smooth gait, and as we raced down the road, it almost felt like we were flying.

Marin turned to me with a smile on her face and I laughed happily. Traveler and I followed behind as they led us off the main road and into the forest, their hooves pounding the ground, and birds taking to the sky in fear, as we bolted past underneath them.

We approached a river and Marin slowed Fire, so I slowed Traveler who walked calmly beside them.

"It's beautiful here," I told her. I preferred the sea, but the forest had its own charms.

"Tilia," she whispered. "Do you feel different after the change?" she asked.

She was referring to us being given longer lifespans by the gods. "No," I told her.

"What if they lied? What if they didn't lengthen our lives, but just told us that so we could defeat whatever this new enemy is?"

I had been worried about the same thing.

"I don't think they would lie to us," I replied as I looked up at the leaves overhead. "I suppose we'll know for sure in about fifty or sixty years when I'll be close to the end of my normal lifespan."

"What if they don't see us living past this fight?" she suggested. "It could be to placate us."

"I don't think they would warn us and order us to train to be ready if they didn't think it was possible. I can't see them tossing our lives away like that."

"They're gods," she reminded me. "We're just another of the millions of lives they will see fade."

"That hurts," her father said as he appeared between our horses.

"I hate when you do that," she told him and slipped her dagger away.

"Is she right?" I asked him.

He turned and looked at me a moment before answering. "We don't see the future exactly. We see certain events or see what might be done to alter an event, but nothing is set in stone."

"And in your visions, are we alive or dead at the end of the battle?" Marin asked him.

"Why would I save your life just to throw it away?" he asked her.

"Because you need someone to save the rest of the world," she replied.

"I would not throw your life away like that," he told her.

"And what about Tilia's?" she asked him. "She's the only one of us who doesn't have a longer than normal lifespan. Are you trying to lure us into a false sense of security just to have the truth come to light when it is too late?"

"You are rather distrusting," he told her.

"Answer, please."

"We would not have put you three through such pain just as a ruse," he told us.

"Why won't you give us any additional information about the enemy we will be fighting?" I asked him. "If we knew more about them we would know what to focus on in our training."

"I don't have any information to give you. What I know is that the enemy you will face will be stronger than any you have encountered before, magic and fighting are their strong suits, and if you do not defeat them, they will destroy civilization as we know it."

"Where do they come from?" Marin asked.

"We're unsure," he replied.

"Maybe they aren't from this world," I told Marin with a smirk.

"Wonderful," she muttered. "Should we practice holding our breaths under water in case they are from the trenches in the sea?"

"Your attitudes are simply delightful," he teased us.

"Do you know what type of magic they have? If it's a certain element we could focus on a counter to it. Or, if it's summoning or curses, we can work on protections for those."

He sighed. "I wish I knew, children. I really do."

"It's almost impossible to prepare for an unknown enemy of extreme magical power," I told him. "There are so many specialties and specific counters to them that we would have to be Faxon to know them all."

"If only we could access his memories like you can after a binding," Marin said. "Then we would have all of his knowledge and we would know the counters and how to use them."

"You can't be bound to more than one person," he said.

"I wonder if there's a spell that would allow us to access his memories," I whispered mostly to myself.

"By the time we accessed the memory and went to use it, it could be too late," she commented.

"But if we could practice enough with various things, it wouldn't be hard. It would be like your own memories and how you recall them quickly and use the same defense or counter against a specific technique or ability," I countered.

"Do you swear that our lifespans were extended and are equal to Favian's now?" Marin asked him.

"I would not lie to you," he told her. "You are the last child I will have and I intend to keep you alive as long as possible. Aquinn feels the same and he would not see his son live for a decade or more without Tilia."

"If only this enemy would wait a few decades, we could be able to fully prepare," I said wistfully.

"Enemies are never accommodating," Marin agreed.

"I'll take my leave now," her father said. "Stop fretting about your lifespans and focus on the present. You two have a wedding to plan after all."

Marin and I groaned and turned the horses around to head back.

"We should make a training plan," I told her. "To ensure we cover every topic and at least have basic knowledge of them."

"Agreed."

"We also need to make a plan for our weapons training."

"Yes, someone needs to learn to use spears," she teased.

"And bows and arrows," I added.

"Finn said something about axes, too," she commented.

"Yeah."

"You think they'll let us get out of wedding planning to plan our training?" she asked me with a smirk.

"A girl can dream," I said with a longing sigh.

We took the horses back to the stables and Alex greeted us. "How was the ride?"

"Traveler was perfect and you're right, his gait is incredibly smooth," I praised as I dismounted.

Alex took the reins and smiled at me. "I'm glad that you enjoyed it. You can take him out any time that you wish while you are here."

"Thank you," I said in shock at such generosity.

I walked with him into the stable and despite his protests, I helped him unsaddle and brush down Traveler.

"Have you seen my brush?" Marin asked Alex.

"It's in your tack box in the back corner," he told her as he picked out Traveler's hooves.

I brushed his tail and was so distracted with the task that I didn't see when one of the horse's in a nearby stall leaned out and nipped Traveler. He backed up and I stumbled backwards to avoid being stepped on.

I started to fall, but Alex caught me.

"You okay?" he asked.

"Tilia," Finn called angrily.

I looked down the aisle and saw him and Favian standing at the end glaring in our direction. I realized when I looked back at

Alex why Finn was mad. I was still in Alex' arms and it looked like he was dipping me for a kiss.

I promptly stood up and brushed my clothes off. "Thank you for saving me," I told him. "I lost myself to the task and didn't pay attention."

"It's my fault," Alex said. "That filly should know better than to bite." I guessed that he meant the horse that had bitten Traveler.

"Time to go," Marin whispered to me.

"Thank you again for allowing me to ride, Traveler," I said and hurried along beside Marin.

"He's pissed," she commented softly to me as we approached the guys with wide smiles.

"What was that about?" Finn asked me.

"Alex saved me from falling," I told him truthfully. "That's all."

"That's all?" he asked. "That didn't seem like that was all."

"Come on," Marin said and grabbed my hand. "You haven't seen the best spot yet."

I let her pull me into a run, away from the boys, and around the stables towards a large sand arena.

"Thank you," I whispered.

"I don't know what it is with them, but for some reason Alex makes them jealous."

"Maybe it's because he's the opposite of them," I suggested.

"How so?" she asked and slowed to a walk.

"They're tough and mostly violent men. They are loud and commanding. Alex is kind, quiet, and non-confrontational, or at least I assume he is for being a Horse Master."

"I guess that's true," she said softly. "I never looked at it like that."

She stopped at the arena fence and said, "This is the infamous Elven fighting arena. It's been here for hundreds of years and I've been the only female allowed to fight in it."

"Impressive," I said as I looked at the arena. As odd as it was to admit, it felt old. Something about it made you think of battles waged long ago and fighters from eons ago.

"Good evening, ladies," King Cesar greeted us.

"Hello, Father," Marin said.

"Hello," I greeted.

"Have you come to spar?" he asked us.

I looked at him in shock. "I didn't think I was allowed in."

He smiled. "We have made an exception for Marin and I will make an exception for you as well. Fighters of your caliber deserve to be in this arena."

"Thank you," I said. I wouldn't admit it to them, but I had planned to sneak out here when they were sleeping just to stand in it.

"Tomorrow morning is the normal practice," King Cesar told me. "You are welcome to join us."

"Thank you."

"You as well Finn," King Cesar said over our heads.

"They caught up," I whispered to Marin.

"You think they're over it?" she asked me.

We glanced back and both were still scowling.

"Nope," we said at the same time.

"Are you ready for dinner?" King Cesar asked. "It should be ready. I actually came out here looking for you two."

"Yes," I said enthusiastically.

"Great, let's head on in," King Cesar said and led the way.

Finn grabbed my hand and pulled me to a stop. "What the hell was that back there?" he asked angrily.

"Finn, you have got to stop being jealous. Nothing happened. I was brushing the horse's tail and another horse bit him which made him back up into me. I was falling and Alex caught me. That's it."

"I don't care if they're elves or not," he whispered. "If they don't keep their hands off of you—"

"Yes, I know," I interrupted him. "You're so jealous." I walked away from him before he could say more and caught up to Marin who was being talked to by a stern-faced Favian. I linked arms with her and tugged her away. "I'm hungry!"

"Me too," she said and squeezed my arm.

We entered the room and the King's chief, Kato, pulled out chairs for Marin and I. "Good evening, Princesses," he greeted us.

"Good evening, Kato," I replied.

"How are you today, old badger?" Marin asked him.

"Growing older every day," he teased her.

"After lunch tomorrow, the seamstress will be here to take your measurements," Queen Amadis told us.

"Have you decided on a style?" Kato asked.

Marin and I glanced at each other and then at Kato.

"We're still discussing it," Marin told him.

"You're running out of time," King Cesar reminded us.

"We know," she assured them. "It's just difficult making a final decision."

"You could show me your favorite sketches and I could help you decide," Queen Amadis offered.

"No, thank you, but we will make our choice. We've almost got it finished," Marin told them.

"How many weapons do you think they're trying to hide in their dress?" Favian asked Finn.

"At least three," Finn replied. "Not counting the one they'll hide in their hair."

"What have you two been up to today?" I asked the boys.

"Comparing various things between our Kingdoms," Finn said.

"Where were you two today?" Queen Amadis asked.

"Marin took me on a tour and then we went for a ride," I answered.

"Oh, who did you ride?" King Cesar asked.

"Traveler."

"Traveler is a wonderful horse. Alex trained him very well," he replied.

"Sebastian should take some lessons from him," Favian muttered.

"What?" I asked.

"Sebastian's horse broke my foot when he first came here," Marin told me. "Favian still hasn't gotten over it."

"Have you started preparations on the island?" Kato asked.

"No, we will start them in a couple days. Faxon and I surveyed the island and found the best place for our houses and began sketching out floor plans, but nothing else has been discussed or planned yet," I said.

"Well, let's focus on one thing at a time," Queen Amadis said. "Once your wedding is over, have you decided where you will travel to?"

The four of us looked around at each other and then we shrugged in unison.

Queen Amadis sighed heavily. "Decisions must be made."

"We will discuss it tonight," Marin assured her.

As soon as we finished dinner, Marin and I raced to her room and finished our sketch of our dresses and our separate sketch which showed where we would be hiding our weapons. The one thing that we were keeping completely secret, even from the boys, was that we would be wearing our swords across our backs.

"You think your mother will try to take your sword off when

she sees it as we go to head down the aisle?" I asked.

"No, I told her already that I'm going to wear my sword."

"Any idea where you'll be taking your wedding trip?" I asked.

She sighed loudly. "None. You?"

I shook my head. "There are some really nice islands that are pretty uninhabited, but part of me just wants to find someplace in the middle of nowhere that will be quiet and that we won't be bothered."

"Yeah, that's our issue as well. I own a house that no one knows its location, but that's also the place that I died, so Favian isn't too fond of it."

"You died?" I asked loudly.

"Oh, right, you guys don't know about that. Yes, I died, but my father brought me back to life and that's why I was dying again when Favian contacted you about the decision to extend my lifespan."

"Wow, that's rough," I said softly.

"Favian's the one who has taken it the hardest. I don't know how to help him get over the pain it caused."

"I imagine it's not easy to get over," I whispered.

"What is that look about?" she asked me.

"I almost died not too long ago," I admitted. "Finn's been very jealous of any guy being near me since."

"Because almost dying means you might have changed your mind about who you want to marry?" she asked with a laugh.

"I don't know what to do about him."

"It can't be easy to get over," she said, repeating what I had told her.

"Perhaps if you ladies would stop trying to die on us, we wouldn't be so worried," Finn said from the doorway.

We quickly hid the dress sketches and turned to glare at him and Favian.

"You should have knocked," Marin accused them.

"You were talking about us, so we thought it was only fair that we be included in the conversation," Favian told her.

"Sometimes we need to talk without you being present," she told him.

"If you want to fight in the arena tomorrow, you need to get some sleep," Finn told me.

"I'll see you tomorrow," I told Favian and Marin.

I let Finn lead the way to our rooms and into his room where he shut the door behind us. He was upset about something, so I sat on the edge of his bed and waited.

"I'm sorry," he said a moment later, which caught me completely by surprise since I expected him to tell me why he was angry.

"About?"

He sat down next to me and let out a loud breath. "About being a jerk today. We have so much going on with this impending threat that I've been on edge. Plus, we had that fight not that long ago that we never really talked about. And all of these elves are—"

"Gorgeous?" I offered.

He growled in frustration and stood up. "Yes!"

I laughed and he spun around to glare at me. "Finley, have you been having doubts about wanting to marry me after seeing all of these beautiful female elves?" I asked.

"No!" he gaped. "Of course not."

"So, then why would you think that I might be doing that exact thing?"

He looked at the floor and said, "Because I haven't been the best fiancé to you this past month."

I walked to him and took his hands in mine. "Would you have left me to go become King of the Pirates?" I asked softly.

"No. I would have taken you with me," he told me.

"Do you want out of this relationship and all of the obligations it gives you for the future?" I asked.

"No."

"Do you love me?"

He looked up into my eyes and rested his hand on my cheek. "More than anything."

"Are you going to leave me if things become too tough?"

"No."

"Do you want to be with me and only me until we both die?"

He nodded.

"Then we have nothing else to discuss," I whispered and leaned forward to kiss him.

"I'll be better," he whispered and rested his forehead against mine.

"As will I."

"Tilia," he whispered. "Stay with me tonight."

"Finn, what else is bothering you?" I asked and placed butterfly soft kisses all over his face.

"I've almost lost you too many times in the short time that we've been together. Favian told me about Marin dying in his arms and I could see the pain that he still felt even though she was alive and he could feel her through their bond. I can't lose you."

I kicked off my boots and led him to the bed where I curled up with my head on his chest. With my Dad's death still so fresh, the thought of losing Finn hurt immediately. "I can't lose you either."

He tilted my chin up and kissed me deeply. I kissed him back and dug my fingers into the muscles of his back. It felt good to know that we were alive. To feel his warm skin and muscles as they flexed and relaxed beneath my touch.

"Tilia," he whispered breathlessly.

"Yes," I told him.

It was the last words we would speak until the next morning.

13

FAVIAN POUNDED ON THE DOOR TO WAKE US UP FOR THE FIGHTS and then went to wake Marin.

"How do you feel?" Finn asked me as he traced random patterns along my arm with his fingertips.

"Happy," I told him and kissed the tip of his nose. "How do you feel?"

He smiled brighter than I had seen him smile in months. "Perfect."

"We have to get dressed," I reminded him.

He kissed my neck and whispered, "We can be a few minutes late."

We ended up being more than a few minutes late, but it turned out, so did Favian and Marin.

Marin and I scarfed down some fruit on the way to the arena, which was surrounded by a huge gathering of Elves.

"Is it always this popular?" I asked quietly.

She nodded. "Word spreads fast here though, I'm sure they heard that you were going to be allowed to fight and wanted to see why."

"Wonderful," I mumbled.

"Marin," King Cesar called when he saw us. "I was wondering if you had changed your mind about sparring today."

"Sorry, we had a late start to the morning," she told him.

"Who are you sparring with?" I asked.

"My dad."

"Who am I going to spar with?" I asked.

"Me," Favian said with a smirk.

"You?" I asked in shock. I hadn't expected to spar against him. He and Finn were better rivals.

"Perhaps the Princess would prefer to spar against Marin," Kato suggested.

King Cesar nodded. "I think that would be a good idea. It would give us a chance to see what her abilities are for future matches."

"Okay," Marin said. "I'll just beat you another day," she teased King Cesar.

He stepped out of the arena and leaned his arms on the fence. "In time, I am certain that you will surpass me."

"I normally fight with two swords," Marin told me.

"That's fine," I replied and drew my sword and a dagger.

"Don't light me on fire," she ordered me.

I laughed. "I'll only use a defense shield if I absolutely need to," I offered.

We stood in the center of the arena and I took a deep breath to center myself and focus on Marin. She raised her swords and nodded. I returned the nod and sprinted forward. She was fast and smart. Her strikes hit hard and I smiled at the first vibration I felt through my arms as our swords clashed.

She liked to fight close and almost knocked my legs out from under me with a kick, but I dodged enough to stumble backwards and then roll out of the way of her strike. We circled each other and I saw her body began to softly glow.

"Pulling out all the stops, huh?" I asked. "If you're using magic, so will I."

"Ready?" she asked me.

I put one hand behind my back and drew a symbol in the air. "I'm ready," I told her.

She ran at me and as soon as she was within five feet, I finished the symbol and dodged. She froze in place and struggled against the spell.

She snarled at me. "Cheater."

"You used magic first," I accused her and flipped my dagger up in the air before catching it again.

"Can it be broken?" Favian asked from the fence.

I nodded. "Once she learns to shield herself, this type of spell won't work on her again. To escape now, she has to find the symbol and erase part of it."

"You drew it in the air," King Cesar said. "How can you erase something drawn in the air with a dagger?"

"A simple swipe of the hand will erase it," I told them, "but she can't move."

"So how does she escape?" Kato asked.

"Can you feel where the symbol is?" I asked her. "It will feel like a hand holding your shirt if that makes sense."

"Yes," she grunted.

"Is your hair near it?"

"Yes."

"Is your hair moving by it?"

"Yes."

"Picture your hair's movement as if erasing the symbol," I instructed.

Marin fell forward a step and righted herself. "But I didn't actually do it," she told me.

"Intent alone is what's necessary," I explained.

"We're going to work on a shield first," she told me.

"Okay," I agreed.

"You could have defeated her with teleportation, too," Finn said.

"True, but that's not very fair."

"Teleportation? How?" Kato asked.

I teleported to Marin with a sword to her throat, but she had her sword raised and blocked it. "She anticipated my move so she blocked it, but others might not. I could also do this." I teleported us both to Finn. "My partner could then kill the enemy for me." I released Marin who put her swords away and leaned an arm on my shoulder.

"How often can you teleport?" Favian asked me.

I shrugged. "I haven't tested it. Until my magic runs out, but that also depends on how much energy I've exerted as well."

"How many people can you teleport?" Marin asked.

"It depends on distance. For example, teleporting from here to my Kingdom is much more difficult with four people than teleporting ten people from here to the front of the castle," I explained.

"We're going to have to do a lot of testing," Favian said.

"And endurance building," I added. Finn cleared his throat. "Except for you."

"Ready, Finn?" Favian asked him.

Finn kissed my cheek and then appeared in the middle of the arena. "What's taking you so long?" he teased Favian.

"This should be interesting," Marin commented.

"Sorry about freezing you. I know it's at terrible feeling," I apologized. There had been a second where she had looked terrified.

"It's fine. I need to learn how to counter things like that so that it doesn't happen from an enemy. I would rather you do it in training than someone else on the battlefield." She looked at me a second and smirked. "If you hadn't done that I would have won."

"I know," I told her. "Your speed and stamina is definitely better than mine," I admitted.

She patted my back and said, "Now we know what to work with you on."

Favian handed me a fan.

"What's this for?" I asked.

"To fan yourself after you see me defeat Finn," he said and winked.

Marin laughed loudly and Finn twirled his sword. "You mean to fan Marin to keep her from fainting," he said with a smirk.

"I think you're the first human to insult me that I've actually looked forward to fighting, and not because I wanted to kill them," Favian said.

Finn bowed at the waist. "What a kind compliment."

"If this was a test of will alone, I think we would die of old age before a winner was announced," Marin whispered.

"I think a test of egos would never be determined and we would have to announce a tie," I told her.

"I'll go half speed to keep things interesting," Finn taunted Favian.

"If you want to walk out with your pride, you should go full speed."

"But then the fight will end so quickly," Finn said with a sigh.

"How fast is he?" Kato asked as he and King Cesar walked to stand next to us.

"He ran across the ocean," I told them. "He ran from dry land to his ship while carrying me."

No one spoke again.

Favian gripped his swords tightly and then I saw nothing,

but flashes of color, heard the clang of their swords, and the grunts of pain when one landed a blow.

I didn't know if anyone else could see them or not, but there wasn't a single noise from the spectators.

Time past as they fought and we stood by tensely waiting for someone to claim the title of winner.

Suddenly, Favian and Finn appeared in the center of the arena with Finn holding Favian in a headlock. A few of the elves gasped and Marin gripped the fence in front of us so hard her knuckles turned white.

"I believe this would be a draw," Favian said.

I looked closer and saw Favian's sword pressed against Finn's side, ready to plunge it in and kill him. I opened the fan and Marin put her face next to mine so that I could fan us both.

The boys saw us and released each other to laugh.

"You were still holding back," Favian accused.

"I was holding back my speed, but nothing else. If I had been in a fight previous to this one, I would likely move at that pace," he explained.

"You could have frozen him, too," I reminded Finn.

"Yes, but that's not nearly as much fun as putting him in a headlock," he teased Favian.

"I'm going to learn how to freeze you and then I'll make sure you can't escape," Favian threatened.

"You have to catch me to freeze me," Finn taunted.

"Are there many people like you in your Realm?" Kato asked.

"Not that I know of. Crilan is pretty unusual for our Realm. There are other mages there, but I think only about one third of the Realm's population are mages and of those not many have the amount of magic that Faxon and Queen Esmeralda have."

"And yourself," Finn added.

"Well—" I didn't want to brag about myself.

"How much magic do you have?" Marin asked.

"She turned an entire ship and its crew into ash," Finn told her. "Twice."

"To ash?" Favian asked.

"It's a fast burn that is so hot, they turn instantly to ash," I explained.

"When you see it, you'll understand," Finn insisted.

"Can you do it to anything?" Marin asked.

I nodded.

"What about that tree?" she asked and pointed at a large tree across the field.

"I don't want to kill your tree," I told her.

"We'll plant a new one," she assured me.

"You sure?" I asked and looked at King Cesar.

"I would like to see it," he agreed.

"Okay," I gave in.

"Do we need to move?" Favian asked.

"No, I'll just burn the tree," I promised.

"Do it like you did with the ship," Finn instructed. "It doesn't have the same effect if it doesn't go up in a poof."

"Fine," I grumbled.

"Let me check to see if there's anyone near it first," Finn said. He disappeared, appeared beside the tree, disappeared again, and then appeared beside me. "It's clear."

"That's creepy," Marin told him.

"Do it, Tilia," Finn told me.

I focused on the tree and then it exploded into ash and rained down to the ground.

"I didn't think she could actually do it," one of the elves in the crowd said.

"They could kill anyone."

"Could you do that to an entire army?" Favian asked me.

"I'm not sure. The ship I destroyed had more than fifty men on it," I said. "But I just focused on the ship as a whole, not the people too. It might not make sense, but focusing on multiple things is harder than focusing on one large thing."

"Why don't you just use this all the time?" Kato asked.

"I've never used it in a battle situation against individual people," I admitted. "And I haven't had the power for very long."

"You have this ability and yet they still think that you all need to train?" Kato asked softly. "What kinds of monsters are coming?"

That was exactly what I had wondered myself.

"The Little Death Bringer!" a male elf said as he walked through the crowd towards us.

"Jovian," Marin said with a smirk. "It's been a long time."

He looked her over and asked, "Have you improved with your twin blades yet?"

"A bit," she said cryptically.

"Care for a match?" he asked her. He noticed me and Finn and his smile disappeared.

"Jovian, this is Princess Tilia of Crilan and her fiancé Finn," Marin introduced.

"Nice to meet you," I said and bowed my head.

"Little Death Bringer?" Finn asked Favian.

"That's Marin's nickname here," he explained.

Finn looked at me and said, "So we've got the Little Death Bringer and the Pirate Princess becoming best friends. I can't imagine how that could go wrong."

Favian laughed and Jovian looked at me harder. "You're human?" he asked.

"Yes."

"Your aura is odd for a human," he muttered.

"Jovian!" Marin chastised. "She's a guest and my friend."

I set my hand on her arm. "It's alright. He is actually correct. My aura looks different than your humans here because of my magic."

"Magic?" Jovian asked. He moved a step closer and suddenly Finn was between us. Jovian's eyes widened in shock and he took a step back. "Where'd you come from?"

"Finn's faster than most," Favian explained and thumped his hand against Finn's back. "And you should reconsider touching someone without asking first or you might lose a hand next time."

Finn sheathed his sword and stepped aside.

"He's so jumpy," Marin muttered to me.

"Says the one who has a dagger in her right hand," I whispered back to her.

"I apologize," Jovian said and bowed low. "I wouldn't dare harm a guest of the Princess's."

"Apology accepted," I said with a smile.

"May I?" he asked and held up his hand.

I held out my hand and he held his palm above mine. I watched as his aura touched mine and sparked suddenly.

Many gasped in shock and Finn, Favian, and Marin had blades drawn.

"You okay?" I asked Jovian.

"That's some odd magic," he whispered and rubbed his hand on his jeans.

"Magic is magic," I told him. "Except for the dark kind."

"What was that?" Faxon asked angrily, appearing behind me.

"Dammit, Faxon," Finn yelled. "Stop doing that!"

"Tilia," he said to get me to answer.

"Jovian here was just inspecting me and our auras sparked," I explained.

Faxon looked at Jovian and Jovian began twitching. He stopped and then Faxon used his sight on me which made me want to rub my arms. "You both seem fine. It could be a defense mechanism your power has that you made subconsciously," he told me.

"I shocked him?" I asked.

He nodded. "Remember when we got shocked when I touched you after you thought that you had lost your powers?"

I nodded.

"I think that was when it came into place."

"But it didn't do it again," I reminded him.

"You must have finished sealing it up then without realizing it," he said.

"How did you know something had happened to her?" Finn asked Faxon with folded arms across his chest.

"I always monitor her when she's away," Faxon told him. He looked at me and something sad crossed his face before he teleported away.

"I'm going for a run," Finn told me angrily and disappeared.

"I'd go after him, but he's moving pretty fast," Favian told me.

"Let him be. He's just blowing off steam. He and Faxon haven't been getting along lately," I explained.

"Makes sense," he said with a nod.

"How? How does that make sense?" I asked angrily. "Nothing happened and yet Finn and Faxon are acting like they suddenly can't stand each other."

"Faxon did tell you to reconsider the binding," Marin reminded me.

"That might be part of it," I conceded, "but I doubt that's all of it. There's something else that neither will tell me about."

It had to do with why Faxon looked sad. I was certain of it.

"Well, now that you've caused more drama, would you like to fight now?" Marin asked Jovian.

"Sorry," he apologized to me.

I waved my hand. "It's fine. They're just on edge from me almost dying like four times last year."

"Wow, I think you beat Marin's record," Favian teased me.

"If we work together," Marin whispered, "we could take him and leave him frozen someplace."

"We could tie him up and eat cake in front of him," I suggested.

"You are cruel women," he teased us.

Marin went into the arena to fight and Favian grabbed my arm as soon as her back was turned and pulled me away. He led me away from the crowd and into grass that was taller than I was.

"What are you doing?" I asked.

"You need to take Finn somewhere away from Faxon for your wedding trip," he told me.

"The plan was to get away from everyone," I reminded him.

"Finn's close to exploding and if he does, it won't end well for anyone," he said.

"What are you talking about?" I asked.

"Something happened between Faxon and Finn, something that made him so mad that he almost lost his mind the other night when we were talking," Favian told me.

"What happened?" I asked.

"I can't tell you. It's Finn's choice whether to tell you or not."

"Favian," I growled.

"Tilia, just listen to me. Finn feels like you're going to leave him. When he saw Alex holding you, he had started to draw a weapon. If I hadn't known that he was in a bad mood, I might not have stopped him in time. He won't tell me everything, but despite your reassurances that you aren't going to leave him, he thinks that you will."

"How can I fix it if he won't listen to me when I tell him that I won't?" I asked in exasperation.

"You need to be bound," he said.

"We are going to at the wedding ceremony," I reminded him.

He shook his head. "You need to do it before then."

"But—"

Favian grabbed my shoulders and stared into my eyes. "Someone is going to die. He is letting this eat at him like a disease."

"Are you sure that will fix it?" I asked.

He dropped his hands and sighed. "No, but it's the only thing that I can think of. Unless—" he paused and looked at me. "Have you guys, you know, slept together?"

"Favian," I blushed.

"You don't need to be embarrassed. Marin and I have already."

"We did last night," I admitted. And this morning, but I wasn't going to tell him that.

"That explains why he was calm until Faxon showed up."

"This is stupid," I told him as I grew angry.

"The death of your mate is harder on you than I hope you will ever know. Having a mate that is sought after by so many others makes your rage barely containable," he admitted. "Even now, I still want to pulverize Jovian when he looks at Marin like that despite knowing that she has no interest in him and that she's mine."

"Why are you men so jealous?" I asked.

"My father said it's common for males of all species to be very protective of their mates, especially within the first few months," he told me. "It's like a claiming time. I know you're not an item to be claimed, but you know what I mean."

"You've been with Marin for so long," I commented. "How do you know that it won't take Finn years to get over this?"

"I don't, but I think this will greatly help."

"Who can perform the binding?" I asked.

"The gods or goddess," he answered.

"So, I need to take Finn to the ocean and ask his dad to do it?"

"Yes, or Marin's dad."

I sighed and ran a hand through my hair. "I hope this works. He's been such a wreck emotionally lately and I don't know how to fix it."

"The wedding trip will help," he assured me. "And hopefully he'll be over whatever happened with him and Faxon when we get to the island. If not, you might need to ask Faxon to wait and we'll focus on our fighting first."

"Okay," I agreed.

Favian pushed my shoulder with his fist. "It'll get better. I will help him. I think our talks are helping him process the emotions and figure out what he is feeling and how to deal with it or what to talk to you about, so he can deal with it."

"Does Marin know about this?" I asked as we headed back towards the arena.

"She knows about me and what I go through because she can feel it through our bond."

"Fun," I whispered. "Something to look forward to."

We went back to watch the fights, but I could hardly pay attention. What had happened between Finn and Faxon? Now that I thought about it, they had been at odds since the trip to Drimla. I needed to know what had happened. I considered asking Faxon, but I knew he wouldn't tell me and Finn would likely be angry that I had asked Faxon instead of him.

"Tilia," Favian whispered.

"Hm?" I looked up and realized that everyone had left and only Marin and Favian were here with me. "Oh, sorry."

"Come on," Favian said and nudged me with his shoulder. "Let's get some snacks and we can brainstorm on our wedding trips."

Marin draped her arm across my shoulders and squeezed me. "We could go find some ogres to kill," she offered. "That always makes me feel better."

I smiled and felt my shoulders relax. "Thanks for the offer, but knowing us, we would get into trouble somehow and then we would have to sit through lectures from the boys about not doing dangerous things without them and blah blah blah."

"True," she muttered.

"You two are definitely trouble magnets. I have a feeling that you two staying in one place too long will draw enough trouble to end the world," Favian teased us.

"Maybe that is why they are making us live together on that island and train. It will draw the enemy to us, which will save the rest of the world from trouble," I said.

"I'm going to get us some snacks. I'll meet you in the room," Favian said and then walked in the direction of the kitchen.

"So, you want to talk about what's bothering you?" Marin asked.

"It's Finn. He's so angry lately and apparently, something happened between him and Faxon, but he hasn't told me. Favian thinks if we perform the binding now it will help mellow him out. Finn thinks I'm going to leave him, which is absurd," I told her and then sighed and dropped my head forward.

"I noticed that his jealousy is getting a bit out of control," she told me.

"When?" I asked.

"When he was about to attack Alex for catching you in the stables," she answered.

"Men are so ridiculous," I grumbled. "Why can't he believe me when I tell him that I'm not going to leave him?"

"It is hard to fully trust another person. You never really know if they are telling the truth or not. Favian could have lied about where he was going for all I know," she said and shrugged. "Trust is hard to give."

"Did the binding help you and Favian?"

She nodded. "Immensely. Although he was, no is, still very

jealous of others being near me. Tradition is that once you begin sleeping together you isolate yourselves or the male will be overly protective and it is difficult for him to distinguish friend from foe. Some call it the mating fog."

"So, that means that there is more reason behind waiting until marriage then just morals," I said and laughed. "Whoops."

She stopped walking and looked at me in shock. "Did you?"

I blushed. "Yes."

"When?"

"Last night."

We resumed walking and she laughed. "He was in a better mood this morning, much more than usual. And he didn't kill Jovian for looking at you like he had. You are right; whatever happened between him and Faxon is really what is eating at him. As soon as he saw Faxon all of his logical thought disappeared. He was gripping his sword as soon as Faxon appeared."

We entered her bedroom and she ran around picking up stray clothing and tossed it all into one corner of the room. I sat on her bed and leaned back against the headboard.

Marin grabbed some paper and a writing utensil and asked, "Where do you think about going when you picture your wedding trip?"

"A small island with clear blue, warm ocean water," I answered immediately. I had a brief flashback to our trip to Carlos the Crusher's island and the one after.

"Warm ocean water?" she asked.

"It's so clear you can see to the ocean floor! And the water is warm, like a bath. We sat on the shore where the water came up to our waist while we sat. It's heavenly."

She wrote down a few notes and then asked, "Where else?"

"Sometimes I think we need to go to the middle of the forest in a cabin where no one else lives within a hundred miles," I replied.

She made some notes and then tapped her fingers on the paper as she thought.

"What do you picture?" I asked her.

"The forest," she said, "but I like the sound of warm ocean water and a beach."

"You started without me?" Favian asked as he entered. He set an assortment of foods on the bed and a pitcher of water on a side table.

"We figured it would help speed the process along," I told him.

"What do you picture when you think about the wedding trip?" Marin asked him.

He smirked at her and a blush rose on her cheeks.

I laughed and she cursed. "You're terrible. We have a guest and you are being crude."

"She laughed," Favian pointed out.

"Come on," I urged Favian. "Answer the question."

"A field of grass surrounding a small house," he said.

Marin made some notes and then handed them to Favian. He read them over and sat on the end of the bed. "Warm ocean water? I've heard of it, but I thought it wasn't real," he said.

"It is very real and very nice," I told him.

"Hey," Finn said from the doorway.

"Come in," Marin urged him. "We are discussing wedding trip locations."

He hesitated a moment and then walked around the bed to sit beside Favian. He took a piece of dried meat and chewed on it.

"It seems that we are tied between the ocean with warm water and a cabin in the middle of the forest," Marin said to update Finn.

"I prefer the ocean, but it might be nice to have a different view for a while," he commented.

"What about the island?" I asked and looked up from the piece of bread I had been mutilating. "We could go there and build our houses and live there."

"The ocean is cold there," Finn reminded me.

"Oh, right."

"We could go back to the island I took you to," Finn suggested.

"I wonder who is running Carlos's island now?" I murmured as I resumed tearing up the bread roll.

"I could find out," Finn offered, "but I would rather go to the island we went to afterwards."

"Bad memories?" Favian asked.

Finn nodded. "Tilia was kidnapped by Carlos. He drugged all of us and sent me and my crew away from the island while he had her. I came back, but she had already tried to escape him and was hurt when I got there." He froze a second and I saw fear, pain, and anger cross his face before he looked up again. "Plus, that wolf might be there still."

I had forgotten about the wolf that Carlos had kept and trained. "He is probably there, unless the crew killed him."

"You have the most interesting stories," Marin told us with a smile.

"Says the woman who fights ogres," I countered.

"You fought chimeras," she countered back.

"You fought shapeshifters."

"Ladies," Favian said to end our discussion. "It seems we have decided on our location."

"We have to find a ship," Marin said.

"I can teleport us," I offered.

"That would give us more time to spend on the island versus traveling," Finn added.

"We could always go to the Isle of Respite," I whispered.

Finn frowned and then said, "There will be too many there who know us. We'd never have a moment of peace."

"There would be a lot of drinking too," I added and agreed. "We will go to Siladen then."

"Siladen?" Marin asked.

"That's the name of the island," Finn explained.

"Okay, Siladen it is," Marin said with a wide smile.

14

AFTER A FIFTEEN-MINUTE BATTLE WITH QUEEN AMADIS, MARIN finally convinced her to let us meet with the seamstresses alone. The two seamstresses were female elves with soft voices and kind smiles. Their smiles never faltered, not even when we showed them our sketches and explained the inner straps and their purposes.

"Will it be solid white?" one of them asked.

"Yes," Marin answered. "I don't want to give Mother a heart attack."

The seamstresses laughed softly.

"We will get to work on it immediately," the second one said. "We will bring it for a fitting in two days."

"Thank you," I said, beaming with excitement coursing through me.

They curtsied and left with our sketches hidden within their bag of tools.

"You think your mother will freak out when she sees us?" I asked softly as Queen Amadis walked in.

"She might, but she should know me well enough to agree that the dress is fitting to my style."

"Is everything set?" Queen Amadis asked.

"They will come in two days to have us try them on and fit them," Marin explained.

"Will I be allowed to see them then?" she asked.

"No, you have to wait until the wedding like everyone else," Marin told her.

"You're impossible," she muttered.

"Ah, a queen never mutters," Marin teased her.

"Have you decided on your bouquet yet?" she asked us.

"Oh, oops," I said and looked at Marin.

"We will go tomorrow to find our flowers," Marin promised.

"Four days until the wedding and they haven't even figured out their flowers," Queen Amadis muttered to herself as she walked away.

"Men have it so easy," I complained.

"I bet they still haven't taken care of the rings," Marin said.

We headed out of the Queen's drawing room and out to the arena in search of the boys. Surprisingly, they weren't there.

"Where could they have gone?" I wondered aloud.

"On a ride maybe?" Marin guessed.

We went to the stables, but Ice, Favian's horse, was in his stall. We walked out and looked around the grounds.

"Can't you sense Favian?" I asked her.

"He is blocking me," she said and slowly turned in a circle as she tried to locate him.

"What could they be doing that he would block you?" I asked.

"I'm not sure. Can't you find Finn's magical signature?"

"I should be able to, but I can't right now. He must be masking it. I didn't even know that he could do that."

She and I looked at each other and I saw the same reaction on her face. They were up to something.

"You think they're in trouble?" I asked.

She shook her head. "Favian would not hide that he was in danger. Plus, I would have felt his fear or anger when a fight began."

"What could they be doing then?" I asked grumpily.

"Well, let's go look for our flowers and if they aren't back by the time we are done, then we will go find my father and ask him if he knows where they went."

I followed her into the fields and pondered over our futures. At some point, we would both become Queen of our Kingdoms. How often would we be able to see each other?

I shook my head.

We had to live through our upcoming battle first. After that we could worry about the future.

We crested a small hill and she asked, "Which colors do you want?"

The ground before us was covered in flowers of every color, more colors than I had ever knew flowers could be. They were beautiful.

"Wow," I said as I continued to take in the beauty of the sight before me.

"Come on," she urged and walked down towards them. "Let's get our bouquets ready."

"If we pick the flowers now, they'll die," I reminded her.

She smiled smugly. "No, they won't."

"Are you going to tell me how the flowers will continue to live once we pluck them from their roots?"

"No, but once you have your bouquet I will show you," she said.

We sat at the edge of the field as neither of us wanted to risk stepping on any flowers, and picked an assortment of colors. I picked teal and white colored flowers while Marin picked red and white colored flowers. We arranged the flowers into the grouping that we wanted and then she pulled out two long pieces of ribbon for us to tie the flowers together with. We each tried to tie a bow, but they were rather pathetic looking.

"Do you think Queen Amadis will be able to fix our bows?" I asked as I looked at the droopy one I had tried to make.

"I am certain that she can," she said and frowned at her small bow.

"Okay, now that we have them, what are you going to do?" I asked her.

She held her hand over my bouquet and then her entire body started to glow. The glow spread to my flowers and then the light disappeared. "Now these will never die or wither," she explained.

"Really?" I asked as I examined them. They did not look any different. I did not sense any magic on them either.

"My dad showed me how to do it," she said and repeated the process on her bouquet. "He did it to a flower and gave it to me. When I came back into the castle with it, Favian started to get incredibly jealous because he thought another man had given it to me. Well, another man had given it to me, but he doesn't count. You should have seen his face when I called him out for being jealous."

"He seems rather calm compared to what you have told me he was like before," I noted.

"Honestly, I think I have you and Finn to thank for that. He was calming down, but after we met you two, and Malavar was defeated, he relaxed fully. I have watched how he interacts with you and I have to tell you that I never thought that I would see him return to the kind, soft-hearted boy that I loved as a girl. My life being in constant danger, and our falling out, put a strain on him that caused darkness to swirl around him like flies around dung. He's no longer bitter or angry, and he let you two into our lives with open arms. I think he feels like Finn fully understands him due to encountering so many similar issues."

"And they're both equally stubborn," I added.

She laughed. "That as well."

"I don't think Finn and I would be in a great spot emotionally, if it weren't for you and Favian. Favian is helping him deal with the emotions and events that he won't confide in me. I'm sort of jealous of Favian for that."

"Every man needs a brother and every woman needs a sister that can share and empathize with their issues. We have each other and I know Finn wishes he could understand you like I do," she told me.

I leaned back on my elbows and looked up at the puffy clouds as they passed by overhead. "Have you heard from Sebastian or Deana?" I asked.

She copied my position and said, "No, but he has been keeping his thoughts to himself lately."

"You can hear his thoughts?" I asked, mouth slightly open.

"We have bracelets that were spelled by the Queen of the Pegasi, Silvermist, that allow us to communicate telepathically while wearing them. He either removed his bracelet or is blocking us."

"Do you think it is because he is worried what your parents will think about him and Deana's relationship?"

She shrugged. "Maybe. He hasn't been back very long and he does not know Amadis and Cesar very well. He might worry that they would not approve of the relationship."

"Will they?"

"I think they will just be happy that he found someone that he loves," she said.

"Will there be any people who rebel at the fact that the royals of the elves are marrying non-elves?"

She sighed loudly. "Definitely, but that won't matter to our parents."

"What happens if your child's children continue to marry

non-elves and the royal family ends up being less elf than anything else?"

"Who knows?" she said nonchalantly. "Our child might end up being with an elf and then returning the lineage to mostly elves. Or Sebastian might not end up staying with Deana. They haven't known each other that long and he hasn't had much time with the elves. There are many beautiful and kind female elves here."

"I saw," I said. "And lots of males, too."

She smirked and looked at me out of the corner of her eye. "See some good-looking elves?" she asked.

"Only constantly," I said and laughed.

"If Finn didn't exist and you came here, who would you seek to court?" she asked me.

"I don't know," I admitted. "There are so many attractive males and I don't know any of them."

"I wish you could have attended an Elven ball when you were single," she told me. "You get to dance with all of the single male elves and I know you would have an amazing time."

"Finn crashed my birthday party," I told her. "He came in a suit and danced with me without letting anyone else cut in."

"Did you dance all night?" she asked.

"No, my Uncle chased him away because he saw us kiss and he didn't like that," I said and laughed.

"That was when he was a pirate, right?" she asked.

"Yes, when he was Captain."

"Do you ever worry that he will miss it enough to leave?" she asked me softly.

I nodded. "He had even considered going to become King after my father died," I told her. "We had a huge fight about it because he didn't tell me until another of our comrades went to take the title."

"He was going to leave you?" she asked in shock.

"He claims he was going to take me with him, but we both know that I couldn't just leave Crilan like that. The King of Pirates travels all over the seas and the new one will be in constant danger of those wishing to take the title from him."

"Do you worry that you will miss being a Mercenary enough to want to stop being Queen?" I asked her.

"Protector," she corrected. "I earned the title of Protector, which is above Mercenary."

"My apologies," I said in a mockingly deep tone.

"I worry that I will miss it, but the way my life is, there are bound to be adventures while I'm queen to keep me busy. If not, you are welcome to ask me to join you when you have grand adventures."

We smiled at each other and I nodded. "Deal. You call on me and I will call on you."

"You ready to head back?" she asked.

I used my power to try to locate Finn, but he was still missing or too far away for me to sense.

"They're still gone," I told her.

"I wonder if they went into the Pegasi lands for some reason," she mumbled.

"Would that make a difference?" I asked.

"Well, it's likely that they have a spell to block people like you from finding magic there. The Pegasi are strict about not allowing humans..." She paused and said, "Finn should not be allowed to go there. Unless..."

"Unless what?" I asked.

"Unless they gave him special permission because he is like me and half-god."

"Lucky," I mumbled.

"I promise to introduce you to Silvermist before you leave."

"What would they be doing there?" I wondered aloud.

"Maybe they're making our wedding rings," she suggested.

"Favian made my engagement ring there," she added and held up her hand to inspect the beautiful ring.

"What about their rings?" I gasped. "We don't have rings for them!"

"Are we supposed to get them?" she asked, suddenly frantic. "We need to ask Amadis."

We stood, grabbed our bouquets and ran to the castle. As we ran inside, we stumbled into someone and I ended up falling on them.

"Sorry!" I said quickly and tried to untangle myself from them.

"Are you hurt?" a male voice asked from the body of the person I had fallen on.

I looked up and my breath caught in my throat. He was the most handsome elf I had seen, the most handsome male I had seen ever. "Uh..."

Marin grabbed my arm and pulled me up. "Sorry, Balon. We were trying to find Amadis."

He stood up and brushed his clothes off. "Well, I'm glad that I was able to save such a beautiful creature from falling on the cold ground." He picked my hand up and kissed the back of it while bowing to me. "I will gladly be available for such service in the future."

"We have to go," Marin said and dragged me away from him. We turned down a hallway and she pinched my cheeks. "You're blushing brighter than my flowers."

"My flowers!" I gasped when I realized that I didn't have them.

She lifted up her hand where she held both of our bouquets together. "You threw yours up in the air and I caught it."

"I can't believe that happened," I whispered in embarrassment.

"Just be glad that Finn did not witness that," she teased me.

"We would have had to chain him up to keep him from murdering someone."

"I'm so embarrassed," I whispered as we resumed our search for Queen Amadis.

"Don't be. When I turned eighteen, Balon gave me a present and I had no idea at the time that it was a courting gift, so I accepted it. Favian was livid and demanded that I give it back and was so smug the next day when I did."

"I didn't know they made men as stunning as that," I told her and laughed.

She joined in on my laugh and then stopped next to a door.

"What's in here?" I asked.

"The war room," she said. "Sometimes they come here to talk in private." She knocked twice and called, "Mother, are you here?"

The door opened and Queen Amadis looked at us in shock. "What's got you girls all rosy cheeked?"

"Uh, we were worried because we realized that we don't have rings for Favian and Finn and we weren't sure if we were supposed to," Marin said and smiled at Queen Amadis.

Queen Amadis looked at us suspiciously a moment and then said, "I thought you had picked out their rings already?"

We both shook our heads.

She sighed loudly. "Come with me, girls." We followed her obediently and I was surprised when she led us out of the castle and towards the stables.

"Where are we going?" I asked Marin in a whisper.

She shrugged.

"Your bouquets look beautiful," Queen Amadis commented. "I will have Alex take them from you and to my drawing room for safe keeping."

We entered the stables and Alex rushed to greet us. "Your Highnesses," he said and bowed low.

"Will you please give us a cart?" Queen Amadis asked. "We need to travel and although I normally would not mind a horseback ride, these two are prone to trouble and I would like to keep them as close to me as possible to ensure all three of us arrive safely."

"Right away," he said and rushed outside.

"I can't remember the last time that I rode in a cart," Marin said.

"Are you as strong as the males?" I asked Queen Amadis.

She smiled wide and leaned close to me to whisper, "When we return for dinner, ask King Cesar about the competition we had."

"What competition?" Marin asked. "How come I don't know about this?"

Queen Amadis brushed invisible dirt off her dress and said, "Although I do not like to discuss my age, I have been alive quite a long time. There are many things that you do not know about me, Daughter."

"Now I wish it was dinner time and not because I'm hungry," Marin said.

Alex brought out a beautiful silver cart with a mare that had a mane and tail that flowed behind her as she pranced.

"She's gorgeous," I whispered in awe.

"Princess is Mother's horse," Marin explained.

"Hello, Princess," Queen Amadis greeted her horse and ran her hand down the horse's face.

"Would you like me to drive?" Alex asked.

"No, thank you. I will drive," Queen Amadis said.

"You're driving?" Marin asked in shock. "You should let Alex drive."

"I am perfectly capable of driving this cart. Now, climb in ladies and we will be on our way," Queen Amadis said and climbed up into the driver's seat.

"Your Highness, I would feel more comfortable if—" Alex began, but the Queen gave him a look and he bowed and backed away.

"Let the King know we will return for dinner," she ordered.

We climbed up into the cart and Queen Amadis clucked her tongue. Princess began trotting and we headed deeper into the elves' territory.

"Do you know their ring sizes?" Amadis asked us.

"No," we admitted.

"When we get to the shop, you will need to take two sizers, teleport to the men, size their fingers, and then teleport back to us," Amadis informed me.

"Okay."

"What if they're still on their secret mission?" Marin asked. "What if they're in the Pegasi lands and she teleports there?"

"If that happens, I will personally give her a pardon and speak to the Pegasi regarding the incident," she assured us.

"How far is this place?" Marin asked her.

"Not too far. I don't think you've been there since you were very young," Queen Amadis said. "Why haven't you returned to visit the villages?"

"I did once," Marin admitted. "They weren't very accommodating."

"What happened?" Queen Amadis asked.

"It's old news," Marin said.

"Marin," Queen Amadis ordered.

"I ran into a few of the female elves who liked Favian. They started insulting me and tried to threaten me to stay away from him, so that they could court him. There were five of them and I had come alone. I was trying to avoid fighting them and then one of them hit me in the back of the head with a log. I was bleeding and I really wanted to tear them apart, but I didn't want them to lie and accuse me of starting it and risk you getting upset at me, so I just came home."

"That was the night Favian burned down the tree house," Queen Amadis replied with shock.

"What tree house?" Marin asked.

"Those girls had a tree house that they used as a secret club. Favian burned it down and didn't even deny it when we asked him. He had made certain that the girls watched him do it and was very proud of himself when we talked to him about it. He wouldn't say why, but now it make sense," Queen Amadis explained and then chuckled. "Those girls cried for a week straight. Had I known what had happened, I would have dealt a harsher punishment out to them and not punished Favian."

"I didn't know that he had done that," Marin whispered.

"You guys are so cute," I said with a wide smile.

"We always knew that they would marry," Queen Amadis said.

"What?" Marin gasped.

"Please, Marin. We aren't blind, and even if you didn't want to admit it to each other, we could see that you were both in love. You forget that I'm well over five hundred."

"Five hundred!" I gasped. I looked at Marin. "Does that mean that we're all going to live to be over five hundred?"

She smiled. "Oh, we didn't tell you how old elves lived for?"

"You said a couple hundred years," I accused her.

She shrugged with a wide smile.

"I wonder if we will run into those girls," Marin pondered.

"Well, now there are two of us, so I think we can take them," I said with a devilish grin.

"You two will behave," Queen Amadis ordered us.

"She is such a downer," I teased.

"If one of those twits says anything, I will handle it," she said.

"Am I the only one hoping something happens?" I asked Marin in a whisper.

She shook her head.

We stayed quiet the rest of the ride and I found myself staring wide-eyed as we entered a village made up entirely of elves. There were businesses and houses and elves of varying ages and appearances walking around.

Queen Amadis stopped in front of a shop and turned around with a wide smile. "We have arrived. Follow me into the shop."

We obeyed, climbed down from the cart, and followed as she walked into the shop with an elegance that I envied. A bell jingled as we entered and a short, rotund elf with silver hair down to his belt walked out of the back to greet us. "Welcome to..." he paused when he noticed who was in the shop and then bowed low. "Your Majesty. I had no idea that you were coming."

"This was an unexpected trip and an emergency at that," Queen Amadis informed him.

He straightened and asked, "How may I help you?"

"We need two wedding bands. One for Prince Favian and one for Prince Finn of the humans of Crilan," Amadis explained. "Their wedding is in two days and the Princesses forgot to purchase the bands."

"That's no problem," he said. "As long as you know their measurements."

"We will take care of that as soon as you give us the sizing tool," she said with a smile.

He looked perplexed, but opened a drawer behind the counter and handed Queen Amadis a silver ring with several smaller rings. "Here is the sizing tool."

"We will be right back," she informed him. She turned and faced Marin. "Stay here and do not cause trouble. You may look for a ring while we are gone."

"Yes, Mother," she replied grumpily.

"When you are ready," Queen Amadis said to me.

I set my hand on her shoulder and focused on Finn's magic signature. This time I was able to find it. Once I locked on to it, I teleported us to him. When we arrived, I was shocked to discover him standing with Favian and King Cesar in the center of a field surrounded by Pegasi and beside his father, Aquinn."

"Tilia!" Finn said in shock.

"She can't be here!" Favian gasped.

"Calm yourselves," Queen Amadis ordered them. "I needed her to teleport me to the boys and it is my fault that she appeared in these lands. We had no way of knowing where you were. Now, Favian, find your ring size and tell me what it is and then Finn, you do the same."

The boys obeyed, while everyone stared at me with disbelief and fear.

"If she didn't come here intentionally, will she still be punished?" Finn asked softly.

"No," Queen Amadis answered before King Cesar could say what he had wanted to. "I pardon her and take the blame for this. We will be on our way as soon as Finn is done."

"I will speak with you later tonight," Aquinn told me.

I bowed. "Very well."

"We have the measurements, so we will be on our way. Be home for dinner," Queen Amadis said and then nodded once at me.

I teleported us back to the shop and Marin. Marin exhaled loudly, her shoulders relaxing at the sight of us.

"That was not fun," I commented.

"What happened?" Marin inquired.

"Nothing, I handled it," Queen Amadis assured her.

"What were they all doing there together?" I pondered.

"Who?" Marin asked.

"Favian, King Cesar, Finn, Finn's father, and a herd of pegasi," I told her.

"That is rather suspicious," she whispered and looked off into the corner of the room as she thought about it.

"Here are the sizes and your sizing tool," Queen Amadis told the shop owner.

"These rings are nice," Marin said, pointing to some in a case near her. I walked to her and looked them over.

One caught my eye and I pointed to it. "That one."

"That one is nice," Marin commented.

"May I see it?" I asked the shop owner.

He hurried over and pulled the ring out for me to examine. "Of course. That one is made of the strongest material in existence, nothing can break it or bend it."

"How is it made then?" I asked as I held the light ring in my fingers and marveled over the dark material that shined and sparkled.

"Magic," he replied as though I should have known that.

"What about this one?" Marin asked and pointed at a silver ring.

"You two have excellent taste," he commented. "This is made from a fallen meteorite."

"A fallen star?" I asked in shock.

"Yes."

"Yours is better," I whispered to Marin.

"Yours is great, too," she commented. "He wouldn't have to worry about it getting ruined in battle."

"Let me see if that one is the correct size," the shop owner said and took the ring from my hand.

"How much is it?" I asked nervously. Something so exquisite was likely very pricey.

"It's the right size," he said happily and then took the one

Marin had to check the size without answering me. "This is Prince Favian's size."

"Prices?" I asked again.

"A gift from me to the new couples," he replied with a wide smile. "Consider it my wedding gift."

"This is too much," I said in surprise.

"It's not every day that the Prince is married. And besides, many will ask where the ring was obtained, so it's good for me, too."

"Are you certain?" Queen Amadis asked.

He nodded and then put the rings into two boxes and held them out to us. "May your lives be long and filled with joy and your union the same."

"Thank you," I said with heartfelt sincerity.

"Thank you," Marin said.

Queen Amadis led us out and then pointed towards a bakery across the street. "Let's stop in there and then the store next to it which has amazing chocolates."

"Sounds like a perfect plan to me," Marin said with a wide smile.

"Me too," I agreed.

We skipped across the street, arm in arm, and laughed the whole way. As we opened the door, a group of female elves exited and ran into us.

"Sorry," Marin and I said at the same time.

"Perhaps you should watch where you are going," one of the females said with disdain.

They looked us over and one asked, "Did you find a friend finally, Marin? I always assumed you would have to turn to a human."

They giggled and another asked, "Did you find her under a rock or does she just naturally smell this horrid?"

My fists were clenched and ready to hit the horrid females,

when Queen Amadis cleared her throat from behind us. We stepped aside and the females paled instantly.

"In my long life, I have rarely experienced such hatred and outright disgusting attitudes towards females you do not know. The fact that you act this way towards your Princess, and soon to be Queen, astonishes and disappoints me. You will apologize this instant and in three days meet me at the castle where I will educate you on the proper ways to act in public."

The females whispered apologies and then hurried away with ashamed looks on their faces.

"Are you certain I can't hit just one of them?" Marin asked her.

"You were amazing," I told Queen Amadis.

"You can order them around in the future and give them awful tasks once you are queen," Queen Amadis told Marin.

"She's so devious and I love it," I said with a wide smile. "I see where you get it from."

Queen Amadis laughed and entered the shop.

Hours past as we ate and talked and laughed and before we knew it, it was dinner time. We hurried back to the stables where Alex took care of putting away the horse and cart. We raced into the dining room to find it empty.

"Where are those boys?" Queen Amadis asked aloud. "I'm going to check the war room. You two sit."

We obeyed and snuck a bite of chocolate while she was gone.

"Can you believe that we are going to be married women very shortly?" Marin asked me.

"No, it is very hard to believe," I agreed.

"Part of me is very excited and part of me is very terrified. Please tell me that you feel the same," she whispered.

"Exactly the same," I whispered back.

"Good evening, ladies," Sebastian greeted us and sat down next to Marin.

"Where have you been?" Marin asked him.

"On a trip," he answered vaguely.

"Tilia," Aquinn said behind me.

I gasped in shock and then growled. "Why does everyone enjoy scaring me?"

He smirked and said, "Your face is rather amusing when you are scared."

"Wonderful. How can I help you?" I asked.

"It is time," he said vaguely.

"Time for what?" I asked.

"The binding," he replied as though I should have known immediately.

"Oh, right."

He set his hand on my shoulder and we appeared next to Finn in a grass field surrounded by trees.

15

Finn smiled at me, but there was tension in the corner of his eyes. I might not have noticed it if Favian had not talked to me.

"Are you ready?" he asked me.

I nodded and gripped his hands with mine. "Definitely."

Some of the tension left and his back straightened a bit. "Good."

"How does this work?" I asked Aquinn.

"Just repeat the words after me and then you'll be bound for the rest of your longer than usual lives."

"Will it hurt?" I asked softly. Finn squeezed my hands in reassurance.

"No," Aquinn said quickly. "Repeat these words: I bind thee to me, from now until my last breath. Joined as one, none will come between us."

We repeated the words and warmth filled me up. A golden thread flowed out of my chest and one out of Finn's. They floated towards each other and then connected. Instantly, I was thrown into Finn's mind and his memories flowed one after the next. I watched everything that had happened to him, right up until the moment we were bound. When the memories disappeared and my normal sight returned, Finn stared at me with shock and tears on his face.

"It is done," Aquinn said.

Love. Jealousy. Sadness. I could feel all of these emotions swirling within Finn.

"I will teleport you to your room and leave you to talk," Aquinn said since neither of us had spoken yet.

Once he left, I wiped my face on my sleeve and asked, "What are you thinking about?"

"Many things," he answered and wiped his own face.

"Well, let's talk about it," I suggested. "I have nothing to hide from you."

"Cristoff kissed you again before he left," he said and sat down on his bed.

I sat beside him. "Yes."

"You...care about him," he answered.

Jealousy spiked in him.

"I love him as a friend," I clarified. "I have no romantic interest in him. You would be able to tell if I was lying right now."

He exhaled and ran a hand through his hair.

"What else?" I asked softly.

"I wasn't prepared for this," he told me and clenched his hands into fists in his lap. "To feel what you felt when I told you that we were taking you home. To feel what you felt when I left. You walked in the rain to the castle."

That had been a very emotional time. "Yes."

"I can't...it hurts me to know that I caused you so much pain," he whispered.

I didn't know what to say to him. I didn't want to placate him with a lie of "it wasn't that bad".

"You were in pain as well," I reminded him.

He shook his head. "I should never have left you. I should have kept you by my side."

I scooted closer to him and leaned my head on his shoulder. "We're together now and we can learn from our past mistakes."

He wrapped his arms around me and hugged me. "I love you."

Love. Regret.

"I love you, too."

"How could you forgive me for all of that pain?" he asked in a whisper.

"The same way that I forgave my father. I love you and I need you in my life. You bring me more joy and love than I expected to find in my life."

"You're my greatest treasure," he whispered and then kissed my jaw.

"I would hope so. I saw the treasures that you owned," I teased him.

He nipped my neck and kissed around it.

Love. Passion. Need.

"Finn," I whispered in shock. I hadn't thought about feeling these emotions from him.

He laid me down and kissed his way up my neck to my jaw and then my mouth while running his hand from my leg to my hip. "You are the most beautiful woman in the world," he told me. "And I intend to show you just how much I think that."

It had been amazing before, but being able to feel everything that he was feeling and thinking was an overload of ecstasy. We lay in each other's arms after, and then fell asleep surrounded by our love.

"WAKE UP!" Marin yelled through our door.

"No," I called back and snuggled closer to Finn.

"The seamstresses will be here soon," she informed me.

"Come get me when they're here," I yelled back.

"Shush," Finn ordered and wrapped his arms around me. "Sleepy time."

Marin didn't talk again so I figured that I had won and began to drift off again.

"Tilia," Faxon said and then gasped.

I started to jerk away, but Finn held me in place and tugged the blankets up a bit higher.

"You shouldn't teleport to someone's room without knowing what they are doing," Finn chastised him. He wasn't mad, quite the opposite, he was very happy and smug. There was also a bit of jealousy which I didn't understand. "What if she had been changing and was naked?" Finn asked him.

"What are you two doing?" Faxon yelled. "Tilia, get up now."

"I'm naked," I informed him. "I am not getting out of bed with you here while I'm naked."

"You shouldn't be naked in bed anyways," he reprimanded me.

"We are bound," Finn told him. "That's more official than a wedding ceremony."

"You're bound?" Faxon yelled. He squinted his eyes and then they widened in disbelief. "What have you done?"

"Faxon, what has gotten into you?" I asked him. "You knew that we were discussing being bound."

"I didn't think you would be stupid enough to do it!" He yelled. Flames flickered along his hands and arms as his anger grew.

"I would suggest that you calm down," Finn told him.

Anger. Fear.

Finn climbed out of bed and I realized that he was wearing pants. When had he put them on?

"You've lengthened your life, increased the time that you will be alive here and experiencing things. Then you bound yourself to someone that you have known only a short time. What happens if he leaves you? What happens when you realize that he isn't good enough for you!" Faxon was still angry and the flames grew.

Pain. Jealousy. Rage.

"Faxon, you need to leave now," I told him. I wished that I had gotten dressed so I could talk to him without being forced to lie on the bed.

"You've poisoned her mind," Faxon accused Finn. "She's blind to what you truly look like."

"I think the only blind one here is you," Finn told him. "You're blinded by your own jealousy and love."

What? What was Finn talking about?

"You don't know what you're talking about," Faxon told him and took a step closer to Finn.

"I don't? So, you aren't jealous of our relationship? You're not in love with Tilia?" Finn asked and took two steps towards Faxon.

"Of course I love her! She is all I have. She is my single greatest accomplishment. She will be my Queen and she deserves better than you as her King!"

"You mean she should have you as her King!" Finn yelled.

Faxon blinked a few times and the flames sputtered in his shock. "What?"

"You are in love with Tilia!" Finn yelled at him. "Admit it!"

Rage. Jealousy.

Faxon stared at Finn a moment and then burst into a fit of laughter.

Finn's anger grew and he grabbed his sword. "What is so funny, Arch Mage?"

Faxon stopped laughing and shook his head. "You stupid

boy, I'm not *in* love with her. She's my apprentice and my protégé. I have no sexual interest in her."

"Then why are you so upset about her decision?" he asked.

"Because I know what heartbreak feels like. I know what it feels like to be betrayed by the one who is supposed to love you forever. I saw her pain and felt it when you left her. I know that you will cause her more pain and more heartache, and I only wish to find a way for her to escape unscathed."

Shock. Sadness.

"I know what she felt then, too," Finn told him. "And I will never make her feel that way again."

"Your binding made you share memories and feelings?" Faxon asked.

Finn nodded.

"So, you saw everything that she experienced and felt it all?"

"Yes," Finn answered through a clenched jaw.

"Good. Perhaps this will keep you from such cruelty in the future."

"Faxon," I called to get his attention. "Why did you come here?"

"To find out when you were coming home," he said.

"A few days," I replied vaguely. "Now, leave."

"We will discuss this later," he told me.

"There is nothing left to discuss," I told him angrily. "Finn and I are bound and will be for the rest of our lives."

"I will see you when you return," he said and then disappeared. He wasn't going to let the topic drop no matter what I said.

Finn threw his sword at the wall and yelled his anger. The sword's tip slid into the stone wall and the sword quivered as it stayed there.

I climbed out of bed and walked to him. "Finn," I whispered

and slipped my hands around his shoulders and hugged him. "Take a deep breath."

He obeyed and turned around to face me. "I'm sorry."

"You have nothing to apologize for," I told him sincerely. "Faxon was out of line."

"He is right," he whispered and closed his eyes tightly. "I don't deserve you."

"Maybe," I said with mock seriousness.

His eyes flew open. "What?"

"All I know is that I deserve to be happy and I want you to be happy. Are you happy with me?"

He nodded.

"Then that matter is settled," I whispered and kissed his cheek.

"Then I guess we have only one more matter to attend to," he whispered as he slid his arms around my back and down.

"Tilia! They're here now!" Marin yelled. "So, get your butt up and get out here."

Finn groaned. "You think she will wait?" he asked and then kissed me.

I pushed him back gently with my hands on his shoulders. "I think she is likely to bust our door down if I make her wait much longer."

He kissed me roughly and whispered, "Hurry back."

I got dressed in record time and followed Marin down the hallway. She repeatedly glanced at me with a smirk on her face.

"What?" I finally asked after the tenth time.

"How was it?"

"How was what?" I asked.

"Your first time after being bound?"

I blushed. "Intense," I whispered.

She laughed loudly and bumped her shoulder into mine. "That is an understatement."

"I can't think of any words adequate enough to express it," I told her.

"Why did he yell not that long ago?" Marin asked.

"Faxon showed up and found us sleeping together, naked, and he sort of flipped out," I told her.

"Oh, wow. Do you think he went back and told your Aunt and Uncle?"

I stopped walking and paused.

Had he? Would he? Oh no.

"I don't know," I admitted. "I hope not."

"That would be a fun conversation," she said and laughed.

"Have you had that conversation?" I asked as we started walking again.

"No. They aren't aware of that," she informed me.

We entered the room where the seamstresses were and they unveiled the wedding dresses.

"They're perfect," I said as I examined mine.

"More than perfect," Marin said while lightly touching her dress.

"Well, let's get them on so we can make final adjustments," one of the seamstresses said with a bright smile.

It took longer than I expected to get into the dress, but once in we were able to get our weapons secured and then checked each other out to make sure they weren't noticeable, aside from the swords that would be on our backs.

"You seamstresses are magicians," I told them.

"We are glad that you are happy with your dresses."

"We will make our final alterations and have them back this evening."

We changed clothes again and then headed out of the room.

"So, have you figured out the mind to mind communication?" Marin asked me.

"What? I can't hear his thoughts," I told her.

"You should be able to," she said with a frown. "Unless you have a wall up."

I focused and giggled. "Subconscious wall," I admitted. I took it down and immediately heard and felt Finn. "So weird," I whispered out loud.

"*Tilia!*" he yelled in my mind. "*Finally! I thought something was wrong with our bond.*"

"Had a wall up," I admitted.

"You don't have to say it out loud," Marin told me.

"Habit," I whispered.

"Well, I'm going to find Favian. We're going to spar in a bit if you two want to join us?"

"Okay. I'll get Finn," I told her.

"*Tell her we will be a bit late to the sparring,*" Finn told me. *Passion. Need. Desire.*

I blushed and was thankful that she was headed the other direction. "Stop that," I ordered him.

"*Come here and make me.*"

"*I'm going to put my wall back up,*" I threatened him.

"*Tilia, hurry up!*"

AT DINNER we enjoyed a fun meal with lively conversation and delicious dessert. I promised to have Faxon teleport the rest of them the following morning. Finn had packed our bags and Marin and Favian were ready when we met them in the hallway.

"Don't throw up on me," I ordered them.

"Where are you going to teleport to?" Finn asked.

"My room."

"Is there enough room for all of us?"

"Well, I guess I could teleport us to the dining room. They should be done eating now," I murmured.

"Sounds good," Finn said.

I closed my eyes and then teleported the four of us into the dining room. We appeared to find it not empty, and in fact they were still eating dinner.

"Hello," Esmeralda greeted us with a wide smile.

"Oh, man. You weren't kidding about puking," Marin said and bent over while drawing in deep breaths.

"Sorry," I apologized. "I can't control it."

"It should pass quickly," Faxon said coldly.

"Where are your dresses?" Esmeralda asked.

"Queen Amadis has them and when Faxon teleports them here, she will bring them," I advised her with a smirk.

"You really won't let anyone see them before the wedding, will you?" she asked with a pout.

"It will be a wonderful surprise," I assured her.

"Are you hungry?" Jared asked.

"No, we just ate," Finn replied.

"Would you like a tour?" I asked Marin.

She nodded and I realized that she was looking around at the dining room. "Yes."

"Well, this is the dining room," I said and led them out to begin the tour.

It took me longer than I thought it would to give them the full tour, but I saved the arena for last since I knew we were likely to spend more time there.

"This is very nice," Favian praised as he slid his feet through the sand.

"You know what it doesn't have?" I asked Favian with a smirk.

Finn's head jerked towards me as he read my thought and he laughed loudly.

"What's that?" Favian asked.

"This sand has never tasted an elf's blood."

He smirked back and said, "I'm afraid it never will, either."

"Well, there is only one way to find out," I said and drew my sword.

Marin and Finn climbed up onto the wall and cheered for us.

Favian drew his sword and bowed to me. "I hate to ruin your hospitality before we have even spent the night."

"The only way to ruin it is by refusing to spar," I told him and then lunged forward.

It was impossible to keep up with him and before I had even tried to strike him, I was on my back on the ground.

"Now my feelings are hurt," I said with a fake pout.

"Why is that?" Favian asked with his sword at my throat.

"You and Finn have been training together and now you are faster. I have no hopes of catching up. It is hardly fair."

"Life is not fair, Princess."

"I know that, Prince."

"Did you also know that the only reason you were moving slower is because you were *thinking* instead of reacting?" he asked me.

"Fine, again."

He pulled me up by the arm and we squared off again.

"*Finn, help me out,*" I asked silently.

"*Left. Right. Down. Forward. Back. Slash.*"

Finn gave me directions in our mind to mind communication and it surprisingly worked. I was able to dodge his attacks and almost landed one of my own.

Favian was glaring at Finn when he finally pinned me again. "You were helping her."

"How could you tell?" I asked out of breath.

"I tested it by trying to fake you, a move you fell for earlier, and you didn't fall for it. Finn has learned my tells," he said angrily.

"I guess you will have to get better," Marin told him.

"Two weeks and I'll pin you," Favian told Finn.

Finn smiled wide. "I hope so. I need some competition."

Finn dodged just in time to avoid the dagger aimed at his head and laughed as he walked towards me.

"I was worried the orders and my responses would be delayed," I told Finn, "but your knowledge of his moves definitely helped."

"It's that shoulder," Marin complained. "He only started dropping it this past year."

"I'll fix my moves," Favian told her and sheathed his sword. "Tilia needs to work on her speed. I think the first thing we will learn on our island is endurance. That means lots of running."

"You guys can wake me up when you get back from your runs," Finn said.

"Oh no," I told him. "If I have to suffer, you have to suffer with me."

"You need to work on your endurance, too," Favian told him. "You aren't as fast as you could be."

"I'm still faster than you," Finn taunted him.

"They are so cute when they squabble like children," Marin whispered to me with a wide smile.

"My heart is beating so fast, I think I might faint from the manliness seeping from these two," I said and fanned my face with my hand and then leaned against Marin as though I were going to faint.

"You two are hilarious," Favian said grumpily.

"And you are stuck with us for a very *very* long time," I reminded him.

"I figured I would find you four here," Jared said as he entered the arena.

"Well, of course," I said. "This is my favorite place."

"Did you need us?" Finn asked him.

"Me, need my Chief? Of course not," Jared teased him.

"I offered to rescind the title since I won't be around much," Finn grumbled.

"I actually came to ask if I might be able to find out why Faxon was so angry when he returned from visiting you?" Jared asked us.

We all suddenly found various spots on the roof interesting.

"No one?" he asked.

"He stepped out of line and I made him mad," I said. "Things were said and Finn almost skewered him."

"Instead he skewered a wall," Favian whispered.

"What happened?" Jared asked with a frown.

"I would rather not discuss it. It is sort of personal," Finn said.

"There are no secrets in this house," Jared told him.

"Please," I begged. "Let this lie, at least for a little while. Either Faxon will get over it or he won't and well...I don't know what will happen then."

Would Faxon stop visiting me? I couldn't think of my life without Faxon in it.

"Well, try to make up. I was enjoying him not being a grumpy mage and now he has reverted again," Jared complained.

"I don't think that will be fixed any time soon," I admitted.

"It's about Finn, isn't it?" he asked softly.

"He does not approve of me being with Tilia," Finn said and then a board on the opposite side of the arena cracked.

Favian's eyes widened and he looked at me in silent question.

"Finn," I whispered. "Why don't we go inside and show them to their room and then get ready for bed?" I suggested.

"Actually, I was hoping to go on a run," Favian said and gave me a look to tell me to let him handle it.

"Well, then Marin and I will go get into our pajamas," I said.

Anger. Regret. Sadness.

"I'll race you to the docks and back," Favian said with a smile and then took off before Finn could answer.

"You got a head start, you cheater!" Finn yelled after him and then disappeared in pursuit.

Happiness.

"I am so glad that we have Favian here," I whispered. "He knows just how to get Finn's mind off of whatever he is thinking about."

"They are two peas in a pod," Marin agreed. "They are so similar that it is sort of baffling."

"And you two aren't similar?" Jared asked with a wide smile.

"Of course not. We are completely different," Marin argued.

"I mean, just because we both like fighting does not mean that we are exactly the same. That is like saying that anyone who likes horses is exactly the same," I chastised.

"So, are you going to tell me what was said?" Jared asked.

"No. I would rather not repeat the awful things that he said. He was incredibly rude and out of line and I may have made it worse by making him leave. It was a huge mess," I said.

"What could have set him off?" Jared pondered and turned around to look at something in the distance.

Marin looked at me and smirked. I glared at her and then Jared turned around so we both smiled at him.

"You are hiding something," he said angrily. "Why won't you tell me?"

"Because you will get mad and I have had enough of people getting mad today. Can't we just forget about it and let it lie? We can discuss it when we get back from our wedding trip."

"Where are you going anyway? You never told us," Jared said.

"We had not decided until just recently," I admitted to him.

"And it is a secret," Marin told him.

"A secret? Why are you all being so secretive?" he asked angrily.

"I'll fight you for it," Marin offered with a wide smile.

"Marin, we have to go to bed," I reminded her.

"Oh, fine. Spoil sport."

"Good night, Jared," I called as I pulled her away.

"Night, girls."

"Why did you stop me?" she asked with a pout.

"Because if he had won, you would have had to tell him and I would rather not have that conversation with my uncle."

"You are no fun," she complained.

"You can spar with him another day."

"Fine."

16

"WHY AM I NERVOUS?" I ASKED MARIN AS I FIDGETED WITH MY dress. We were already bound, so this was really just a formality.

"Perhaps because there are over a hundred people present for our wedding," Marin whispered. "And, they are all going to watch us."

"Fight an army, not nervous. Walk down the aisle for a wedding and you're scared?" Deana asked.

"You're nervous, too," I reminded her.

"Well I didn't have as long to prepare as you!" she snapped and tugged on one of her curls.

Sebastian and Deana had surprised us all by returning, engaged. Marin and I had immediately agreed to a triple wedding. The seamstresses worked all night to create a dress for her that somewhat matched ours.

"How did your father react when you told him?" Marin asked Deana.

"He was relieved, actually," she admitted.

"Is he coming?" I asked her.

She shook her head. "No, but he gave us his blessing. He has an urgent matter to attend to or he would have come."

"Wait, she's going to upstage us by not wearing a sword," Marin gasped in fake horror.

I smirked. "Her wedding present was a shiny new sword from Finn and I."

"Not sure why a shifter needs a sword," she muttered.

"You can't always shift," Marin argued.

"I promised to wear the sword as well as learn to use it," Deana explained.

"Are you two coming to the island as well?" I asked. It would be great to have two more people to help us fight whatever it was.

"No, Sebastian is going to take up Favian's duties while we are training," Marin explained.

"Oh, so she's going to be stuck around all those beautiful elvish men? Poor thing," I teased.

We all laughed together and then the seamstresses came in to help us get into our dresses. It took us longer than ever to get ready, but once we were all dressed and our weapons were on, the three of us stood before the mirror in shock.

We looked like warrior brides.

"The Princess Triumvirate," The Goddess said happily as she appeared in our room. "You've finally formed."

"Princess, what?" Marin asked her.

"You three are the Princess Triumvirate, the three most powerful princesses in the world. By working together, you can make this world a better place," she explained.

"I'm not powerful anymore," Deana reminded her.

"You're a shifter, my dear, you are powerful and perhaps if you worked at bringing the shifters together and starting your own territory, you would again have that power."

"Shifters have a longer than human lifespan, don't they?" I asked suspiciously.

"Yes, we do. How'd you know?" Deana asked.

"You are very sharp," The Goddess commended me.

"You've been planning this, haven't you?" I accused her.

She beamed proudly. "I plan a great number of things. This has been my favorite, by far. You three will show the world the power of women once again. I bestow my blessings upon you and will be here to guide you as needed."

"It's time!" someone called through the closed door.

"I'll see you out there," the Goddess said with a wink and then disappeared.

"Gods and goddesses are incredibly tricky," I whispered.

"Yes, they are," Marin agreed.

"Ready, ladies?" Deana asked.

We nodded and then had one group hug before we walked out of the room and towards the back of the Markleville castle where the wedding ceremony was being held. The ocean would be behind us as we took our vows, a place I had found perfect and the others found charming.

Instead of having fathers walk us down the aisle as tradition called for, we decided to walk each other down. It eased the pain of my father not being alive to see me being wed. Plus, Deana's father wasn't here so it made convincing the Queens even easier. We checked our swords and weapons once more, linked arms with Deana between Marin and I, and headed down the aisle.

Everyone stood and turned to face us.

Love. Pride. Joy. They filtered through the bond as Finn and the two elven princes watched us walk towards them.

"Do not cry," Marin growled.

I wasn't certain if she was ordering us or herself, but I agreed.

A simple wooden arch had been built on the edge of the cliff with flowers placed along the poles. The two gods and the goddess stood between us and the men. They had decided that they wanted to officiate the wedding and no one had objected.

"Swords?" a woman whispered to our right. "How brutish."

"What would you expect from those three?" another sneered.

"Do not attack them," I ordered Marin.

"Afterwards," she promised.

We made it to the front and stood before the most powerful beings in existence. They were not holding back their power and it was almost unbearable to be there.

"Sit," Aquinn ordered the attendees.

"We come before you this day to marry Marin and Favian of the Elves, Deana of the Shifters and Sebastian of the Elves, and Finn and Tilia of the humans. The Princess Triumvirate have made their choices for mates and we approve and give blessings to each couple," the Goddess said in a voice that made me worry she was going to give a prophecy at any moment.

"Marin and Finn are the last two demigods in existence," Aquinn began, "and these six will be your last hope against enemies in the future."

Several people began murmuring nervously.

"Today, we set aside those disconcerting discussions," Aquinn said with a wide smile. "And rejoice as they finalize their unions as husbands and wives."

"Men, please take the hand of your mate," Marin's father instructed.

The men stepped forward and we took a collective breath as we admired our men approaching us. They were dressed in white just as we were, but they each had a handkerchief that matched a color of our flowers, red for Marin, teal for me, and forest green for Deana.

"We did well," Marin whispered.

Deana and I stifled our laughs, but all three men raised their eyebrows at us in question, which caused the three of us to lose it and laugh loudly.

"They can never be serious," Favian complained.

"It's part of what makes us charming," Marin reminded him with her own raised eyebrow.

They each took one of our hands, and stood to our rights. We faced the supreme beings hand in hand with our mates and it felt right.

"Do you men promise to protect, love, and cherish your mates for the rest of your existences?" the Goddess asked them.

"I do." All three men answered.

"Do you women promise to protect, love, and cherish your mates for the rest of your existences?" the Goddess asked us.

"I do," we answered.

"Exchange rings," Marin's father ordered us.

The ring Finn slid on my finger was the most beautiful I had ever seen. Silver with a bright teal gem and two small diamonds on the sides. I put his ring on and his smile widened.

"As Goddess of this world, I proclaim Marin and Favian, Deana and Sebastian, and Tilia and Finn, husband and wife, Prince and Princess, and blessed of the Gods!"

"You may kiss your mates," Aquinn said with a broad smile.

In unison, the men grabbed us, spun us around their fronts, dipped us, and kissed us.

The crowd cheered and after separating from kissing, we all began hugging each other.

"Celebrate well, children," the Goddess said with a wide smile and then the three of them disappeared.

A cannon fired at sea. We spun towards it, expecting someone to be firing at us, with swords drawn. Instead, we found Finn's, my father's, and Cristoff's crews aboard two ships, firing out to sea and cheering for us.

"All hail the Pirate Princess!" Cristoff and his crew cheered.

"All hail Prince Finn!" Finn's and my father's crews cheered.

Finn pulled me against his side with an arm around my waist. "I told you that our family would come."

I was crying now as I raised my hand to them and they continued to fire cannons in celebration.

"You guys sure have an interesting family," Deana said with a smile as she leaned against Sebastian.

"You don't know the half of it," I told her and smirked as Finn smiled down at me.

"Go on," he encouraged me.

I stepped away from our group, stood up on the railing, raised my sword in the air, and shouted, "All hail the Pirate King, Cristoff!"

Everyone grew silent a moment and then they began cheering for him. Cristoff met my eyes, misty just like mine, and bowed to me.

"Treat her well or I'll steal your treasure!" Cristoff threatened Finn, though we both knew, there was no true threat there.

"All hail Pirate King Cristoff!" Finn yelled and raised his sword in the air.

The crews sailed away and Esmeralda cleared her throat. "Now that the pirate side is gone, let's reconvene to the reception."

"Cake!" Marin yelled.

"Cake!" Deana and I yelled back. We sheathed our swords, linked hands, and ran towards the reception.

"Never a dull moment with them, is there?" Sebastian asked.

"We wouldn't have it any other way," Favian replied as he draped an arm around Finn's shoulders.

THANK YOU

Thank you for reading my book. If you enjoyed it, won't you please take a moment to leave me a review at your favorite retailer?

Thank you!

~Catherine Banks

CONNECT WITH CATHERINE BANKS

I really appreciate you reading my book! Here are some ways to connect with me:

www.catherinebanks.com

Follow me on BookBub:

https://www.bookbub.com/authors/catherine-banks

Join my newsletter for deals and snippets:

http://catbanks.co/newsletter

Like my author Facebook page:

http://www.Facebook.com/CatherineBanksAuthor

Follow me on Twitter: http://www.Twitter.com/catherineebanks

Follow me on Goodreads:

http://www.Goodreads.com/catherine_banks

Purchase items handmade by Catherine:

http://Etsy.com/shop/TurboKittenInd

ABOUT THE AUTHOR

Catherine Banks is a USA Today bestselling fantasy author who writes in several fantasy subgenres under two pseudonyms. She began writing fiction at only four years old and finished her first full-length novel at the age of fifteen. She is married to her soulmate and best friend, Avery, who she has two amazing children with. After her full-time job, she reads books, plays video games, and watches anime shows and movies with her family to relax. Although she has lived in Northern California her entire life, she dreams of traveling around the world. Catherine is also C.E.O. of Turbo Kitten Industries™, a company with many hats including being a book publisher and Etsy store full of nerdy fun.

facebook.com/catherinebanksauthor

twitter.com/catherineebanks

amazon.com/author/catherinebanks

bookbub.com/authors/catherine-banks

goodreads.com/catherine_banks

ALSO BY CATHERINE BANKS

Song of the Moon (Artemis Lupine, Book One)

Kiss of a Star (Artemis Lupine, Book Two)

Healed by Fire (Artemis Lupine, Book Three)

Taming Darkness (Artemis Lupine, Book Four)

ARTEMIS LUPINE, THE COMPLETE SERIES

Pirate Princess (Pirate Princess, Book One)

Princess Triumvirate (Pirate Princess, Book Two)

Mercenary (Little Death Bringer, Book One)

Protector (Little Death Bringer, Book Two)

Royally Entangled (Her Royal Harem, Book One)

Royally Exposed (Her Royal Harem, Book Two)

Royally Elected (Her Royal Harem, Book Three)

Royally Enraged (Her Royal Harem, Book Four)

HER ROYAL HAREM, THE COMPLETE SERIES

The Demon's Fair

True Faces (Ciara Steele Novella Series, Book One)

Barbaric Tendencies (Ciara Steele Novella Series, Book Two)

Demonic Contract

Anja's Secret

Daughter of Lions